Praise for Kelly Killoren's first novel

A
Dangerous
Age

"This novel is the crown jewel of Kelly's extensive career in fashion. I am so proud to have been able to see her morph from a young, fresh-faced twentysomething into the woman she is today. This novel is a celebration of past, present, and future set against the fabulous backdrop of New York City!"

—Calvin Klein

"Kelly Killoren invites us behind the seams of three industries she knows a heck of a lot about: the fashion world, the art world, and the magazine world. Fashionistas, you are in for one fab ride!"

—Giuliana Rancic, *New York Times* bestselling author and host of *E! News* and *Fashion Police*

"[*A Dangerous Age*] explores the New York art, fashion, and publishing world[s] few women have access to. Kelly is an insider; Lucy Brockton is, too."

—Zac Posen

"It's wonderfully hard to figure out the real from the unreal in superstar model Kelly Killoren's fun and hot novel—which makes for an irresistible read."

—Lucy Sykes, author of *The Knockoff* and former fashion director at *Marie Claire* magazine and Rent the Runway

"A delicious guilty pleasure from the glorious Kelly Killoren. I loved it."

—Elizabeth Hurley

"A sophisticated take on what it means to be a contemporary woman in this day and age, this sultry, fiery novel will have you wishing you could pack your bags and move to Manhattan with your best girlfriends. Bubbly and compelling!"

—Brandi Glanville, *New York Times* bestselling author of *Drinking and Tweeting*, entrepreneur, and former *The Real Housewives of Beverly Hills* star

"Kelly Killoren is an inspiration to us free-spirited bitches of the world, and this book is all kinds of major. Yes, Kelly. Yes."

—Babe Walker, *New York Times* bestselling author of *White Girl Problems* and *Psychos*

"This is the REAL Kelly—not the TV construct."

—Jill Kargman, program creator of smash hit television comedy series *Odd Mom Out* and author of *The Ex-Mrs. Hedgefund*

"[A] sharp novel . . . it's *Sex and the City* meets *The Age of Innocence*."

—*In Touch* magazine

"Killoren weaves together the tangled threads of their four stories to produce a conclusion that exhibits the drama and immediacy of a reality show in novel form. Fans of *Sex and the City* and the Real Housewives franchise will enjoy the rarefied atmosphere."

—*Booklist*

"This is the next beach book, especially for chick-lit fans and those who enjoy the TV show *Sex and the City.*"

—*Library Journal*

"Intriguing and twisty."

—*Kirkus Reviews*

"*A Dangerous Age* walks us hand in hand throughout the inner sanctum of the New York social world only few are privy to. The clothes, the food, and the pampering are right out of a *Vogue* magazine must-have . . . [a] fun read."

—Melissa Odabash, American swimwear designer and former fashion model

"Kelly is back on the scene in a major way. Iconic, sexy, and smart, this supermodel redefines the rules of the game for all women of a dangerous age."

—John Demsey, executive group president of Estée Lauder

the Second Course

a novel

Kelly Killoren
with Maia Rossini

G

GALLERY BOOKS

New York   London   Toronto   Sydney   New Delhi

G

Gallery Books
An Imprint of Simon & Schuster, Inc.
1230 Avenue of the Americas
New York, NY 10020

First Gallery Books trade paperback edition August 2017

GALLERY BOOKS and colophon are registered trademarks of Simon & Schuster, Inc.

For information about special discounts for bulk purchases, please contact Simon & Schuster Special Sales at 1-866-506-1949 or business@simonandschuster.com.

The Simon & Schuster Speakers Bureau can bring authors to your live event. For more information or to book an event, contact the Simon & Schuster Speakers Bureau at 1-866-248-3049 or visit our website at www.simonspeakers.com.

Interior design by Davina Mock-Maniscalco

Manufactured in the United States of America

10   9   8   7   6   5   4   3   2   1

Library of Congress Cataloging-in-Publication Data

Names: Killoren, Kelly, author.
Title: The second course : a novel / Kelly Killoren.
Description: First Gallery Books trade paperback edition. | New York :
   Gallery Books, 2017.
Identifiers: LCCN 2017012590| ISBN 9781501136153 (softcover) | ISBN 9781501136238 (ebook)
Subjects: LCSH: Female friendship—Fiction. | Women cooks—Fiction. | BISAC:
   FICTION / Contemporary Women. | FICTION / General. | FICTION / Literary.
Classification: LCC PS3611.I4519 S43 2017 | DDC 813/.6—dc23
LC record available at https://lccn.loc.gov/2017012590

ISBN 978-1-5011-3615-3
ISBN 978-1-5011-3623-8 (ebook)

Some say to leave the past behind; I say take it right with you. To my beautiful girls, who have taught me how to love unconditionally. To my foodies, who taught me to eat, love, add salt, repeat. And to my four friends: Lucy, Billy, Sarah, and Lotta, who continue to surprise me with their relentless ability to fight really hard for friendship.

First we eat, then we do everything else.

—M. F. K. Fisher

chapter 1

East Hampton, NY
Lotta Eklund's wedding day

I took a bite of caviar and rolled it around in my mouth, enjoying the crisp saline snap and mineral tang as the tiny eggs exploded over my tongue.

Pop Rocks for the rich, I thought to myself, not for the first time.

"Don't you think," I whispered into Sarah's ear, "that this is getting a little fucking ridiculous?"

Sarah took a sip of her Negroni and cocked her head. "I think it's kind of sweet."

I took another bite and followed her gaze across the room. "It's like their own private romance novel. I don't understand how those two haven't just melted into a permanent puddle of champagne, rose petals, and empty Tiffany boxes."

We were watching our dear friend Lucy as she sat in her husband Titus's lap. Her arms were twined languidly around his neck as he looked into her eyes with what could only be described as a blazing hunger.

"Maybe used condoms, too. Add that to their puddle."

Sarah wrinkled her nose. "Gross, Billy."

I didn't begrudge them their happiness. They had gone through some rocky times lately, and we were all relieved to see them on the other side of things. But it was starting to border on irritating. The two of them had been married for almost twenty years, and they were acting like horny teens who had just discovered dry humping.

We were supposed to be helping Lotta get ready for her wedding. She was due at the altar in twenty minutes, but Titus, legend of the art world and hopelessly besotted husband, had crashed the bridal suite with a tray of drinks and toast points, and a giant tin of osetra.

"Compliments of the groom," he'd said, but I had a sneaking suspicion that he had conjured it all up himself as an excuse to see Lucy.

The suspicion had grown even stronger after he'd taken one look at his wife in her semitranslucent slip of a dress and pulled her onto his lap.

"This gown is exquisite on you," he murmured. "Who designed it?"

"Lotta did," said Lucy. "Isn't it wonderful?"

"Oh, well," said Lotta in her smoky Swedish accent. "Zac Posen helped, you know. I just told him the general gist of what I wanted and we created it together."

"Well, kudos to you and Zac," said Titus.

"Thank you. Now please get out before you further wrinkle my bridesmaid with all your manhandling."

Titus stole one last quick kiss from his wife before he rose to exit. "You all look beautiful," he said, gracing the room with a warm smile. "Most especially the bride, of course."

Lotta returned his smile and then waved him out with an imperial gesture of her perfectly manicured hand. She did look beautiful.

The rest of us were wearing filmy white linen, but Lotta was wearing blue silk. The shimmering color turned from summer sky to stormy with the smallest shift in her movement.

"This is not my first rodeo," she had explained when she'd unveiled her gown to us, "and it's ridiculous for me to pretend to be some blushing virgin. You all can wear the white for me—I will wear a color that actually flatters."

Of course, Lotta, with her waist-length platinum-blond hair, sleepy Nordic eyes, and six feet of Brigitte Bardot curves would have looked spectacular in any color—but blue was her particular signature, and she refused to be a generic bride.

The wedding was simple. Which did not mean cheap. It was at the groom's summer cottage. And by cottage, I mean ten-thousand-square-foot mansion with a private Hampton beachfront. It was small—which meant only 250 of the couple's nearest and dearest friends and family. And it was "beach casual," which meant the bridal party would not be wearing shoes.

"Are you absolutely sure about the barefoot thing, Lotta?" said Sarah as she gazed longingly at a shoebox on the floor. "It just seems like a missed opportunity to show off those cute Gucci ankle straps."

"I told you," said Lotta, "you can wear whatever you like at the reception. But no shoes on the beach. I have a vision."

"Okay, then!" said Lucy, bouncing up and dusting off her hands. "Let's get this vision out the door! Only fifteen minutes left to go! Sarah—you do one last hair check. I'm on makeup. Billy, you get that headdress on."

We all sprang into action. There had been a squad of professionals here before us, of course. Hair and makeup, the photographers, and the florist, with the wedding planner hovering over the room like a mother cat tending to her newborn kittens. Lotta had let them do their work and then dismissed them all, demanding a few moments of privacy for the four of us before the ceremony began.

I carefully lifted the fine web of linked platinum chains that Lotta would be wearing in lieu of a veil. The metal all but disappeared into Lotta's silvery-blond hair, just leaving the hundreds of inset sapphire chips glinting through her tresses like the world's most expensive glitter. Sarah moved a few stray strands from the front to the back. Lucy dotted the barest amount of powder over Lotta's chin and nose.

"Enough," said Lotta. "Let's have a toast."

The bridesmaids picked up our Negronis. The bride was drinking sparkling water. She'd been 98 percent sober for almost six months now.

When Lotta had first come out of rehab, she was 100 percent sober and had stuck with the usual twelve-step plan. So we'd tiptoed around her sobriety, thinking of things to do together that didn't center around alcohol or other, more illicit, substances. We doubled up on our already challenging exercise classes. We saw a lot of movies. Took a lot of walks. Drank a lot of coffee. Watched a lot of television. We even took up group knitting at one point, much to my horrified dismay. And then, after we spent our requisite amount of time sober, Lucy, Sarah, and I would kiss Lotta good-bye and sneak off to the nearest bar.

It ended about six months in. Lotta had marched into Lucy's town house and slammed a large bottle of tequila followed by a small, hand-rolled joint on the kitchen table.

"New plan," she announced. "I appreciate how supportive you've all been. I really do. But I can't live through another fucking night of polite chitchat and *Scandal* reruns."

We all looked at each other with alarm. Lotta had been in the teeth of a terrifying addiction before she'd finally gotten help. No one wanted to go through that again.

"This," she said, picking up the marijuana, "is for me. And this"—she pushed the bottle of alcohol toward us—"is for you. You girls are going to party, and I am going to smoke this joint, and you will see that I am not made of spun sugar. I will not melt down or break just because you are having a little fun."

We all stared at her. "But Lotta—" said Lucy.

"No," said Lotta. "I will be ninety-eight percent sober from here on out. I am not going to start snorting coke again just because I smoke a little pot, but I will definitely fall off the wagon if I have to spend one more minute dealing with how fucking boring we've become. Now drink. Please. I beg you. Drink. I can take it."

After that, things went back to relatively normal. We cut back on the coffee and restarted the dinner parties and girls' nights out. We went to all our old favorite bars and restaurants and drank all our old favorite drinks. We tried not to overindulge too much, and Lotta kept her glass full of tonic and lime, and after, she'd go home and enjoy her small daily break from sobriety.

It seemed to work for her. I asked her once if it was hard, and she shrugged. "Almost dying was hard," she said. "Detox was hard. This . . . this is just maintenance."

I thought she meant it. I hoped she meant it. But I still couldn't help feeling a pang of guilt as I raised my fragrant glass full of gin, vermouth, and Campari and prepared to clink it against her boring bubbly water.

Lotta paused a moment, looking at us. Then she put her glass down.

"Tell me the truth, you guys. Am I crazy to be getting married?"

I think the three of us must have bitten our tongues in unison.

It wasn't that we didn't like her fiancé. Because we did. There was almost nothing not to like about Omari Scott. If Lenny Kravitz, Jay-Z, and a young Quincy Jones managed to combine themselves into one glorious person, you'd get Omari. He'd started out as a neo-soul musician and rapper, which was hot enough, but then he'd switched over to producing and now he owned his own ridiculously successful record label. He was gorgeous, talented, rich, kind, and brilliant, and he absolutely adored Lotta.

But Lotta was barely a year sober. And she had only known Omari for four months total. Plus, he had a college-age daughter who, from everything we'd seen and heard, completely *loathed* Lotta.

Of course she was crazy to be getting married. We had talked about this behind her back nonstop since the day she had announced her engagement.

But before anyone could work up the balls to answer, Lotta laughed and picked her glass back up.

"Fuck it," she said, grinning. "Don't tell me. I don't care. Here's to my wedding!"

And so we all raised our glasses and wished her the very best.

chapter 2

We made a pretty picture, I'm sure, all lined up at the altar, silhouetted against the sparkling sea, skirts billowing in the breeze: slim, dark-haired Sarah with her strong patrician features and porcelain skin; model-tall, model-gorgeous, model-everything Lucy; and me, doing my best to hold my own, the ugly redheaded stepchild of our little group, just happy that we were all wearing the same thing and that for once, I hadn't had to borrow my designer clothes. We all smiled and clutched our massive bouquets of lavender and hydrangea and pretended we didn't think this wedding was a disaster waiting to happen.

I will admit that I almost cried when Lotta turned to Omari's daughter, Sage, a gorgeous nineteen-year-old in Adele eyeliner and Bantu knots, and told her sincerely that she wasn't just marrying Omari, that she felt so lucky to be getting such a wonderful daughter—a *family*—as well.

I knew what it meant when Lotta said that. She had been short on a loving family for most of her life. Only the sour expression on Sage's pretty face and the fact that I could see her just barely managing not to roll her big brown eyes saved me from completely breaking down.

The reception was in the ballroom (yes, the "cottage" had a ballroom), a huge, soaring space with banks of French doors that opened up onto a mammoth terrace that overlooked the ocean.

Lotta had us seated at the bride's family table, right next to the wedding couple's table, because, up until today, we were basically all the family she had. She hadn't talked to her parents in years, and although she kept up a cordial relationship with her ex-husband, it wasn't the kind of cordial that necessitated a wedding invitation.

So it was me and my kind-of, maybe boyfriend, Brett Walker (*Brett. Brett. Could I really fall for a guy named Brett?*); Lucy and Titus, who would probably fricking hand-feed each other strawberries dipped in chocolate all night long; and Sarah and her fiancé, Brian.

Though she had managed to cover it up during bridal prep, Sarah was in a shitty mood and was now letting it all hang out. She was pissed at Lotta and Omari for not allowing any cameras in from the reality show—*Under the Plaid Skirt*—that she was a cast member on. Her first season had been a hit, and now the pressure was on to top herself. She had initially planned that her second season arc would be all about her own wedding, but now she felt that Lotta had stolen her thunder.

"I can't get married *now*," she said, gesturing around the ballroom. "I mean, we just finished planning all this. It would be so boring to do it all over again."

Brian frowned and buried his nose in his drink. He was known to be a man of endless patience, but sometimes I wondered if the end to that endless was closer than we thought.

"So it's going to have to be the baby first," continued Sarah. "But I'm not unthawing the embryos yet. My doctor wants to see if we can just make one the old-fashioned way. And I think the longer we can draw out the tension, the better for the show, so we're willing to give it a try, right, Brian?" She smiled sweetly at her fiancé.

He cleared his throat and then gave her a smile back. "Of course," he said.

"But we'll need a B-plot while we're trying to make a baby. Did I tell you that Penelope Hanover is doing a cancer scare this year? I mean, it's a melanoma, for God's sake. Not even real cancer, but she's going to milk it for all it's worth."

I laughed. "Jesus, Sarah, a little heartless, maybe?"

She ignored me. "So I was thinking, maybe I'll sell my apartment and find a new, more kid-friendly place in Brooklyn. We can do a house hunt. Everyone likes real-estate porn."

Lucy's head jerked around. "What? Brooklyn? What are you talking about?"

Sarah waved her hand airily. "Prospect Park. Brooklyn Heights. Hey, do you think your mom could help me? Think what great TV Cheri would be! She's the hottest real estate agent in New York. She must know all kinds of gossip."

"Leave Manhattan? Why would you do that?" Lucy sounded genuinely bewildered by the idea.

"Matt Damon just moved to Brooklyn for the schools, you know. It's the responsible choice to make for my family, Lucy."

"Well, if Matt Damon says so . . ." said Brett.

I laughed.

Sarah turned to me. "You should consider it, too, Billy. I mean, obviously not the Heights or Prospect Park, but somewhere cheaper. I don't see how you're keeping up the rent on your place."

"I still have royalties coming on my book," I said, stung.

Sarah lifted a dubious eyebrow, letting me know exactly what she thought of that plan.

She was right, by the way. I couldn't afford my place. At least not for much longer. I still had a little chunk of money from the initial book sale, but it was disappearing fast, and royalties were pretty much a delusional pipe dream. It seemed that fewer people needed a cookbook on obscure cocktails than I had initially thought.

It was embarrassing. Even before Sarah was a quasi-celebrity making bank from her TV show, Brian had already been an extremely successful hedge fund manager. And of course Titus and Lucy had all of Titus's world-famous-artist money plus whatever Lucy had socked away when she was still doing *Vogue* covers and Marc Jacobs campaigns. Lotta used to be my comrade on the edge of poverty—we'd joke about how we were going to end up sharing an efficiency in Queens—but now she was married to Omari frigging Scott, who probably had more money than the rest of us put together. And Brett? Well, Brett had underwritten Instagram—and made many other wise investments—so he wasn't exactly hurting for cash, either. With all this around me, being on the verge of broke somehow seemed even more pathetic than usual.

Brett took my hand. "Hey," he said quietly, "if you ever need help . . ."

I jerked my hand away. "I'm fine," I hissed.

I immediately felt bad. I knew he was only trying to be kind.

"I mean, thank you, but I'm fine."

He laughed. God, he was good-looking. Like a Hollywood throwback—Burton or McQueen. His eyes gleamed with an irreverent, wicked sense of humor that got me every time. "Heaven forbid Billy Sitwell admits that she needs any help."

I deflected. "When is the waiter getting here? Lotta promised me that my mind was going to be blown by this food. She said she found this chef when they had a private dinner with John Legend and Chrissy Teigen. It's supposed to be like nothing I've ever tasted."

Brett shook his head. "Hard to imagine there's anything you haven't tasted, B.," he said.

He was correct again. Actually, it was starting to make me a little jumpy, just how well he seemed to know me, but he was right—I couldn't imagine that there was much left under the sun that I hadn't already put in my mouth.

Food became my everything when I was six years old and my mother died. She killed herself, knocked off this earth by the kind of depression that probably could be controlled with a couple of Zolofts and a gluten-free diet these days. But back in 1982, it was basically a choice between being a lithium zombie or shock therapy, so she took what I'd eventually come to accept as the most sensible way out.

My father was left at sea in a million different ways, but cooking was maybe the most tangibly difficult thing for him. So he drew up a never-changing menu, mostly based on ground meat. Burgers on Monday. Tacos on Tuesday. Spaghetti Wednesday. Frozen-pizza Thursday. Grilled cheese on Friday. Breakfast for dinner Saturday. And Sunday, we went to Denny's. He was doing his best, but it was unrelenting.

I started out small—changing it up just a little bit. Adding a slice of Swiss cheese to the burgers, a couple dashes of Tabasco to the tacos, making an iceberg salad to eat alongside the spaghetti. But soon I put my precocious reading skills to use by wading my way through the cookbooks that my mother had left behind (starting with *Joy of Cooking*, every Midwestern mom's bible).

I'll never forget the first time I really cooked for my father—like, a full meal: vegetable, main course, and dessert. It was simple. I blanched some green beans, sliced some tomatoes from our neighbor's garden, and broiled a steak. And then for dessert, I made homemade chocolate pudding. Everything turned out. The beans were crisp and tender, the tomatoes perfectly ripe and sprinkled with salt. The steak was juicy and pink inside, just how we liked it. And even the chocolate pudding—which took real effort on my part—was smooth and delicious.

I was nine. And my father cried after he finished eating.

"Sweetheart, this was as good as anything your mother ever made," he said, smiling through his tears.

I have spent my lifetime chasing the overwhelming pride and happiness I felt at that moment.

I finished high school and followed Lucy, who had been my best friend since grade school, to Manhattan. By the time I arrived, she was already well established in the fashion world. She was everybody's favorite model, and she assured me that I could be, too.

I thought she was insane. I had frizzy red hair, boobs that were way too big, and an ass that you could serve dinner on, but I also had nothing to lose. It was that or stay in the Midwest bagging groceries. And to be fair, Lucy supported me in almost every way possible. She let me sleep on her couch, she loaned me her clothes, she introduced me to everyone she knew, and she pulled what strings she could to get me a few small jobs. Me as a model was basically a disaster. Makeup artists labored to cover up my thousands of freckles. Stylists split dresses down the back at the seams and then safety-pinned them to get me into sample sizes. One hairstylist told me cheerfully that I had the kind of face that was perfect for radio (I still fantasize about cock-punching that asshole). Even with Lucy's sponsorship, I wasn't tall enough, or thin enough, or striking enough to get far. And there is a world of difference between the cover of Paris *Vogue* (Lucy, twice) and modeling clogs and a midi-skirt for a Chico's catalogue (me, once. It was the apex of my career, and I was never called back again).

But I still had food. Maybe I wasn't going to get to go to a culinary institute like I had once dreamed, but I had waitressed my way through high school and was more than willing to start at the bottom of the Manhattan food chain.

I bussed tables. I was a hostess. I did time behind the bar, and in a tiny skirt and fishnets as a cocktail waitress. I got into the kitchens anytime I possibly could (which was not very often—in those days, a woman in the back was considered poison). And in my downtime, I read everything I could lay my hands on. I read Calvin Trillin and Ruth Reichl and M. F. K. Fisher and Laurie Colwin. I read Jeffrey Steingarten and Julia Child and James Beard and Madhur Jaffrey. I read, and I shopped at the farmers' markets and the Village cheesemongers and the Italian butchers and the fish places in Chinatown. I cooked in my tiny little galley kitchen with a two-burner stove and inconsistent oven, turning out dish after dish and meal after meal.

And, even more importantly, I ate. New York City is the best place in the world if you are hungry. And I was starving.

I never agreed to a date unless there was food involved. A man could have had an IQ of five and smell like infected feet, but if he offered me a meal at some place above my pay grade, I was in. I cut a swath through the New York restaurant scene, eating out at every meal I could manage. And then one day I just happened to go out with the right guy—a guy who watched me put away seven courses while I kept up a running commentary about everything I shoved into my mouth—and who just happened to edit an up-and-coming little magazine that just happened to need a food critic.

Those were the glory years. An expense account and open access to any restaurant in the city. I tried to remain anonymous at first, but word got out fast, and it was a little hard to hide my head of flaming curls and girl-next-door, Midwestern face in a sea of sophisticated New Yorkers. So I gave up and let restaurants do their best by me, and wrote about them based on that.

But, maybe precisely because I was eating the best food all the time, I got jaded. It was all so over the top. The rich sauces and the strange cuts of meat and the tiny, jewel-like vegetables and the teetering architectural presentations . . . Chefs were tripping over themselves to impress me, and after a while, nothing really did.

So I quit. I got the idea for my book, resigned my position at the magazine, and started doing guerrilla dinners in my apartment to make ends meet while I wrote it. The dinners were a carefully choreographed freak show and I hated them. Every night I would cook for wealthy voyeurs and aesthetes, people whose palates were as jaded and overtaxed as mine was. They didn't really care about what actually tasted good, just as long as it was new and exotic and they could brag about eating it later. I swear, I could have pissed in a bowl and called it bone broth and those assholes would have lapped it up and asked for seconds.

I thought I was done with all that when my book came out. I thought I had finally caught up—at least a little bit—with my friends. But lately it was looking to be as much of a failure as anything else I had ever tried. It didn't even get a second printing.

And so now here I was, once again having to reinvent myself. But this time I was in my forties. And I was worn-down, and I was disappointed, and I was tired.

And, honestly, I just wasn't that hungry anymore.

The waiter put a bowl of soup down on the table in front of me.

The soup was a light green, almost white. There was a small, brighter green, quivering square of gelatin floating in the center. I brushed my finger against the dark blue bowl. It was chilled. I rolled my eyes. *Vichyssoise.* Cold potato and leek soup. Not a terrible thing at all, but certainly nothing new.

So much for this chef blowing my mind, I thought as I dipped my spoon in and took a bite.

It was not vichyssoise.

It was . . . it was creamy and cold but also slightly sweet and spicy. There was fruit—I was almost certain it was some kind of melon, but damned if I knew what kind of melon it was. I took another bite. Cucumber? Ground almonds? So, a white gazpacho? No. I wouldn't call it gazpacho, either. I spooned up the green square, which instantly melted as it touched my lips, and my entire mouth was filled with the brightest, most intense herbal flavor. Basil, for certain. And mint. And Jesus, was that lovage? And then, after I took the next bite, I realized that the green square had changed the entire flavor of the soup. Now the spice was stronger than the sweet, and I could definitely taste apple, not melon. It was like that scene in *Willy Wonka* when Violet chews the gum and she has tomato soup that turns into roast beef that turns into blueberry pie. I scraped the bottom of the bowl, just barely keeping myself from licking it clean. Then I stood up.

"Where's the kitchen?" I called over to Lotta.

She smirked at me. "I told you so," she said.

"Where's the kitchen?" I repeated insistently.

Omari pointed out one of the doorways. "To the left," he said.

I turned and starting marching out of the room.

"Hey, Billy!" Omari laughed. "Please tell Ethan that we very much enjoyed the soup!"

chapter 3

I followed the crowd of waiters down the hall. I was pretty sure that I was heading for the second kitchen—the restaurant-grade, working kitchen that some wealthy people kept for catering and parties, and that was nothing like their main kitchen: the sun-drenched, showboat everyday kitchen with the pretty little AGA that they used to put the kettle on for tea each morning.

I made my way into the cavernous room and noted the twin ten-burner Vulcan stoves; the enormous, steamy dish machine, where a white-aproned busboy was expertly stacking dirty glassware; the double sinks where you could hose down a half-grown child if necessary. The stainless-steel wall of refrigeration. The workstations all set up with their *mise en place*. The bright, fluorescent ceiling light. The no-frills, spray-it-down floor and tile. Yes. Definitely the second kitchen.

I stood back for a moment, enjoying the noise and smell and fire and choreography of what was, essentially, a working restaurant. I had been the audience for so long now, it felt like years since I'd slipped backstage.

This crew was no bored housewife's hobby catering company. This crew moved with precision and grace. Knives were flying, red-hot pots were being flung into the air, cooks were missing each other by inches as they ducked and swerved and moved around each other, avoiding collision with the built-in sonar of longtime professionals.

I tried to pick out the chef. Usually it was easy—look for the burly older dude (and nine times out of ten, he was a dude) who moved from station to station tasting, pointing, barking orders, and getting his way. Usually this guy charged around acting like he had a two-foot dick and balls the size of cantaloupes. In my experience, there was no one more unbearably macho than a chef in his own kitchen. But as my eyes flicked around the room, I didn't see that guy.

In fact, there were quite a few women here. I knew this had become an increasingly common sight since my days behind the scenes, but it still surprised me to see that nearly half the staff was female.

And young. Everyone was very young. Which was even weirder. Aside from the typical masculinity, restaurant kitchens were usually pretty diverse places. There were always multiple languages being spoken, a wide range of races and cultures—because every society in the world produced cooks—and definitely a span in age. There were teens and young adults—porters and stewards and dishwashers and prep cooks cleaning and organizing and chopping piles of onions and paying their dues. There were the cooks in their prime—the sous-chef and the pastry chef and, of course, the executive chef himself. And there were usually a few old-timers around, as well, people who had put in a lifetime in the kitchen, who knew no other way. They had various jobs but were often kept around out of pure sentimentality, because, let's face it, cooking is fucking hard on a body and it will break you down if you do it for too long.

But this crew was uniformly young. No one over thirty-five, if I had to guess. And there was something else—they worked as if no one had to be told what to do, each a completely competent expert in their own task.

This kitchen lacked *fear*, I suddenly realized.

"Can I help you?" came a soft voice from behind me.

I turned to face someone I assumed to be a busboy. He was probably twenty-five, tall and slim, with longish, straight black hair; a large, sharp nose; dark eyes under heavy eyebrows; and smooth, golden skin. His arms were, incongruously, full of pink roses. He was wearing jeans and a pristine white T-shirt and apron, and he smiled at me politely while at the same time tracking the room over my shoulder.

He had large tattoos on both of his sinewy forearms. A swirling, colorful, phoenix-like bird on his left arm, and a photorealistic, life-size black-and-white image of a chef's knife on the other.

I was startled to feel a sharp throb of lust in my belly. Ink was not usually my thing.

"I'm looking for the chef," I said. "I think his name is Ethan Something?"

"Ethan Rahimi, that's me."

Not fair, I inwardly groaned. *This dude is a fucking child.*

"You're too young," I blurted.

He raised his eyebrows. "For what?" he said.

I shook my head. "Shit. Sorry. That was rude. I was just expecting . . . Never mind. I'm Billy Sitwell and I—"

"Chef! Chef!" A short, round woman with a blue fauxhawk shouldered past me. "Are those my roses?"

He handed the bunch over to her. "Straight from the garden, Marta."

She bent her face to inhale their fragrance and then looked up at him. "Took your time," she snapped as she hurried back to her station.

He rolled his eyes. "Despite my childlike demeanor," he deadpanned, "I obviously have the full respect of my employees."

"You know how long it takes to make a rose jam?" challenged Marta from across the room as she frantically plucked petals. "We're going to be lucky if the guests get their dessert before midnight!"

"I'm sure you'll get it done," he answered. He looked back at me. "Pastry chefs, so temperamental."

"Fuck you, Chef!" called Marta cheerfully.

"Anyway," he said, stepping past me, "if you'll excuse me, I should really get back to my kitchen. I just wasted fifteen minutes stripping Omari's rose garden." He looked back. "Don't tell him it was me."

"Wait," I said. "Your soup. What—"

He nodded. Not surprised. "It was melon. Persian melon."

"But," I said, "I've had Persian melon before and I've never tasted—"

"I'm sorry," he said, picking up a spoon and heading for a stove, "I would love to talk to you about this some other time, but I really need to get back to work right now."

"Of course," I said. I knew he'd already been patient.

"You've never tasted anything like that because he grew it himself," said the burly guy standing next to me chopping walnuts. "He crossbred it—Persian melon and some weird Japanese honeydew he smuggled home from Tokyo. He has his own goddamn greenhouse. There's nothing happening in this kitchen that he doesn't have a direct hand in. We call him the fundamentalist foodie." He snickered.

Intrigued, I looked at Ethan's back as he stirred and tasted something on the stove.

As if he could feel my gaze, he looked over his shoulder. "Hey, wait," he said, "are you the same Billy Sitwell who used to review for *Gastro Eat?*"

"I am," I said.

"I have a restaurant in Kingston—you know, in Ulster County. It's called Huma. You should come up and see it sometime."

I wrinkled my nose. *Kingston? Ulster County? What the hell?*

"I will," I said.

And I was surprised to realize that I really meant it.

chapter 4

Manhattan

Ever since we were girls, Lucy had always found it easy to talk me into things.

"It will look amazing," she assured me as I wrinkled my nose at the bright pink color her hairstylist, James, was mixing up in front of me.

"It looks like a flamingo ate a shrimp cocktail and then puked it all up again," I said.

James put the tips of his fingers on my temples and turned my head one way and then the other. "Don't worry, it will be incredibly subtle."

"What's the process called again? 'Sober'?"

"Ha ha," said Lucy dryly. "It's called 'sombre.' Like, a softer version of ombre."

"Except it's pink."

"That's because your hair is red and there needs to be gradations of color."

"What if we don't color it?" I said, a little desperately. "How about we just cut it?"

"Billy," said James sternly, as he ran his fingers through my hair, "do you know how much I cost?"

I actually didn't, because Lucy was paying. "A late birthday present," she had insisted, and when I reminded her that she had bought me a perfectly nice bracelet for my birthday, she said, "Okay, an early Christmas present then. But something has to be done with your hair."

"No, I do not know how much you cost," I said to James, "and I don't think I want to know."

"A lot. I get paid a lot."

"A ridiculous amount," agreed Lucy.

"And do you know why I get paid this ridiculous amount of money?"

Because you're super-hot, and lonely society women like to pretend you're going to go down on them in the salon chair? I thought.

"Because you're good?" I said out loud.

"Because I'm the best," he assured me. "So just sit back and let me do my thing."

"Just don't make me look like fucking Strawberry Shortcake," I grumbled as he tipped my head back and started brushing on the color.

"It's unacceptably hip," I said later as I gazed into a mirror across the bar. "And it's totally, totally pink."

Lucy shook her head and sipped her martini. "It's barely pink and it looks absolutely cutting edge."

"Yes, exactly. It looks like I'm trying too hard. I don't have any desire to look like a twenty-two-year-old DUMBO douche."

Lucy handed me a menu. "Want to get some food?" she said. "What's good here?"

"Don't try and change the subject. I know what you're doing." But I bent my head and studied the menu.

Seared foie gras with aubergine foam and—

I slammed the menu down. "This is bullshit."

Lucy raised an eyebrow at me.

"Pink hair, fucking eggplant foam. This city is driving me nuts."

Lucy took another drink. "Would you rather be back in the Midwest?" she said.

"No, I would rather be someplace that actually surprised me once in a while. I feel like I've seen this menu all over town. Fusion this and foams that. Tea-smoked bullshit. Liquid nitrogen edible balloons of pretentiousness. All this food, and nothing I want to eat."

My mind flashed back to Lotta's wedding. It had been two weeks, and I had thought about that meal—and the chef who'd prepared it—more times than I could count.

I pushed the menu away. "Let's go get some pizza."

Lucy's phone beeped and she quickly checked it and shook her head. "Actually, I can't. I have to get home. Titus needs me."

"Oh, come on," I said, suddenly feeling a little guilty. "I promise I won't bitch anymore. I'm sorry I've been such a whiny cunt."

Lucy laughed. "You really have been," she agreed. "But I honestly need to go."

My bad mood returned. "Fine," I said. "He calls. You answer. Go home to lover boy. I'll stay here and eat a lollipop made out of octopus or whatever the fuck they're serving."

Lucy smiled at me and gathered up her things. "Your hair really does look fantastic, Bill," she said.

I waved her out the door, and picked up the menu again.

Apricot gelée over medallions of—

I groaned, tilted back the rest of my drink, tossed some money on the bar, and left.

It started to rain on my way back home. The kind of late-summer New York rain that appears out of nowhere and comes down in sheets. I didn't care. I just kept walking and let myself get drenched. New hair be damned. I was hot and annoyed, and despite the big, greasy pepperoni slice I had bolted down, I still felt hungry and dissatisfied.

Impulsively, I waved down a cab and instructed the driver to go uptown, ignoring the censorious look he gave me as I soaked his backseat.

You home? I texted.

Yup, came the instant answer.

I'm coming over . . . now.

Lucky me.

Brett smiled when he opened the door and found me wet and dripping all over his doorstep.

"You're a mess, Sitwell," he said. Then he squinted at me. "Is your hair pink?"

"Shut up and make me a drink," I ordered as I stalked past him.

He laughed and headed to his kitchen.

"Can I borrow a towel?" I called out to him.

"In the hall closet," he called back.

I opened up the closet and smiled. Stacks of soft, thick, Egyptian cotton towels and pristine, perfectly folded sheets were piled in front of me. I grabbed a big, thirsty bath sheet and sighed happily as I wrapped it around my hair. Maybe Brett wasn't perfect, but he was the only man I knew who kept his linens in such good order.

"Here," he said, handing me a whisky and water as I walked into his kitchen.

I took a greedy gulp and closed my eyes in pleasure as the smooth drink burned down my throat and warmed me from the inside.

"Feel better?" he asked.

I gazed at him suspiciously. "Who said I was feeling bad?"

He laughed again. "You looked like you were ready to kick a puppy when you marched in here."

I couldn't help smiling a little before I took another drink.

"Come on," he said, draping an arm over my shoulder. "Let's go sit down."

"I've got a better idea," I said, turning toward him and fitting my body to his. "Let's go lie down."

"You know what's wrong with you, Sitwell?" said Brett as he lounged in his bed, the sheets pulled up just enough to make him barely decent. "You're always in a hurry to get out of here."

I shot him a look as I was pulling on my still-wet jeans. "I told you, I have somewhere I need to be."

He stretched his arms behind his head and the sheet slipped. Oops. No longer decent.

"You don't have anywhere you need to be."

I kept pulling on my clothes, not looking at him. He was right, but I didn't want him to know that. "Yes, I do."

He shook his head. "It's not that I mind being used for sex. I mean, hell, you know that I pretty much *love* being used for sex. But you also know that's not all this is, right?"

I paused. "What do you mean?"

He smirked at me. "'What do you mean?'" he said, pitching his voice into an innocent little squeak.

"Was that supposed to be me? I don't sound like that."

He sat up. "You know, I have dated a lot of women."

I snorted. "Yeah, well, congratulations."

"And I've never had a relationship that I could see past a month. I mean, I was willing to make plans for weekends out of town, or to be someone's date to a wedding, but I never thought, *I wonder what we'll be doing in ten years.* Except with you. I think that kind of stuff about you all the time."

I stilled. "Do you?" I tried to keep my voice neutral.

"And I know you don't feel the same way. Or at least I know you want to believe that you don't feel the same way. But I also know that you will. Eventually."

"Oh?" I said. I fought back my impulse to bolt out of the room.

"Yup. I'm just waiting for the moment when you come to your senses and take one-tenth of the passion you feel about food and your work and direct it toward me. Once that happens, it's going to be fucking fireworks."

I looked around desperately. "My purse. Do you know where I put my purse?"

He laughed. "It's in the kitchen."

I started toward the door.

"I don't mind waiting, Sitwell!" he called as I escaped out into the hallway. "And I've got all the time in the world!"

As soon as I got back to my apartment that night, I bought a bus ticket to Kingston.

chapter 5

The River House, Airbnb
Kingston, NY

I was in the kitchen of my dreams.

The kitchen of my dreams was not made of granite and polished cherrywood and filled with the latest stainless-steel gadgets. Nor was it a cold, scientific, industrial lab, either. The kitchen of my dreams had soul and history and wear. The kitchen of my dreams had quirkiness and comfort. The kitchen of my dreams had a view.

With its sweet little Magic Chef stove, its squat Frigidaire, and its deep, enamel farmhouse sink, you could never comfortably cook for two hundred people here. But this kitchen was warm, and obviously well loved, and at least five times the size of my tiny galley in Manhattan. The floors were of wide-board pumpkin pine, mended here and there with patches of hammered copper; the ample countertops were scarred butcher block; and the island was made out of a giant slab of sealed bluestone. I touched the cool surface, imagining generations of women rolling out perfect piecrust and working chilled butter into a delicate puff pastry.

Sarah would have turned up her nose, I thought, and Lotta simply had zero interest in kitchens. But Lucy would have liked it. She would have recognized it. It felt like one of the kitchens we'd grown up with.

The late-afternoon sun poured through an enormous window and sparkled off the glass-fronted cabinets. There was a fireplace practically big enough for me to stand up in, topped with an ancient and pocked piece of lumber, which served as its mantel. I walked to the sink and looked out over the plumy green of the treetops. I could see the Hudson River rolling down below like a slow-moving giant.

I turned around. "Pardon my French, but this is fucking amazing."

The owner of the kitchen, a tottering little woman named Portia, grinned at me in return and patted her sparse gray hair in a pleased sort of way. "Know anyone who's looking for a long-term rental?" she said. Her voice was rusty, as if she didn't use it very often. "Now that the summer season is almost over, I'd like to have someone more steady renting here. Vacation bookings really drop off once the weather changes."

I shook my head regretfully. "Not really. I'm only here for the weekend. But just out of curiosity, how much?" I asked.

She named a price that was a third of what I paid for my one-bedroom in Manhattan.

"Per week?" I wondered aloud.

She laughed. "Per month. You've obviously lived in the city too long, darlin'."

I gave her a rueful smile. "Apparently. Anyway, I'll let you know if I think of anyone. Is there anything else you need to show me about the place?"

She had already given me the tour. Four bedrooms upstairs. Two bathrooms, one up, one down. Twin parlors up front, separated by a wide hallway. There was a cheery red woodstove in one and a small fireplace in the other. And off the kitchen was a formal dining room with built-in breakfronts and a round, claw-foot table that could easily seat ten.

There was a small dock at the river, Portia explained, and if I was comfortable in a boat, there was even a little canoe I was welcome to use.

I was not comfortable in a boat, but I wondered if maybe I could learn to be.

You know how sometimes you see a house and it instantly feels familiar, like the place has just been waiting for you to show up? That was this house. Even the smell, a fecund odor from the river outside and the accumulated scent of years of sweet woodsmoke and lemon furniture polish on the inside, made me feel like I was in exactly the right spot for once.

"I think that's all," said Portia. "But I'll just be at my place in town if you need me."

"Do you live there all the time?" I asked.

She nodded. "Yes, ever since my husband died about ten years ago. This was meant to be a family house. I never felt right living here alone. So I moved into a little cottage in the village and started renting this place out."

She left me with the key and a list of instructions.

I started unloading some groceries I'd brought up from the city. Not knowing what I could buy here, I'd visited the Union Square greenmarket before coming up and procured a glass bottle of whole milk, cream floating on the top, from Ronnybrook Farm, a chunk of oozy goat cheese, a half dozen duck eggs, some early apples, and a nice loaf of Balthazar's sourdough bread. I pulled a bottle of Tibouren rosé out of my bag and hesitated for a moment, knowing it would taste better if I was patient enough to let it chill, but instead, I poured myself a small glass, admiring the gorgeous apricot-pink color and slightly floral scent, and then put the bottle in the fridge.

I carried my glass out onto the wraparound porch and perched on a chipped wicker chair. The river sparkled and roiled, reflecting the sinking sun in little gold glimmers and sparks. It was still technically summer, but the light had the low, syrupy quality of autumn already. A pleasant breeze ruffled through the bright green trees all around me. A bit upstream, I could make out a small, white lighthouse on a tiny island.

A bird— *No wait.* I shuddered. *A fucking bat* swooped through the yard in front of me.

I hurriedly downed the wine and went back inside.

I went into food-critic mode when I slipped into Huma that night. My plan was to come in, eat, and then sneak back out again. I wore my usual uniform: dark jeans with ankle boots, and a black bodysuit. I just wanted to fade into the background and enjoy my meal, but I touched my hair, self-conscious. Those fucking sombre "rose-gold highlights" were still distinctly pink. I felt like mutton dressed as lamb.

I was also slightly embarrassed that I had taken the chef up on his offer with such alacrity. It had only been three weeks since Lotta's wedding. The poor guy was probably going to think I was stalking him. But I'd needed to get out of the city. Even before Brett had spooked me with his crazy talk about ten years down the line, I had been ready for a break. And I just couldn't shake the wedding meal. I'd spent almost every night since lying in bed and soothing myself to sleep by reliving every haunting, delicious bite (I might have also dwelled upon Ethan's muscular, tanned, and tattooed forearms, but that was an entirely different kind of self-soothing).

It was late, nearly nine, but the restaurant was still crowded. It was a small space—it couldn't have seated more than two dozen people—and the décor was something I immediately termed Industrial-Country. There were wooden tables that looked like someone had nailed them together in their backyard, and they were flanked by neon-orange metal chairs and benches. The stemware and the cutlery was purposefully mismatched, and I almost laughed to see the ubiquitous blue mason jar of wildflowers crowning every four-top.

"Just you, ma'am?" asked the hostess. She was tall and dark-haired and beautiful, and had ear gauges large enough to poke a baby's fist through.

I nodded, and she led me to a small table tucked into a corner. It was half in the shadows, which suited me just fine.

I ran my hand over the rough surface of the table. *Splinter city*, I thought as I shook my head. I'd seen this before. Some restaurants were definitely taking this whole "raw, real, and authentic" thing way too far. If you could potentially get tetanus from eating at a place, they should probably rethink the décor.

I looked at the menu. It had been handwritten by someone who could not claim penmanship as their strength and it seemed to be laid out in a narrative form. I squinted in the dim candlelight. *"The night my father taught me to shave . . ."*

Wait, what? Surely that can't be right . . . Then I thought, *Fuck it, no one's looking at me*, and dug into my bag for my cheaters.

I had only started wearing glasses about a year ago. I hadn't told the girls. I didn't want to tell anyone. I mean, there were things I had control over when it came to aging. I was merciless with my body, beating back the years with hours at the gym and on the running trails of Central Park. I had dyed my hair regularly since I was in my twenties, so I didn't even actually know if I had any gray. And my round, Midwestern cheeks had actually turned out to be an asset as I'd aged. I mean, I'd been carded just last month. But I'd noticed more and more often that things were starting to change—an ongoing twinge in my knee, a certain subtle slackness to the skin at my elbows, and my optometrist had laughed in my face when I'd tried to read the small print at my last exam, so I'd started carting the glasses around for emergencies like this.

"Can I get you a predinner drink?"

I dropped the menu. The waiter, a muscular twenty-something with a blinding smile, had apparently materialized out of nowhere. I snatched the glasses off my nose and stuffed them under my thigh. "Um, yes. What would you recommend?"

He smiled even wider. "The house cocktail is called the Kingston. It's our own kitchen-infused rosemary vodka with triple sec and fresh-squeezed Meyer lemon juice. The lemons were grown in the chef's greenhouse, and the rosemary is from the chef's own garden."

I laughed. "Of course it is. I guess I better start with that, then."

He beamed back at me. "Excellent."

After he turned his back, I reached for my glasses again, only to realize that I had cracked one of the lenses. I shook my head in disgust. That's what I got for being so fucking vain. I pushed the broken glasses back into my purse and groped for my phone, scrolling. Five unanswered texts from Lucy.

The waiter returned with my drink, and since I wasn't about to admit that my eyes were too old to read the goddamn artisanal, probably handmade, hemp-paper menu, I played my fail-safe hand.

"Chef's choice," I said.

His face lit up with the kind of beatific grin that belongs on a newly converted religious fanatic. "Oh," he said breathlessly. "Oh, that's wonderful. You won't regret it, ma'am."

He hurried away as I shook my head over being called "ma'am" for the second time that night.

I was well into my second Kingston cocktail and feeling pretty good when Chef Ethan Rahimi plunked himself down at my table.

I blinked at him, relieved that I had shattered my glasses beyond repair. He looked at me, a puzzled smile on his face.

I realized, with a little sting, that he couldn't figure out how he knew me.

"Billy Sitwell?" I said. "We met at Lotta and Omari's wedding? I invaded your kitchen?"

He instantly relaxed. "Ah, that's right. Your hair is different."

I touched a pink curl, embarrassed. "The result of an overzealously hip hairstylist," I said.

He cocked his head, examining me. "I like it. It's cool."

I felt a rush of pleasure and then instantly was disgusted with myself. *What did I care what this infant thought was cool?*

"So, anyway," he said, "what brings you up here?"

For a moment I considered lying, but then I thought, *Why bother?* "You invited me," I reminded him. "And I was hungry."

A slow, sexy smile blossomed over his face. Man, his lower lip was hot. Full and pouty. I wanted to bite it.

Then I heard Lucy's voice in my head. *Cut it out, Grandma. He's a child.*

I had dated plenty of younger men. In fact, there had been a time, not so long ago, when pretty much *all* I had dated was younger men. And I loved dating those men for lots of reasons. I loved them for their cheerful sexual willingness, stamina, and almost instant recovery time. I had dated some guys whose ability to fuck was akin to one of those endless scarves that magicians just keep pulling and pulling out of their sleeves. I loved that none of these men came with ex-wives or half-grown kids, I truly appreciated that none of them had yet had the chance to develop years' worth of bad bachelor habits that they had let fester into rigid, unattractive eccentricities and compulsions. And I absolutely loved the easy emotional simplicity of a younger man, the way that I was almost 99 percent certain that I was going to have a good time, enjoy myself, and then happily walk away, because I never, ever fell in love.

But see, the reasons I knew I would never fall in love with these guys were the same reasons I had finally decided to stop dating them. Younger men were clingy and addled and benignly thoughtless. They were like adorable puppies whom no one had bothered to house-train yet, and I was not willing to be the one who walked around with a bunch of freeze-dried liver treats in my pocket, rewarding them every time they managed to piddle outside. After the last younger guy I'd been dating (a firefighter, for fuck's sake!) had pouted for a week when I refused to come take care of him while he was in bed with a cold (I had a major deadline, I could not risk getting sick, and he had a goddamn *cold*; it wasn't like he was dying of cancer), I'd decided I was done. I was nobody's mommy, and I wanted to keep it that way.

But this guy . . . with his dark sloe eyes and genius sense of cuisine, his burn-scarred hands and sly smile . . .

"I came out here to meet the woman who ordered chef's choice," he said. "I like to talk to my customers before I cook for them." He leaned back and cocked his head. "But you know what? I have a better idea. We're only about half an hour before closing. Can you wait it out? I'll feed you, I promise. But there's something I want to show you first."

I shrugged, trying not to show how the words *I'll feed you, I promise* made the breath hitch in my chest. "I guess I can have another drink," I allowed.

He reached over and briefly squeezed my wrist and then stood. "Good, good. I'll make it worth your while."

It took much, much longer than half an hour, of course. The last customers, a pair of twenty-somethings in matching horn-rims and lumberjack plaid, lingered over their coffee and shared dessert (some sort of peach, almond, and meringue concoction that I eyed enviously from my table). The staff were blowing out the candles and sweeping up and wiping down and stacking the chairs. I nursed my drink and watched uncomfortably, feeling the need to explain to every passing waiter that I was waiting for Ethan.

I wondered what the girls would think if they saw me, hanging around like a foodie groupie in this weird little restaurant in this strange little town.

They would laugh, I thought, *and make merciless fucking fun of me.*

I decided to leave. It was ridiculous. It was almost eleven o'clock, I was starving, a little drunk, and this kid hadn't even bothered to come out and apologize for making me wait. I threw some money on the table to settle my bill and then marched over behind the bar and stuck my head through the kitchen doors.

"Hey, Chef," I called, "I think I'm going to go."

Ethan jerked his head from where he was hunched over the stove, stirring something in a pot. He blinked his eyes as if he had just woken up. "Oh, shit. Billy," he said. "God, I'm so sorry. I didn't realize how late it was. It's the stupidest thing, one of my cooks broke his sauce . . . and we need a ton of it for brunch tomorrow . . . and I'm just trying to fix it before we leave."

I walked over, noting that the kitchen was much smaller and more ill-equipped than Omari's second kitchen had been. There were half a dozen people wedged in there, each diligently cleaning their stations and packing up their leftovers.

"What is it?" I asked, craning my neck to see into his big stainless-steel saucepan.

"Just a simple butter sauce," he said. "I can fix it with beaten egg yolk, but it's a pain in the ass because you have to add the warm sauce to the egg spoonful by spoonful."

I wrinkled my nose. "Why not just start over?"

His cheeks flushed and he shrugged. "Why waste four pounds of butter?"

I raised my eyebrows. Most places I'd worked at wouldn't have thought twice about pouring that sauce into the garbage. "Where's another bowl?" I asked, and he handed me a copper bowl, a whisk, and three eggs.

We must have spent thirty minutes standing side by side, companionably adding warm sauce, drop by drop, to the egg mixture, beating it, careful not to let the eggs scramble, and then adding some more. We didn't talk much, focusing on the task at hand, but I didn't mind. I liked repetitive, time-consuming tasks in the kitchen. Stirring risotto, shelling peas, pitting cherries—it all relaxed me. It was the closest I ever got to meditation.

Finally, we had a saucepan of gorgeous, creamy, sun-yellow sauce.

Ethan scooped up a spoonful. "Here, taste it."

I closed my eyes and accepted the bite.

Maybe it was because I was well past starving, but the sauce was extraordinary. Smooth and unctuous, but with just the right little explosion of acidic tang at the end. I imagined it drizzled over a whole feast of dishes—it could go sweet or savory: on apple crepes or replacing hollandaise on eggs Benedict, poured over roasted asparagus or brushed onto warm baking-powder biscuits . . . I took another taste and decided I could probably just sit down and eat a bowl of it plain.

"Needs salt," I said, not quite willing to tip him off to my total admiration.

Ethan tasted it himself and laughed. "It does not," he said.

I rolled my eyes. "Okay, it doesn't. It's perfect."

"Awesome," he said. "Hey, Kai?"

A tall, pretty, blond woman with a glittering nose ring turned from the back of kitchen, where she had been stacking glasses. "*Oui, Chef?*" she said.

"This is Billy. Billy, this is Kai. She's our bartender and resident wine expert."

I nodded at her. She nodded back. Her expression was cool and I could feel her large blue eyes sweep over me curiously.

"Anyway, Kai, can you hang around until this hits room temp and then pack it up?"

"*Oui*, Chef."

He snorted and shook his head. "Kai just spent some time working in Europe," he said to me. He raised his voice. "You don't have to say *oui*, Kai."

She gave him a smirk and turned her back to him. "*Oui*, Chef."

He met my eyes, just barely containing a smile. "Okay?" he said.

I nodded and followed him out.

chapter 6

I am an idiot, I thought to myself as we hurtled up a dark mountain road, cutting through mist and blaring around corners. Ethan operated his Dodge Ram truck like he was a teen out joyriding in his parents' car. I was fairly certain that I was not going to live to see morning.

"Deer! Fuck! Deer!" I screeched as a doe and two fawns skittered across the road in front of us.

Ethan didn't even blink as he expertly swerved around them.

"Okay," I said, my heart still pounding, "I may have underestimated your driving skills, but I'm still pretty sure you're taking me somewhere to chop me up and feed me to your morning rush. Where the hell are we going?"

He laughed. "You'll see." He glanced at my feet. "Are those shoes comfortable to walk in?"

"How far?" I asked suspiciously.

"Just a little way. But it might be kind of damp."

I shook my head. "Dude. I just wanted dinner."

He smiled. "I swear, I'll feed you soon."

He pulled into a little inlet on the side of the road and turned off the truck. There was nothing but the dark shadows of trees and road as far as I could see.

I heard Lucy's voice in my head.

Are you fucking crazy, Billy?

"Um," I said.

He scrunched his nose at the darkness outside the windows. "Okay. I can see why you might think I'm going to chop you into little pieces."

I sized him up. "I have a brown belt in Krav Maga and I can bench one-sixty."

He held up his hands. "And I was kicked off my peewee soccer team when I was a kid because I sat down and refused to play."

I laughed and swung my door open with a creak. "All right. Let's see which one of us makes it out alive."

I shivered in the cold autumn air, stretched my arms, and threw back my head. I had never seen a more perfect sky. There was only the tiniest sliver of a moon, and it was half covered in tattered wisps of clouds. Other than that, it was brilliantly clear and the sky was spread so thick with minute, glimmering stars that it seemed to me I could see the actual layers of the universe hanging above us. I was used to the New York City sky, where only the brightest stars shone through. This made me dizzy.

"Wow," I said.

"Yup," said Ethan. "We give good sky up here."

"And where is here again, exactly?" I said. "Are we still in Kingston?"

"No. We're in the Shawangunk Mountains."

I looked at him. "Seriously?"

"They say once you stand in the shadow of the 'Gunks," he intoned, "you will always return home to them."

"Who the fuck is 'they'?" I asked.

He looked at me and laughed, and then grabbed a paper bag from the cab of his truck, took out his cell phone, and switched on the flashlight app. "Okay. You ready? You trust me enough to take a little walk in the woods?"

I shook my head. "Just remember, Chef, you try anything, and I'm taking you down."

The woods were damp, as he had promised. They smelled sweet and green. My heels kept sinking into the soft ground, and if he hadn't had his flashlight, I wouldn't have been able to see my own hand in front of my face.

"I should probably blindfold you," said Ethan. "But I figure you don't live up here, so I can let you in on my secret."

"Wha—" I began to say, but the words died on my lips as his light swept over what looked like a sea of bright orange. "Oh my God," I said. "Are those chanterelles?"

Ethan turned back toward me with a huge grin on his face. "Worth it, right?"

"There must be hundreds!" I was dizzy, calculating how much these mushrooms would go for at a greenmarket in Manhattan.

"It's my secret spot," said Ethan. He took a paring knife out of his pocket and handed it to me. "Have you picked before?"

I shook my head. "Are you sure these are edible?"

"Positive. Don't worry. Just cut them off at the base, and be gentle when you put them in the bag." He took out another knife and kneeled down, propping up his phone so we had light.

I bent down next to him. "But why are we doing this at midnight?" I whispered as we both started harvesting.

"Because it's my secret spot," he repeated. "And if I parked here during the day, other mushroom hunters would find it, too."

"We should take them all!" I enthused, popping a 'shroom the size of my fist into the bag.

He shook his head. "That wouldn't be fair. We'll just take what we can eat tonight." He paused for a moment. "And maybe a few more for the restaurant tomorrow."

We lapsed into silence, making our way through the tiny forest of orange fungi. My eyes adjusted to the darkness and I started seeing details in the woods: the rumpled shapes of ferns, the sprays of little purple asters edging the path. I squinted at the trees looming over us: they looked to be mostly oak, but I could make out the ghostly gray and white peeling bark of a few river birches as well.

A breeze rattled through the leaves, and I heard a distant hooting.

"Oh my God!" I said, grabbing Ethan's arm. "What was that?"

He squinted his eyes and listened. "I think that was a great horned owl."

"Seriously? Can you actually tell them apart just from their call? How long have you lived up here, anyway?"

He shrugged. "I grew up in L.A., but I came here for school across the river. The Culinary Institute of America."

Of course, I thought as I removed my hand from his arm. Suddenly, I felt a little out of my league. When I had first come out to New York, I had dreamed that I would find a way into culinary school. If not the CIA, which was top tier, at least one of the smaller ones that dotted Manhattan. But though I'd taken a few basic knife and sauce classes here and there, I'd never had the time or the money to do a full program. I'd learned on the job (or jobs, I should say) instead. But it truly bugged me that my formal education had ended in high school.

After she was married and quit modeling, Lucy got bored and went on to get her MFA (or, as I liked to call it, Master of the Fucking Arts) at New York University—completely financed by her husband, of course. It's not like she shoved it in my face or anything, but if I thought about it too much, I couldn't help feeling a little gnawing mouse of jealousy in the pit of my stomach.

"Did you like it there?" I asked. I imagined it was heaven.

Ethan cocked his head and considered the question. "Sure," he said at last. "I mean, yeah, of course. I learned a lot, and practically my whole kitchen crew are people I met over there, and they're like my family."

Ah, I thought, *that explains why everyone you employ is so damn young.*

"But sometimes," he went on, "I felt like I was wasting my time and money. That I should have just spent all that tuition on travel, you know? That I could have learned just as much, maybe more, working my way through some great restaurants."

I smiled ruefully. "That's funny, I was just feeling sorry for myself because that's the way I learned. I mean, I didn't get to travel, but I worked at a ton of places in Manhattan."

He cut another mushroom and dropped it in the bag. "I think we've taken as many as we can carry," he said. "Are you hungry?"

"What, are we just going to sit out here in the woods and gnaw them raw?" I asked.

"Would it be weird if I took you back to my place and cooked for you?" He tucked the top of the bag under his chin and placed his arms behind his back. "I promise to keep my hands to myself. Just cooking. Nothing else."

That's too bad, I thought.

Billy! I heard Lucy's voice. *What about Brett?*

We never said we were exclusive, I argued silently.

"I'll chance it," I said to Ethan. "Let's go."

Watching Ethan slice mushrooms was like poetry.

I ached, and not just because his hands were strong and graceful and his smile was sweet and sly. I ached because every slice of mushroom he cut was exactly the same uniform thickness as the one before and the one before that as well, and he wasn't even trying. He was just casually talking to me, taking sips from a small glass of iced vermouth, not even looking at his hands. And then he took a clove of garlic and minced it into perfect, tiny cubes without breaking eye contact with me, and I swear to God, my whole body went up in flames.

But once he handed me a shallow bowl of tagliatelle, tossed with a tangle of the sautéed chanterelles, swirled in a garlic cream and sprinkled with fresh parsley, I forgot about wanting to have sex with him. I mean, I still definitely wanted to have sex with him—no question there—but not before I ate.

"Oh my fucking God," I groaned through a forkful of pasta. The mushrooms were perfect: earthy, slightly spicy, and almost fruity, with the faint taste of apricots. They were crisp on the outside and tender on the inside. They tasted like the forest floor in the best possible way. I had never had mushrooms so transcendentally *wild* before.

I had watched every move Ethan had made, catalogued every ingredient, tracked every technique he had applied, but the dish had still come together in a way that completely surprised me, thrilled me, made me feel I was tasting something altogether *new.*

When I had first moved to New York, not a day had passed when I hadn't had the pleasure of trying something unfamiliar. I had grown up in the suburbs of Middle America. My town was pretty and safe and deeply homogenous. There was one sad little Chinese place, a couple of German restaurants that specialized in various sausages, and any fast food your heart could desire. Mexican food tasted like Taco Bell, pizza was from the Hut, and there was no sushi, no falafel, no Thai, certainly no ramen or soup dumplings. Italian food was a jar of Ragu over spaghetti. And so, my universe exploded when I got to Manhattan and realized that there was a whole world of amazing food that had never passed my lips. It was the gift of novelty, and one that I had sorely missed as of late.

"I don't understand," I said between bites. "It's not like you did anything so special. But this tastes . . ." I was at a loss for words, so I hungrily took another forkful instead.

He smiled. "Maybe it's the context."

I raised my eyebrows. "Sure. Starving me for two hours and then making me think I was going to get murdered in the woods certainly added a delicious frisson."

But he had a point. My most memorable meals hadn't been ten-course extravaganzas loaded with truffle foam and foie gras. If I looked back on the meals I remembered with the most pleasure, they had been as simple as toast, tea, and perfect, glowing, ruby-colored raspberry jam eaten in bed on a rainy morning, or a thick, tender, cornmeal arepa smeared with savory black beans and sprinkled with cotija cheese in a little restaurant in the East Village, where I could see and hear the elderly women in the back gossiping in Spanish while they patted out and grilled each savory little cake by hand.

Ethan took a bite and chewed thoughtfully. "The garlic and parsley are from my own garden. The cream is from a farm down the road. And these mushrooms were literally just growing in the forest."

"So it's all about local for you, huh? Is that what drives your restaurant?"

He wrinkled his nose. "Everyone knows that a sun-warmed to-mato picked from your backyard garden is always going to taste bet-ter than one flown halfway across the world and then left to sit in a refrigerated truck. A pig who grew up foraging for acorns in the woods down the street is going to produce better chops than some poor factory-farmed thing that's never even seen the sun. The Hud-son Valley is the bread basket of New York. Everything you could ever want can be sourced here."

"Sure, sure," I said. "But what about Parmigiano-Reggiano? What about jamón Ibérico? What about a really good Vietnamese fish sauce? Do you go without?"

He shook his head. "You can. There's plenty to eat without hav-ing to resort to imports."

I eyed the tangle of noodles in his bowl. "Is this pasta local?"

His mouth quirked up. "Okay. You caught me. I make a few ex-ceptions. No one around here makes dried pasta like the Italians. Not yet, anyway."

I smiled and took another bite. I was getting full, but I wished I could have ten more bowls.

"Not that I actually ate there, but I liked your restaurant."

He looked at me, searchingly. "Did you? Nothing you'd change?"

I dipped my fork back into my bowl, hesitating. "Well, from what I could see, the food looked amazing but—"

He raised his hand to stop me. "The design. The interior. I know. We're still working on it."

I nodded, relieved that I didn't have to tell him. I could only imagine bringing my friends there. Lotta's sultry voice echoed in my mind. *"Really, Bill? What is this, amateur hour?"*

"It was a choice between what I could make perfect," he said, finishing his drink, "the design or the food. I chose the food." He sighed. "It kills me, honestly. I have so many ideas—but we're so limited by budget."

"Is that why we spent an hour saving the broken sauce?"

He nodded. "I can't afford to waste anything. I have to make every penny count. I had this whole vision when we leased the space, not just for this restaurant, but for a whole cluster of them. I want to go bigger. I want to expand. I can't afford to do anything right now, but I just feel like this isn't enough, you know?"

I considered this. "How long have you been open?"

"Two years."

I laughed. "Have some patience! You have plenty of time. Are you even in the black yet?"

He colored. "I think we'll break even this year," he mumbled.

I nodded. "That's better than most places do."

He shrugged, put his bowl down, and picked up a bottle of wine from the counter. "You want a glass?"

I squinted. "I dunno, what is it?"

He laughed. "Ah, you're a wine snob, eh?"

I cocked my head. "You're not? You had a pretty impressive wine list at Huma."

He shrugged. "I leave most of that to Kai. She's my wine guy."

He popped the cork and poured me a glass. I tasted it. A nice pinot noir. Just right for a cream sauce. "Hmm," I said, "either you got lucky or you're not as dumb as you say."

He leaned toward me. "I like to think of myself as a lucky guy," he said meaningfully.

I sat back and considered him for a moment. He was gorgeous, all lashes and smooth caramel-colored skin, and strong, able hands. I looked at the tattoos on his arms.

"What's this supposed to be?" I said, lightly tracing the phoenix-like bird on his left arm.

He looked at the place where my fingers had touched him. "A Huma bird," he said.

I nodded. "The name of your restaurant."

"It's Persian. Kind of like a phoenix—but it's forever in flight. It doesn't have feet or legs, so it never leaves the air. It's considered extremely lucky to even glimpse one, but if you catch a Huma, it will die. It can't live in captivity."

"You're Iranian?"

He rubbed the tattoo. "Just half. My father immigrated from Iran after the shah fell." He stood, taking our dishes to the sink. "You want dessert?" he asked as he turned on the faucet. "I have some of the last peaches of the season in my pantry."

I couldn't remember the last time someone cooked for me like this—even just a grilled cheese sandwich or an egg. I looked at the way he was standing at the sink, his broad back and slim waist, the way his jeans clung to him in just the right way. I imagined what he would smell like—sweet cream and fresh herbs and a wide-open future.

I stood up, on my way over to where he was doing the dishes, intending to kiss the back of his neck and slowly slide my hands down his chest . . .

Then I heard the sound of the front door opening and a woman's voice calling. "E?" she said. "You still up?"

I sat back down, mortified.

Ethan turned around. "In the kitchen," he called.

Kai—the blond nose ring from the restaurant—walked into the

room. She was out of her white dress shirt and apron and wearing a formfitting tee and jeans that reminded me, once again, just how young this whole crew was.

"Hey, Billy," said Ethan, "you remember Kai, right? My bartender?"

I nodded stiffly as Kai shot me a look of pure malice.

"Hey," she said.

"Kai is just back from out of the country, so she's renting my spare room until she finds something she likes on this side of the river."

I sighed inwardly. *Okay, so he isn't a total asshole. Just . . . twenty-five . . . with a roommate . . . who has a body like Rihanna . . . and is clearly in love with him.*

"It's late," I said. "Maybe I should get back to my place."

Kai blinked innocently. "Oh, don't go on my account. I'm just going to grab a glass of wine and then go to bed." She peered into the pan on the stove. "Oh my God, are those chanterelles?"

"Yeah. You want some?" said Ethan and turned to serve her.

I felt a rush of ugly territorial ownership. I truly didn't know if it was over Ethan or the mushrooms, but I did know that either was entirely unacceptable.

"Yup, okay," I said, "I'm definitely going back to the rental. Can I call an Uber or something?"

Ethan handed the plate to Kai and turned back to me. "Don't be silly," he said, "I'll give you a ride."

chapter 7

S o you didn't even kiss him?" asked Lucy.
She was standing in her kitchen, wearing a kelly-green vintage Diane von Furstenberg wrap dress and a pair of nude Dior peep-toe pumps that made her legs look ten feet long.

"No, I did not kiss him," I said as I arranged a platter of deep-fried sweetbreads. I myself was wearing my trusty black American Apparel dress and sensible flats, and I was doing something I had sworn I would never do again—another private supper club.

Lucy had begged me. She and Titus were hosting a dinner to celebrate a biography that had just been released about his early years in the New York art scene. The guest list was a virtual who's who of Manhattan cognoscenti, and for some reason, Titus had insisted that instead of his usual way of entertaining—a big table at an upscale restaurant where his art hung on the walls and all the waiters knew his drink order—they needed to celebrate at home.

Lucy didn't cook, except breakfast, and Titus sure as hell wasn't going to lift a finger, so she had turned to me, not hesitating to dangle the fact that I needed the money.

Which I did. But that didn't make me any happier to be back in someone else's kitchen, trying, once again, to excite a bunch of food-weary Manhattanites who would probably just pick apart my artfully prepared dishes while they gossiped and got drunk.

"Not even a kiss on the cheek?" asked Lucy. She poked doubtfully at my sweetbreads. "What are these? They look like chicken nuggets."

"Taste one," I said, dipping it into the green goddess dressing and shoving it into her mouth. Her eyes rolled back in her head with pleasure as she chewed. "And no, not on the cheek. Not even a quick blow job in the car."

Lucy swallowed and reached for another sweetbread, but I swatted her hand away.

"Good," she said. "I'm glad. You would have just messed things up with Brett."

I rolled my eyes. "Brett," I said. "I don't know about Brett."

Lucy looked at me sternly. "And what is wrong with Brett? He's funny, he's rich, he's great-looking, he obviously adores you. He's pretty much perfect."

I shrugged, trying to sound nonchalant. "He's great. But haven't I dated fifty different versions of him before? In fact, I was thinking, I need a new photo for online dating. Something younger, edgier. And I wouldn't say no to a wee bit of Photoshop. Can you hook me up with one of your photographer friends, maybe?"

Lucy frowned. "Why would you do that to yourself? Some guy is going to pick you out based on a totally airbrushed, unrealistic picture and then just be disappointed when he actually meets you."

I drizzled the sauce over the sweetbreads. "Well, that's what the dark corners of a bar are for. Camouflage." I shoved the platter at her. "Here. Take these out before they get cold."

Lucy shook her head. "You're just self-sabotaging again, Bill. I like Brett. I think you do, too."

I wrinkled my nose. "He's a money manager."

"So? You could use a money manager. And you know he's more than that."

I shrugged. "Maybe."

"Well, he's better than some baby hipster cook who lives out in the boonies."

"It isn't the boonies. Kingston actually seemed like a cool little town. Ethan told me it's one of the best places in the U.S. for up-and-coming artists. And he's a chef, by the way, not a cook."

She waved her hands. "Cook. Chef. Whatever. You spend one night with this guy, you eat some pasta, but you don't even sleep with him, you'll probably never see him again, and then you come home and decide to upend everything good in your life. Don't you see? You do this every single time. You're afraid something real will happen with Brett, so you find a reason to end it before it even be-gins. Don't be stupid, Bill. You have a real chance at something ap-propriate and secure for once."

And then she popped another sweetbread into her mouth and clacked out of the kitchen carrying the tray.

I blew out a puff of exasperated air and attacked the endive with an overzealous chop. She had done this since we were children—acted like she knew me better than I knew myself. Alternately cod-dled and scolded me and bossed me around. And I suppose I'd needed that. My dad was gone, my mom was long gone. Lucy was the only real family I had.

But . . . what if she was wrong? I'd been letting Lucy call the shots for years—and it wasn't like I had ended up in a great place. Easy for her to talk—easy for them *all* to talk, actually. Lotta, on her monthlong honeymoon in Bali; Sarah, off being trailed by her camera crew and the paparazzi—and here was Lucy in her West Village brownstone, with her world-famous husband, being doted on by the elite of the elite, wearing her six-hundred-dollar Dior shoes, passing off my food as her own. And then me—wearing the same raggedy-ass American Apparel dress, hiding in the kitchen, sweating over a job that made me feel like I was running in place.

I dropped the quartered endive into a dish, added a little water, dotted it with butter, and added a pinch of sugar, a shake or two of white wine vinegar, and salt and pepper, and then slid it into the oven to braise.

For a moment I stood still, remembering the way the light had swept over the golden chanterelles in that dark forest. Remembering the look in Ethan's eyes when he dropped me off back at the rental.

Thank you, he'd said. *This night was kind of magic.*

So fucking corny, and yet when I'd woken up the next morning and cooked myself breakfast in that glorious kitchen, the eastern light streaming in from the river, I had smiled thinking of him saying that to me. And I'd kept smiling as I sat on the porch and ate. Scrambled duck eggs spooned over sourdough toast smeared with goat cheese, and slices of crisp, mottled apple that tasted like autumn. A cup of hot coffee with cream. The morning had been cool and sparkling. The air smelled like woodsmoke and late-blooming roses. And I'd felt hungry and content at the same time . . .

"Billy?"

I jerked my head up. Lucy was back in the kitchen, frowning at me, looking worried.

"What's next?" she asked.

And for a moment, I truly didn't know.

We were running down the West Side Highway toward Battery Park. It was our regular Tuesday girls' night out and even though everyone else had just wanted to head straight for Apothéke—a hip botanical bar in Chinatown—I had talked them into coming out early for a quick run.

I glanced back, annoyed. We had started together, but this always happened. Lucy was the only one who could almost keep up with me. She was about five paces behind. Lotta was maybe half a block behind her, and Sarah trailed way behind us all, walking with her hand clutched to her side like she had a stitch.

I rolled my eyes. This was why we always set an ending point. I usually spent the last fifteen minutes of any run jogging in place, waiting for everyone to catch up.

I had compulsively exercised since I was a teen. I ran track in high school, lifted weights and boxed before it was cool for girls, rode my bike everywhere, swam at the local YMCA, and cross-country skied when it got too snowy to run in the winter—anything to keep moving. Now I did a regular series of weekly classes (SoulCycle, barre class, hot yoga) along with a daily two-hour run or swim.

My friends just took it for granted that I worked this hard to stay a solid size eight (even when I had mono for a month and a half and had to eat all my meals through a straw, I had never dipped below a size six. I came from good, solid peasant stock, and I had the ass and hips to prove it), but I had other reasons for working out the way I did.

First of all, I wanted to eat without guilt. I never wanted to turn away a single bite of food because I was worried about the calories. And so my motto was, Work out like a marathon runner; eat like one, too. I figured that if I kept myself in top physical shape, I could always have that warm beignet; that crusty, golden slice from the bread basket; that steaming, fragrant dish of risotto, that extra glass of cabernet. I fucking loved carbs, and I could write an ode to gluten, and sugar was like my bad, fun, irresistible boyfriend, and I wanted the freedom to eat them all without feeling like I was supposed to apologize for every bite I took.

And second, I could hardly be good at what I did for a living and not eat. A good chef regularly tastes what she's cooking, but I had met more than one restaurant worker with food issues. In fact, I had met tons of chefs with food issues—anorexics, orthorexics, bulimics, compulsive overeaters . . . Restaurant kitchens lured them all in like flies to shit. But if a chef isn't tasting, you can tell, because their food sucks. I guarantee it. And I never wanted to be that kind of chef.

But the biggest reason I worked out like I did was that I was pursued by what I thought of as my own small, vicious demon. My mother had literally died of despair, and I knew that I had inherited her tendency toward depression. I beat that monster back in all sorts of ways: therapy, a nice, dependable SSRI when I needed one, getting a certain amount of sunlight each day, a regular sleep schedule, my own version of meditation—but the best, most consistent way of keeping the devil at bay was to keep moving. To literally outrun that motherfucker. I had no intention of giving up. I was not going to get knocked out like my mother had been. And if I had to wear holes in my shoes to keep myself intact and alive, that's what I was going to do.

"Billy," pleaded Lucy, "slow the hell down!" She was breathless and red in the face.

I shook my head. "I'm just going to sprint this last bit," I said. "I'll meet you guys by the bridge like we planned."

"Argh! You suck, you fucking hag!" she shouted as I took off.

I felt a little guilty, but I needed it. I needed to flat-out run. Ever since I had come back from Kingston, I had felt my monster breathing down my neck. I was worried about everything. I was running out of money—I only had twenty thousand left, including the money Lucy and Titus had paid me for the supper club. At one point in my life, twenty thousand would have seemed like a small fortune, but that was before I lived in Manhattan. Now twenty thousand might last me four months, maybe five, if I was very, very careful. And I had come to accept the fact that I was really, really bad at being very, very careful with my money.

Plus, I had just received notice that my rent was going up again, I had nothing on the horizon work-wise, my agent wasn't taking my calls because my publisher had shot down every idea I had pitched for a new book, and even though I knew that they'd all help me if I just asked, the last thing I wanted to do was feel beholden to my friends—or worse yet, Brett—by taking a loan.

I ran even faster, determined to outpace the jagged feeling of anxiety that was opening up in my chest.

What did I want? I wondered as I pounded the sidewalk, pushing my lungs to bursting.

I wanted . . . to work because I loved it, not because I had to. I wanted to feel like I was ahead for once, not struggling to keep up. I wanted to stop waking up at three in the morning caught midway in a sharp, painful gasp for air, my stomach filled with a leaden sense of dread. I wanted to sleep through the night like an exhausted child.

When was the last time I had done that?

I knew the answer without even thinking about it.

It had been that night, that night in that house, after spending time with Ethan. I had fallen asleep the moment my head had touched the pillow, and I hadn't moved until I woke up, rested and relieved, to a view of that sparkling blue river, eight hours later.

I reached the bridge and doubled over, gulping for air. I hung that way for a moment, slowly getting my breath back; then I straightened up and squinted. I could barely even make out the girls, I had left them so far behind.

chapter 8

"The honeymoon was glorious," said Lotta as she stretched out against the red velvet banquette, a cat-with-the-cream kind of grin on her face. "We ate and fucked and slept and then fucked and ate some more. We didn't even leave the villa for the first week. I had no idea, ladies, no idea at all, that sober sex could be this good."

I snorted. "Um, this is just a guess, but maybe sober sex is that awesome because you are having sober sex with Omari frigging Scott. I mean, he was literally voted the sexiest man alive, like, less than six months ago."

Lotta *tsk*ed and shook her head. "He was so embarrassed by that. His publicist threatened to quit if he didn't do it, though." She took a sip of her lurid green cocktail.

Apothéke billed itself as a "cocktail apothecary." It was like a cross between an absinthe den and an upscale juice bar. Lotta was drinking the virgin version of some concoction called Spa Day—

muddled cucumber, aloe, rosewater, lemon, and agave. She said it tasted like the tail end of summer.

"The only fly in the butter," she went on, "was that his ex called ranting about how Sage is having trouble at school. She said that she's on the verge of getting kicked out, but Omari said he's sure she's just exaggerating for effect."

I raised my eyebrows and looked at Sarah and Lucy. "Are you two hearing this?" I demanded. "Lotta's got stepdaughter trouble. Sarah? Lu?"

Sarah looked up from her phone. "I'm sorry," she said peevishly, "but I'm waiting on a text from my producer. He brought the pregnancy story line to the network today. If it doesn't fly, it'll be a whole thing. I'm going to have to call my PR company, BWR, and start from scratch."

"I'm listening," murmured Lucy. She had been staring off into space, and I could tell that she hadn't heard a word Lotta had said.

Lotta looked at Sarah, her brow knitted. "But you're going to have a baby no matter what, right? I mean, you're not actually deciding whether or not to have a child based on the whims of a reality TV show, are you?"

Sarah rolled her eyes. "Of course not. I'm deciding on the timing of when I have a baby based on when it is best for my career."

I laughed. "And what does Brian think about that?"

Sarah shrugged. "He's fine with whatever I want to do."

I dipped my face into my glass to disguise my look of disbelief.

I was drinking something called the Suzuki Method. It had chocolate and smoked artichoke leaves listed among its ingredients, but I mostly tasted the rye and Campari. This drink was strong. I was already feeling pleasantly stoned.

I poked Lucy's arm. "Where'd you go?" I asked.

She half smiled. "Right here the whole time," she said. "Just getting my girls' night on and drinking my Tokyo Drift." She toasted me before taking a large gulp of her foamy cocktail.

I took another drink for courage and cleared my throat. "So, you guys," I said quickly before I could lose my nerve. "I'm thinking about making a serious change."

Lucy blinked. "What do you mean?"

"You know how I went up to Kingston last week? To check out that restaurant?"

"Yes, yes," said Lotta. "And didn't even sleep with my cute chef."

"Well," I said, "I've been thinking that maybe I'll go back up. Maybe stay awhile, actually."

Sarah wrinkled her nose. "In Kingston?" she said incredulously. "Why in the world would you do that?"

"How long is a while?" asked Lucy.

"I don't know," I admitted. "A few months? Maybe longer?"

Lotta pursed her lips. "So you'd give up your apartment?"

I shrugged. "I'm probably going to have to do that anyway. My rent is going up again."

"She's running away from Brett," said Lucy. She sounded angry. "She's afraid that it might actually work out with him, and so she's showing him her ass."

I shook my head. "Jesus, Lulu. I just thought I would take some classes at the CIA, maybe pick up some restaurant work if I found a place I liked. Everything is so cheap up there. I could take my time. My savings would last, like, four times as long."

Lucy's face cleared. "So this is just about money? Well, then you don't have to go. We can always help you with that."

"I don't want to borrow money."

"Then I'll just give you some," said Lotta with a cheerful wave of her hand. "I have more than I know what do with now. I'm sure Omari wouldn't mind."

I sighed in exasperation. "I don't want that, either."

"This is about that boy, isn't it?" said Lucy. "That cook?"

"Chef," I corrected again. "And no. It's not about him. I mean, at least, not like you're implying. I think maybe I want to work with him, though."

Sarah picked up her drink. "You want to work for a twenty-year-old?"

"He's twenty-five."

She raised her brows in response but kept her nose buried in her cocktail.

"Well, you were the one who was talking about Brooklyn," I said defensively.

"I don't think that's a good idea, either!" blurted Lucy.

I looked at her. "Why are you being so weird? You can get to Brooklyn faster than you can get uptown."

She pushed her glass away and stood up. "I'm getting another drink."

"You're not done with that one," I pointed out.

She ignored me. "Anyone else want something?"

We all shook our heads as she stalked away.

Sarah's phone chimed.

"Oh, shit, it's Nelson," she said. She stood up. "I have to take this."

I looked at Lotta, who stared back at me with an amused look on her face. "You should probably get yourself another cocktail." She reached over and picked up my drink. "I'm going to have the rest of this."

I had sex with Brett before I told him about my plan to move. I'd seen him a couple times since he'd announced he'd wait for me, and he seemed to have taken the hint—no more conversations about our future. So I'd relaxed a bit. But I'll admit, I was afraid of telling him about my plans, and hoped that if I threw something hot and fun into the mix, he'd be distracted enough not to get too emotional. Plus, sex with him was generally awesome and I wanted to have it at least one more time before I was completely cut off. I didn't see Brett as the type of dude who would jump on a ninety-minute Trailways bus ride just for a booty call.

We were in bed, naked, slurping pho and drinking whisky sours. Brett couldn't cook, but he was very good at ordering out, and there was an excellent Vietnamese restaurant just down the street from his place. We had been giving it a lot of business lately.

I loved pho. The warm, comforting smell of beef broth spiked with cinnamon, cloves, and star anise; the satisfying slip of the rice noodles; the chewy beef and strands of ribbon tripe; the peppery taste of charred onion and ginger. Brett always had an extra bottle of sriracha around so I could double up on the heat. We were making a mess and getting drips of soup all over the bed, but Brett wasn't picky about things like that. I didn't often sleep over, but if I did, I knew he'd just grab an extra set of (really nice, of course) sheets and remake the bed so we wouldn't have to roll around in lime juice and stray bean sprouts all night long.

"That," I said with satisfaction as I polished off my last bite, "was a great bowl of noodles."

He laughed at me. "You always say that." He reached over and casually brushed a leaf of cilantro off my breast.

I flopped back against the pillows and sighed. "That's because it always is. A well-made bowl of pho is basically my beau ideal of soup."

"Hmm," he said, leaning back beside me and resting his drink on his abs. "I dunno. What about a really good French onion? Or how about that bowl of beef borscht we had at Coney Island that one time? Remember that? That was pretty much nirvana in a spoon."

"Those are good," I allowed, "but think of all the things they lack. They don't have the savory spice, or the heat, or that chewy sweet-and-sour thing like pho does."

He seemed to consider this for a moment. "But the French onion has got cheese," he said. "And I mean, come on, it's *melted cheese.*" He fished the cherry out of his drink and held it by the stem, offering it to me.

I greedily took it. I had already eaten my own cherry.

"No," I pronounced, "you're wrong. Even cheese isn't as good as a good pho. My soup wins. End of discussion."

He shook his head, laughing at me. "Fine. Vietnam wins again. I feel like we just had this conversation about banh mi sandwiches last week."

"Oh, come on, you said yourself that banh mi was the hands-down winner. We didn't even have to discuss it."

He smiled and looked at the clock. "It's still early. You want to catch a movie or something?"

I shook my head. "Nah, it's too cold out."

"Yeah?" he said looking at me slantwise. "You just want to stay in bed, then?"

I felt a little thrill in my stomach. *I could do that,* I thought.

"I gotta tell you something," I forced myself to say instead.

He brushed a lock of hair off my forehead and scooted closer to me: he obviously hadn't given up on the staying-in-bed idea. "Okay," he said. "What's up?"

I bit my lip and looked away from him for a moment; then I looked back.

"Uh-oh," he said, reading the distress in my face. "You're not going to break up with me and ruin pho forever, are you? Because that would just be fucking cruel."

"How can we break up?" I asked. "We were never officially together."

He knit his brows. "We weren't?"

"Well," I said, pulling the sheet up over my chest. "Not officially."

"Huh," he said. "Okay. So are you unofficially breaking up with me, then?"

"No," I said. "I'm not breaking up with you. But . . . I'm thinking about moving. Upstate."

His face relaxed. "Oh. Well, that's not so bad. I mean, how far upstate?"

"Kingston."

"Pssht, that's not upstate. That's just the Hudson Valley."

"Yeah," I said, pleased. "How did you know?"

"My family has a camp in the real upstate—the Adirondacks," he said. "We'd pass through every summer on our way up."

"Seriously? Why didn't you ever tell me?"

He smiled. "There's plenty you don't know about me, Sitwell."

I bit my lip again. "Well, now I guess I might not ever find it all out."

He cocked his head. "Why?"

"Because . . . because if I move up there—"

"I'll come visit," he finished. "Often. What's the point of being my own boss if I can't take some time off and see my girl once in a while?"

I stiffened. "I'm not your girl," I said.

He laughed. "God, you're the worst. Okay, if I don't call you my girl and I bring you some pho, will you let me visit you?"

I looked at him out of the corner of my eye. "And sometimes the borscht?"

"Aha!" he said, grabbing my waist and pulling me on top of him. "I knew you liked the borscht."

chapter 9

Ditmas Park, Brooklyn
House hunting

O h my God, I love it," breathed Sarah. "I mean, it's actually more expensive than my apartment in Manhattan, but, like, three times the space!"

"And," said Lucy's mother, Cheri, "just look at that courtyard!"

It was a gorgeous courtyard. Right off the kitchen, through double French doors, surrounded by a brick wall draped with bright red ivy. There were raised garden beds stuffed with oakleaf hydrangea and massive ostrich ferns, and an inset wall fountain that tinkled musically into a small reflecting pool.

This was the third place we had looked at today. Sarah had insisted on dragging us all on her house hunt through Brooklyn, and the other girls had been surprisingly amenable to the idea. Cheri was obviously having a blast. She had just expanded her real estate business into Brooklyn and was eager to explore the possibilities. So far we had seen an attached five-bedroom brownstone in Cobble Hill and a giant industrial loft in Williamsburg: now we were looking at a stand-alone wood frame in Ditmas Park.

"I don't know." Lucy wrinkled her nose and poked at the kitchen counter. "Tile? So hard to clean."

I snorted. "As if any of you ever clean your own kitchen," I said.

Lucy put her bag on a bar stool so she could try out the gas range. I squinted at it. "What *is* that?"

She picked it back up. "It's Hermès. One of their new 'zero waste' designs. It was stitched out of Birkin scraps."

I wrinkled my nose. "How noble. It looks like a Frankenstein purse."

She rolled her eyes. "It's very green."

"You know who just bought in this neighborhood?" Sarah interrupted with a little trill. "Michelle Williams."

"Yes!" enthused Cheri. "Eight bedrooms. Two point five million. I heard the renovations are going to be spectacular." She turned to Sarah eagerly. "Just think what a great neighbor she'd be. Her and little Mattison."

"Matilda," corrected Lotta. She was lazily sprawled on a chaise longue, wearing a short denim jumpsuit that showed off her long, tan legs to perfection.

Cheri rolled her heavily mascaraed eyes. "All these old-lady names," she said. "What's wrong with Jennifer or Emily?"

"How many bedrooms again?" asked Sarah.

"Hang on." Cheri dug in her bag for her glasses. I turned away, afraid someone would see my telltale blush as she put them on. Don't get me wrong—if I look as good as Cheri does when I hit my sixties, I will count myself one lucky woman, but my cheaters burned in my purse like a guilty secret.

"Yes, okay," she said, squinting at the printout she carried. "Looks like three bedrooms. But the master is an entire floor."

Sarah frowned. "Just three?"

I laughed. "Oh, but wherever shall we put the maid?"

She ignored me. "Do you think the owners would be okay if we came back with the camera crew? Look at that light in the garden. So flattering."

Cheri took out her phone. "I'll ask right now."

I sat down on a stool at the kitchen island. "Where next?" I asked Sarah.

Sarah gave me a strange little smile and shot a glance at Lucy. "You'll see."

"Come on. How many more places are you going to drag us to? I'm starving."

She raised her eyebrows. "Just one more, and then you can eat."

"You know what? The hell with this. I'm about to pass out." And I stood up to check the refrigerator.

"Billy!" hissed Lucy, shocked.

"What kind of sick people are these?" I said, peering into the depths of the Sub-Zero. "They have nothing but mayonnaise, jam, and cranberry juice."

"Probably because some weirdo lookie-loo already ate all their food," volunteered Lotta from her spot on the chaise.

I leaned in and looked more carefully. "Oh, here we go," I said. "Jackpot." I pulled out a white takeout box that smelled like sesame chicken and started to open it.

"Billy Ann Sitwell," barked Cheri as she came back in from the courtyard, "just what do you think you're doing?"

I almost dropped the box. Cheri hadn't been a perfect mother to Lucy by any means—she had been inattentive and inappropriate and inconsistent—but since the fourth grade, she had been pretty much the only mother I had spent any real time with. One time, she had come home early from a date (and by early, I mean before morning) and caught Lucy and me smoking weed in her basement. The stern look on her face as she glared at the box of takeout in my hand made me relive the exact same feelings of panicked guilt that I'd felt as a fourteen-year-old clutching a homemade apple bong.

"Put that back this instant," she ordered.

"But I'm hungry," I whined, even as I meekly complied.

She actually shook her finger at me. "That's no excuse." Then she turned to Sarah, all sweetness again. "The owners are thrilled to be on the show."

Sarah nodded. "Well, of course they are. Who wouldn't be?"

I saw the Airstream as we trudged down the street in Red Hook.

I had no idea why Cheri would even take Sarah to this neighborhood. It was not her style at all. It was arty and gritty and still not entirely gentrified. It had a strong, distinct smell, like industrial debris. It wasn't entirely unpleasant, but I could taste it on my tongue and practically feel it seeping into my clothes and hair. The twenty-something hipsters in carefully torn jeans and ironic T-shirts milled around with working-class families who had obviously lived there for generations. It was the kind of place where one block was crumbling Section 8 housing and the next was filled with young couples who kept chickens in their backyards and beehives on their rooftops. If you wanted to get to Manhattan, you had to take a water taxi.

There was exactly zero chance that Sarah would ever live here.

But just as I was about to point this out, I saw the Airstream parked up against the waterfront, like a giant, gleaming, silver bullet that smelled like melted cheese and cinnamon.

TAMMY'S PLACE, read the sign.

I swerved, heading for the truck.

"Billy!" called Lucy. "Where are you going?"

I ignored her and examined the menu propped up on the counter. *Yes. Perfect.* Grilled cheese sandwiches ("heirloom apple and cave-aged extra-sharp New York cheddar, fig chutney and Gruyère, Gouda, roasted hen-of-the-woods mushrooms and caramelized Walla Walla onions . . .") and fresh apple cider donuts.

"What's your favorite?" I asked the young Asian woman behind the counter. She had a shaved head and a tattoo of a string of musical notes that wound their way around and up her neck and disappeared behind her ear.

"Oh, the fried green tomato and pimiento," she said without hesitation. "I can also split open a warm donut and make you an ice cream sandwich that will make you want to weep, it's so good."

"Yes, and yes," I said, leaning in closer to get a look inside the rig. It was as neat and organized as a ship—with built-in wood cabinets, a sink, and a six-burner stove.

For a moment, Ethan flashed into my mind. The way his knife had flown under his hands while he minced a mound of parsley. The clean, grassy smell of the herb. His grin when he caught me watching him . . .

"Billy," said Sarah as they caught up with me, "can't you wait? I told you we had plans."

"No," I said, shaking aside the memory. "I skipped breakfast." I turned back to the counter. "So, are you Tammy?"

The girl shook her head. "No, I'm Mei Fang, but no one wanted to buy grilled cheese from Mei Fang's Place."

I laughed. "It's a really cool setup," I said.

She shrugged. "Food trucks are on their way out. I'm thinking about selling this and just doing pop-ups instead."

"Really?" said Lucy as she shouldered her way next to me. "No more food trucks?"

I looked at her.

"What? I'm writing an article for *Grub Street.*"

"About food?"

She nodded. "I met the editor at a party and we hit it off. He wants fifteen hundred words on a new food trend. The death of the food truck could be just the thing."

I tried to keep my face neutral, but inside, I was annoyed. Lucy had absolutely no culinary background. Art, fashion, pop culture, maybe—sure. But her writing about food was like me writing about cars. She knew how to eat and I knew how to drive, and that was about it.

She and Mei Fang were already in a spirited conversation about tiffin delivery.

"How much?" I interrupted. "For the Airstream?"

Mei Fang pursed her lips. "Ten thousand dollars. Twelve thousand and I'll throw in my 2001 Kia to tow it with."

For a moment, I imagined doing it. Plunking down more than half my savings, setting up the truck in Battery Park, and selling fancy cheese sandwiches for the rest of my life. Maybe it would solve everything. Maybe it would be exactly what I was looking for.

Or maybe you wouldn't even be able to afford the tolls to get it back to Manhattan, you idiot.

"Are you actually thinking about buying this thing?" asked Lucy. She sounded hopeful.

"Don't be ridiculous," I said. "I'm just buying a sandwich."

chapter 10

Lucy's hand felt cool over my eyes. The air smelled like beeswax and Nag Champa incense. I thought I could detect carpet under my feet.

"Surprise!" said Lucy as she removed her hand. "It's all yours!"

I blinked, looking around. "Wait," I said, confused. "You bought me an apartment?"

They laughed.

"Only for the night," said Lucy. "We Airbnb'd it to give you a chance to really get to know Brooklyn."

"But why?"

Lucy smiled. "I just want you to really consider all your options. Go ahead—check it out."

I walked through the apartment. It was a gorgeous place. Two bedrooms with a sunroom up front; inlaid hardwood floors scattered with worn Turkish carpets; a huge, airy kitchen that opened to a small balcony out back . . .

"Nice," I said. "But—"

"Hey, just think, we can all get filthy drunk tonight and not have to drag our butts back to Manhattan," said Sarah. "Except you, Lotta. Your butt will be sober, of course."

Lotta gave her a wry little smile. "Lucky me."

"So you guys are staying the night, too?" I asked.

Sarah shook her head. "Not here. We booked at the Wythe. You get this place to yourself."

"And I've got plans tonight, too, so I'm going home now, chicks," said Cheri as she kissed us each good-bye. "But have a wonderful time!"

"Um. You all know I've been to Brooklyn before, right?" I said after Cheri left. "Remember how I got lost in Vinegar Hill on that date with the dude who smoked pot and talked about how much I looked like his sister the whole time? And just last month I came out for that vintage show in Carroll Gardens, and it rained and everything smelled like wet wool and I bought that little plaid kilt?"

"That's a great skirt," interjected Lotta. "So fresh."

"And anyway, isn't Airbnb illegal in the city now?"

"Listen," said Lucy, ignoring my questions, "I do not accept that you're leaving the city. I mean, I get that maybe you've been priced out of Manhattan for now. But that doesn't mean you have to get all dramatic and move all the way to Hudson."

"Kingston," I corrected.

"Even worse," said Sarah.

Lucy gestured around the place. "There are lots of other options, and I just think you should explore some of them."

I blinked. "But weren't you bitching about Sarah moving to Brooklyn just last week?"

She shrugged. "That's different. Sarah doesn't need to move to Brooklyn."

"The show needs it," said Sarah. "Duh."

I shook my head. "So this whole day—it wasn't really about Sarah?"

"Oh," said Sarah, "it was really about me. But it just happened to coincide with Lucy's plans for you as well. It was basically a win-win."

"Bill, you can get everything you want without leaving the five boroughs," said Lucy. "Cheap apartment, cool neighborhood—"

"Great restaurants!" piped in Sarah.

"Hot young lumbersexuals," added Lotta. "This place is dripping with single hipster men, and I know how you like a nice bushy beard, Billy."

I laughed. "You guys, this is really sweet but—"

"Shush," said Lucy. "Just give it a chance." She handed me a bag. "I packed everything you'll need. Now let's get ready to go out."

The clothes in the bag weren't mine. Which wasn't unusual. I borrowed clothes from my friends all the time—especially when we were all going out together. Because if I didn't, I'd either have to choose from a few good pieces I had accumulated over the years (things that everyone had seen over and over and yet over again) or slap on something from American Apparel and hope that my accessories and sterling personality could hide the cheap Lycra-and-cotton blend.

It wasn't as if everyone I knew ran around in head-to-toe couture. There were plenty of women who totally pulled off the high/low fashion trick. A six-dollar T-shirt from Target paired with eight-hundred-dollar Frye boots. A Lalo cardigan over an Old Navy slip dress. As long as your hair was right, your skin was good, your abs were firm or firmly tucked into some Spanx, and (here was the tricky part) at least one thing you were wearing cost as much as most people's grocery bill for a month, it worked.

But more and more, lately, I could only afford the low end of the high/low teeter-totter. The few nice things I had—things I had splurged on when I was even more stupid with my money than I was now, things I had been gifted, things I had begged, borrowed, and stuffed down my pants when no one was looking back in the day—the ancient Burberry jacket, the Prada mini, the Valentino booties—were starting to show their age. They were pieces that were meant to be wrapped in acid-free tissue paper and taken out once in a blue moon, not worn barhopping every Saturday night.

And listen, I know I sound like an asshole. I really do. I know that plenty of people would have laughed at my stupid fucking existential fashion dilemma and told me to put on some Gap jeggings and be thankful. But those people were not my friends. My friends bought ten-thousand-dollar Fendi bags as often as they sneezed. My friends believed in fashion like some people believe in prayer, and I can't pretend that some of that zealotry hadn't rubbed off on me over the years.

So that bag full of borrowed finery in my hand was a bit of a loaded gun. On one hand, I was grateful because I loved well-made pretty clothes. I appreciated their artistry and I liked how I felt when I wore them. And then, on the other hand, I was as resentful as a moody teenager whose mother still insisted on dressing her, because *these clothes weren't fucking mine.*

I pulled out a cream-colored bandage dress and a fitted black leather jacket to wear over it, along with a pair of chunky black motorcycle boots. No six-dollar T-shirt here.

"Lotta?" I called. "Are these yours?"

"They're mine," came Lucy's voice. "Brand-new! Enjoy!"

I shook my head. I would, I knew, look spectacular in this outfit. Lucy always did the best job of dressing me. But sometimes my friends made me feel so *handled*. Like the household cat who gets caught and forced into doll clothes and stuffed into a toy buggy. And it didn't help that I was changing into these borrowed clothes in the middle of a borrowed apartment (and let's not kid ourselves: there was no way I could afford this place, either) in the middle of a neighborhood my friends had all collectively decided I should live in. They were arranging my life. Again.

Still, I thought as I slid on the dress and admired the way it showed off my curves, they meant well. And just because I was borrowing their clothes didn't necessarily mean I had to listen to them about anything else. Fashion was fashion. My life was my life, right?

I shrugged on the jacket. Damn. I looked good.

Okay. I will admit, Red Hook was cool. We were in Bait and Tackle— a seedy-chic little corner bar decorated with an overabundance of taxidermy. There was a stuffed donkey on the bar, a trio of friendly (live) pit bulls wagging their tails under a table, and a bartender who seemed to be an ace at his job. I was drinking a Guinness and admiring the view of two young men in skinny jeans and beanies playing darts.

"What the hey?" muttered Sarah. Her face was eerily lit with the blue light from her phone. "Brian is being so weird."

"How so?" said Lotta. Her hair was pulled back in tight braids like some pornographic version of Heidi of the Alps.

"I just told him that the network finally okayed the baby story line so we can throw away my birth control pills and start getting busy, and he took fifteen minutes to respond and then just answered with a thumbs-up emoji."

I laughed. "That's hot."

She rolled her eyes. "I think something's going on with his work. He's not himself lately."

"Or," I suggested, "perhaps he doesn't like his sex life dictated by a bunch of TV producers?"

She stood up. "I'm going to get another drink. Anyone want anything?"

"Bring a round of tequila shots," said Lucy. "We have to show Billy just how fun Brooklyn can be."

"I know that Brooklyn is fun," I protested. "What I don't know is how I can afford it."

"Are you kidding me?" said Lotta. "It's the land of six-dollar shots and two-dollar beers!"

"If only my booze budget was all I had to worry about," I said. "How are things going with your new stepdaughter, Lo?"

She shrugged. "Not good. Turns out the ex wasn't exaggerating after all. Sage is getting kicked out of college. And when she does, I think she'll land back with Omari."

"How old is she again?"

"Nineteen."

"So what's the problem?" asked Lucy. "Just set her up with her own place. Nineteen is plenty old enough to be on her own. Look at what we were all doing at nineteen!"

I shook my head. "Um. You were still living with your mom, as I recall, Lulu."

Lucy tossed her hair dismissively. "Only between modeling jobs."

"Anyway," said Lotta, "it's not that we don't have the room, of course. And I do want to get to know her better. But Omari and I are just so happy, you know?" She smiled to herself. "Really, ladies, I never thought it could be this good."

I felt a little knot in my throat, looking at her. Out of all of us, I never would have guessed that wild Lotta would be the one who fell this hard.

"Okay," trilled Sarah, returning with a tray of shot glasses and a bottle of tequila. "I bought the whole thing. Line 'em up!"

We were already drunk when we got to Brooklyn Crab. Even Lotta had downed a shot or two, and the rest of us had finished off the bottle.

Brooklyn, I decided, was *glorious*.

I no longer had any idea why I had ever wanted to move to Kingston, or anywhere else but Red Hook, for that matter. Red Hook was full of cute boys and cheap drinks and loud music. In Red Hook, they gave you a delicious *bucket* of crab legs and French fries, and you could gaze happily upon the Statue of Liberty while you sucked down a margarita served to you in what looked like a motherfucking goldfish bowl.

Lucy and Sarah were across the booth from me, both giggling uncontrollably as they took turns slurping clams out of their shells and sharing a gigantic piña colada. Lotta was next to me, picking at my fries with a less-than-happy look on her face.

"Brooklyn is the best, you guys!" I exclaimed. "It's got every-thing!"

"I told you!" Lucy slurred back at me. "I told you! Now you don't have to leave me alone in the city!"

"Brooklyn's got hipsters and bodegas and delicious grilled cheese sandwiches. It's got candy stores—did you guys see that awesome candy store we passed?" I was babbling, but I didn't care. "And it's got at least twelve million tattoo parlors. Maybe we should get tattoos?"

"That is a great idea!" crowed Sarah as she tried to stand up.

Lotta grabbed Sarah's wrist and yanked her back down. "Stay where you are," she snapped. "Don't you dare move."

"I mean, it's even got an Ikea. How fucking awesome is that? Manhattan doesn't have any place to get cheap Swedish furniture. I wonder how late it's open? If I'm going to live here, I should probably get a Poäng chair."

"Okay," said Lotta, slamming her hands down on the table. "Okay, we've had enough fun. I think this night is over. Let's get an Uber and take Billy back to that apartment and then—"

"Oh my God, you guys!" I yelped. "Guess what else Brooklyn has got? Guess! Guess!"

"What?" said Sarah happily.

"It's got my ex-boyfriend Marcus!" I pointed at the stocky dark-haired man who was rapidly approaching our table. "You guys remember Marcus?"

"I do remember Marcus," hiccupped Lucy. "He was good in bed. I remember you said that. And he was very needy."

"Hi, Billy," said Marcus.

"Hi, Marcus. You were very needy," Sarah intoned seriously.

"But good in bed," piped in Lucy.

Then she and Sarah slid down the booth together, cackling wildly as Marcus blinked down at me, a bemused smile on his face.

Marcus had been a mistake that I'd let continue far too long. He was a not-very-successful musician whom I'd met on a dating site. He had indeed been both good in bed and incredibly needy. It had been two years since I'd seen or heard from him, and honestly, I don't think he'd crossed my mind even once in that time.

"Hi, Marcus. How's Daisy?" I said, struggling to keep a straight face. Daisy was his tiny little dog who had regularly pissed on my hardwood floor.

His smile vanished. "She got hit by a car about six months ago," he said, shaking his head.

"Oh noooo! Noooo," I said. "That's terrible! I'm so sorry." I suddenly felt awful for poor Marcus. "Do you want to come sit with us?"

Lotta gave me a sharp poke in the side, but I ignored her.

"Cool," said Marcus as he slid in next to me.

"Crab leg?" I offered.

Lotta sighed loudly as Marcus helped himself. "Don't mind if I do," he said happily.

"So," I said, taking another slurp of my margarita. "Are you still living in Queens?"

"No, actually," he said. "I have a place about five minutes from here."

"And do you still have four roommates?" asked Lotta (rather nastily, I thought).

Marcus smiled. "No. Only three now."

"See!" I said triumphantly to Lotta. "See! He's moved up in the world!"

Marcus laughed and scooted closer to me. I caught a whiff of his familiar smell—orange Tic Tacs and clove cigarettes.

"And are you still playing drums?" asked Sarah.

"Bass," he corrected her with a frown.

"In that band—Booty Patrol?" asked Lucy.

"Boogie Patrol." I giggled. "Boogie! Not Booty!" I leaned against Marcus and laughed. Then I turned my head and he was just . . . right there—so I kissed him. And, after a second of surprised hesitation, he started to kiss me back.

"Ah, for fuck's sake, Billy!" hissed Lotta as she stood up and yanked me with her. "Come on, girls. We're leaving now." She loomed over Marcus. "Move," she commanded.

"But—" he protested.

"No buts! Move now!" And she pushed me so hard against Marcus that he slid out of the booth and onto the floor.

"Hey!" he yelped as he tried to get back up.

Lotta shoved him out of the way with her booted foot and dragged me past him. Sarah and Lucy held on to each other as they scrambled to follow, laughing merrily all the way.

Lucy tucked me in that night while Lotta and Sarah waited in the other room.

"You have five minutes, Lucy!" yelled Lotta through the door. "I want you guys back at that hotel before anyone starts puking!"

"Why don't you guys just stay here?" I asked as I snuggled down into the bed. "You can share this bed. It'll be like our old middle-school sleepovers."

Lucy sat down next to me. "No, I want you wake up here and see how peaceful it is, to feel what it will be like when you live here. I don't want you to change your mind."

I blinked sleepily. "Oh, wow, I know that I was saying that I wanted to live here, Luce, but—"

"Shhh," she said. "We don't have to talk about it now. Just—just give it a chance, okay? Pretend that this place is yours. Imagine all the things you could do in Brooklyn." She brushed the hair off my forehead. "Because I really need you not to go, okay? I don't want you to leave."

"But why?" I asked.

She glanced away, shaking her head. "Never mind. Forget I said that. Just—just have a nice night's sleep and we'll meet you at the Good Fork tomorrow for breakfast at ten, okay?"

"Okay," I said, my eyes already sliding shut. "Thanks, Lulu."

I was asleep before she left the room.

chapter 11

And then suddenly I was awake again two hours later, because someone was pounding on the door.

"Oh my God. Holy fucking Jesus," I said as I bolted out of bed, my heart pounding and my head still fuzzy from the tequila. I grabbed the only thing I could find to protect myself with—my borrowed motorcycle boot—and crept toward the door.

"Who is it?" I yelled as the pounding continued.

"Billy Sitwell?" A woman's voice. "I'm Jenny Kadinsky! It's my apartment!"

I hesitated. "But how do I know it's really you?"

"Lucy Brockton rented it from me."

I let out a sigh of relief, dropped the boot, and unlatched the door.

A small woman with dark, messy hair blinked up at me. She was wearing what had to be her pajamas and had a smear of zit cream on her cheek. "You gotta go right now," she said, shoving past me into the apartment and slamming the door behind her.

I followed her back in. "What? Why?"

"The person who owns this apartment is coming back any moment."

"But I thought this was your apartment?"

"I'm house-sitting for her. She was supposed to be in California, but apparently she had a monster fight with her boyfriend and she caught the red-eye home. I just got her text."

"But you rented it to me."

"I needed the money. She wasn't supposed to be home until next week. She'll kill me if she finds out. She'll probably call the police and we'll both be fucked. You have to leave right now."

"It's four in the fucking morning."

She shook her head. "I know. I'm sorry. Please, I'll send you your money back. I'll even send extra for your trouble. But you've got to get out of here."

I blew out an exasperated sigh. "Okay. Hang on. Just let me get dressed." I was wearing sweatpants and an oversize T-shirt that Lucy had provided for me to sleep in.

She shook her head again. "No time. Just get your stuff and go."

"Fuck!" I swore as I hustled back to the bedroom, crammed on Lucy's motorcycle boots, threw the leather jacket over my giant tee, and stuffed the rest of my things into the plastic bag Lucy had handed me earlier.

"Hurry!" Jenny shouted. "Oh, no," she groaned as she rushed in. "I can hear her coming up the stairs. You're going to have to go out the fire escape."

I froze. "What?"

She was already forcing open the bedroom window. "It's safe. I've done it before. Just climb all the way down and then jump the last five feet."

"Five feet?" I squeaked.

There was a knock on the door. Her eyes bulged with fear.

"Go! Now!" she hissed.

And so I threw my bag out the window and then climbed out after it.

Thank God for all-night diners. I was sitting in Jim's 24 Hour Eat Shop, nursing a cup of coffee and a sore ankle from that five-foot (more like eight) drop out the window, and I was pissed.

I had managed to grab my phone before making my exit, but I'd left my wallet behind. All I had on me was the four dollars in change that I'd stuffed in my jacket pocket earlier that night after I'd paid for my first beer.

I didn't have enough money to get back to Manhattan. I didn't even have enough to make it back to where my friends were staying in Williamsburg because there were no frigging trains that ran out to Red Hook. I was stuck.

I had been calling and texting Lucy, Lotta, and Sarah nonstop, but no one was answering.

This is just like Lucy, I thought to myself. *Trying to control my life and then landing me in even worse trouble than before.*

It had been this way since we were kids. From the first day I met her, in the fourth grade, when she had walked right up to me and asked if I liked Matt Henderson. I had been so flattered that this pretty, obviously cool girl would even bother talking to me, I had instantly spilled my guts and told her that I actually thought I was in *love* with him.

She nodded knowingly. "I could tell. The way you watch him play kickball."

"What should I do?" I whispered, mortified to have spoken all my innermost secrets aloud.

"You should tell him," she said with no hesitation. "You should tell him that you love him and see what he says back."

My little preteen heart had fluttered in a mad panic at the thought. I almost never talked to Matt. I had once worked up the nerve to ask him when a homework assignment was due, and I swear I'd been sick for a week after.

"I can't," I whispered, agonized. "I can't possibly say that."

"Then I will," said Lucy, and I watched in horror as she marched off to talk to him.

"Bad news," said Lucy when she returned.

The really bad news, I thought, *is that I am about to throw up right here on your shoes.*

"He says he doesn't like redheads."

My heart cracked. I turned away to hide the tears in my eyes. But then I felt a slim little arm slip through mine.

"He's a total idiot," insisted Lucy. "I think your hair is beautiful. And, by the way, his breath kind of smelled like tuna fish. Ew, right?"

The waitress passed by me and didn't even ask if I wanted more coffee. I couldn't blame her. I must have looked insane. I had gone directly into the diner bathroom and seen that last night's eye makeup was halfway down my face. I scrubbed off as much as I could, but that didn't change the giant sweats and T-shirt crumpled under the expensive leather jacket or the fact that my hair was so big it was approaching *Dynasty*-era Joan Collins.

Red Hook wasn't nearly as appealing at this time of night. What had been a fun, gritty, but accessible vibe when I was drunk and with my friends now felt much more sinister. It was raining. The streets were empty. The shadows seemed darker. And despite the dirty looks the waitress was giving me as I rounded my second hour drinking one bottomless cup of coffee, I was pretty sure I would be murdered if I ventured outside. So I kept my butt firmly in place at the counter.

My phone beeped. Shit. It was out of juice. I waved over the waitress. "Excuse me," I said, "is there a place I can plug my phone in?"

She shook her head and pointed at a sign on the wall that said PLEASE RESPECT OUR PATRONS. TURN OFF ALL DEVICES.

"Seriously?" I said. "But there's no one here but you and me."

She shrugged. "Them's the rules."

Well, there goes your twenty-five-cent tip! I thought vengefully.

Just then Lucy, Sarah, and Lotta burst through the door, shaking off the rain.

"Billy! Oh, thank God!" breathed Lucy. "We got your messages and came right over."

"What happened?" asked Sarah.

I glared at Lucy. "It seems that I was in an illegal housing situation," I said stiffly.

Lotta wrinkled her brow. "What?"

"Jenny Kadinsky showed up and kicked me out at four in the morning. She doesn't even own the place. I had to jump off her fire escape."

Lucy burst out laughing. "Oh my God!" she breathed between giggles.

"It's not funny," I protested. "I hurt my ankle and I left my wallet in her apartment and I've been sitting here for two hours with one cup of coffee, and the waitress fucking hates me!"

Now all three of them were laughing.

"Why didn't you just come to the hotel?" asked Lucy. "We would have paid the cab fare."

I felt my face grow hot. Of course, I had thought about doing just that, but then I had imagined what if, for some reason, I hadn't been able to find my friends or they didn't answer their door? I'd be stuck with a pissed-off cabbie, and no way to pay him. When I was younger, I had actually been in that situation more than once, and I did not want to relive a moment of that particular youthful humiliation. It was the same sinking feeling I got when I ran my debit card at the grocery store and found out I was short on funds. Or when we were all splitting a dinner check and I knew that by paying it, I would be late on the rent again that month.

But these women would not understand that feeling. I was sure that none of them had ever been in my shoes.

"Forget it," I said. "I'm going back to crazy Jenny's apartment and getting my wallet, and then I'm taking the Ikea boat back home."

"But what about breakfast?" said Lucy. "Aren't you hungry? Our time in Brooklyn isn't over yet."

I turned toward her. "It's done, Luce. I mean"—I struggled not to sound angry—"thank you for setting this up. Last night was fun—"

"Last night was more than fun!" she cried. "You said you wanted to move here!"

I shook my head in exasperation. "Just how much do you think an apartment like that would cost to rent? This is Brooklyn, not Iowa. I can't afford to move here. And even if I could, what am I supposed to do then? Just because it's not Manhattan doesn't mean everything suddenly changes. I still have to work."

"I'm sure you could do more supper clubs—"

"I don't want to do any more supper clubs," I snapped. "I thought I made that pretty clear when I did *your* supper club."

She blinked, hurt. "Oh, well, so sorry I hired you, then."

I felt my nostrils flare in exasperation. "You know what I mean. I'm out of the business. I was just helping you guys out."

"Um. Titus is personal friends with Jean-Georges Vongerichten, Bill. If it was such a burden, I think we probably could have managed to find someone else."

"Lucy," said Lotta. There was a warning in her voice.

She threw her hands up. "No. I don't see why I have to tiptoe around this anymore. She has a history of this. She keeps making bad decisions and we have to keep bailing her out and then she's totally ungrateful."

I felt the heat rise in my cheeks. "Jesus Christ, Lucy. I'm not a child. I don't need you to take care of me."

"But you do," she returned. "From the moment you arrived in New York, I've had to follow you around and pick up your pieces."

"You mean try to run my life. And I never asked you to do that."

"You would have ended up homeless on the street if I hadn't done it. You still might. I just want you to make a smart decision now and then, Billy. To be less reckless. Try acting like a grown-up for once."

I exploded. "Are you fucking kidding me? What do you know about being a grown-up? You moved here with your mother! You had the cover of Paris *Vogue* before you even turned twenty."

"I worked hard for that cover!" she interjected.

I laughed. "Um, let's not forget that I was actually there, Lu. You got the cover because you let Helmut Newton do blow off your tits in the bathroom at the Limelight. We all know the story."

"That is not how that happened!"

I barreled on. "Then you met Titus. Who was rich and famous and powerful and treated you like you were the prize in his fucking

Cracker Jack. And you went straight from your mother's to your hus-band's fucking West Village town house and you've been a kept woman ever since. You've never once been on your own. You've never had to work for a fucking thing your whole fucking life. You've just been lucky. Lucky to have been taken care of every step of the way."

"That is not true!" said Lucy. Her face was red.

I was breathing hard now. My voice was shaking. "You don't get it. You don't get how hard this city can be. You've never felt how it wears you down. Everything has always just been handed to you. Everything gets dumped into your lap because you look the way you do. You never even have to ask. Because of some freak genetic luck of the draw, people scramble to give you what you want before you even know you want it. You were just born this way—you never had to work for any of it."

Lucy flinched as if I had slapped her.

"Billy!" whispered Sarah, shocked.

I knew I'd gone too far as soon as the words flew out of my mouth. We all knew I'd gone too far. If Lucy had a weak spot, it was the idea that she had nothing more to offer than her beauty. She was terrified that people would never look past her surface, that she'd be judged as an empty vessel. I knew this. But still, I had hit her with her worst fear.

"Luce," I said, trying to soften my voice, but she cut me off.

"You know what, Billy? Fuck you. You go ahead and move to some hick fucking country town so you can chase a kid and work for tips, and then let me know how that fucking goes for you, okay?"

She stood and gathered her things, then headed for the door. I followed her and grabbed her arm.

"Lucy—" I said.

She shook me off. "No. I'm done. I'm done taking care of you and

I'm done giving a fuck. I don't need this shit. I've got enough to deal with. You fucking do you, Billy. Have a great life."

And with that, she slammed through the door and disappeared.

I stood, frozen.

We'd argued over the years, sure, but we'd never had a fight like that before.

"Damn," breathed Sarah, echoing my thoughts.

"Billy," Lotta started. Her voice was pained.

I shook my head. "I'm—I'm gonna go, guys."

And I followed Lucy through the door.

I stood in the drizzling rain, waiting. It was a warm, end-of-summer rain, but I still shivered.

Finally, she pulled up and got out of her car, wrenching some heavy, covered pans out of her trunk before turning around to look at me, eyebrows knitted.

"Can I help you?" she said squinting uncertainly.

I took a step toward her.

"Mei Fang?" I said. "We met yesterday? I want to talk to you about your truck."

chapter 12

En route to Kingston

I almost missed the Kingston exit, and as I turned hard and screeched through two lanes I felt like the Airstream was going to come crashing through the back window of my car.

"Fuck! Fuck! FUCK!" I yelled as I swerved into the shoulder, over-compensating to right myself. Cars pushed past me, honking angrily.

Finally, I straightened out and carefully nosed out into the road again, stopping to pay the toll.

What was I doing? I felt like I was completely out of control, and it wasn't just the car. It had been only three days since I had cut my savings in half, officially bought the Airstream and the Kia, called up Portia to ask if the River House was still available for rent, told my mercenary landlord to stuff it, and packed up whatever shit I thought was necessary to take upstate. I'd dragged the rest of my things out to the curb. There was nothing I was particularly attached to, and the house in Kingston was furnished.

My little apartment suddenly felt huge with all the furniture emptied out of it. The scratches on the hardwood were more obvious; the hidden places I never bothered to clean were dust-coated and glaring. I traced my hand over the wall in the bedroom, remembering when Lucy had helped me paint it this soft, dove-colored gray. I had been doubtful about the color, saying I wanted something more cheerful, but she had insisted that I needed something calming for the bedroom.

I hadn't talked to Lucy since Brooklyn, which might have been the longest we'd ever been out of touch. When we were girls we did almost everything together, and even when we were apart, we'd spend hours on the phone, checking our homework, talking about boys, combing over the details of the day we had just spent together. Since texting came into existence, there were some days when I heard from Lucy practically every hour.

The silence was strange and it made me sad, but it was freeing in a way, too. Of course, Lotta and Sarah had been in touch, worried about the rift between me and Lucy. They had even offered to help me pack and move, but I turned them down and said I was sure I'd see them soon enough.

I wanted to do this alone.

I'd said good-bye to Brett in person. One last bounce in his bed for the road. He had been remarkably cheerful about it all, merely saying that he hadn't expected me to leave quite so soon, but that he'd be up to visit as soon as I wanted him.

I hadn't felt much when I left my apartment, still fueled by righteous indignation from my fight with Lucy, but I have to admit that I did feel a little pang as I shut Brett's door behind me. There was a tiny part of me that would have liked to have turned around and crawled right back into bed with him.

But now I was here. Starting over, all alone, just like I had planned. I had meant to go directly to the River House and unpack first, but instead, I found myself heading for Huma, my nerves jittery with excitement. I needed to get this part of the plan out of the way before I did anything else.

Parts of Kingston reminded me of (dare I say it?) Brooklyn. There was a waterfront, where cheerful Victorian houses sat high on the hill side by side with the jutting steeples of several converted churches overlooking a small but bustling business district.

There was also uptown Kingston, which changed from block to block. Crowded and worn row houses ran into enormous stone mansions until they all converged into a historic village center of restaurants, wine bars, and small, funky shops. The LGBTQ center was cheek by jowl with a high-end bridal shop and a coffee place that roasted its own beans. I saw a lively farmers' market in progress and made a mental note for later.

It wasn't one of those quainty-quaint, perfectly groomed, Hudson Valley towns filled with antique shops and genteel luncheon places. It was more rough around the edges, a little bit industrial, arty, but still filled with history. Old stone churches and their tottery graveyards, historical markers on every other building, more than one GEORGE WASHINGTON SLEPT HERE proclamation. There was a broad mix of people who had obviously lived there for years, mingling amidst the artist hipsters, weekend Manhattanites, and old hippies and farmers—all wandering the streets together.

I pulled into the parking place behind Huma. It was late afternoon on a Sunday, and I was pretty sure that Ethan would be in the kitchen by now, but I sat in the car for a moment, feeling nearly as hopeful and foolish as I had ever felt. I hadn't called ahead. In fact, I hadn't been in touch with him at all since I had last seen him here. I had convinced myself that I would make more of an impact with a big gesture, that once he saw me in person, he wouldn't be able to turn me down. But now I wasn't so sure.

The back door to the restaurant banged open and I recognized Marta, the young pastry chef with the blue hair, as she dragged out a bag of garbage nearly as tall as she was and heaved it into the Dumpster.

She glanced over at me with a curious look on her face and we locked eyes.

It was now or never.

"Hey," I said, getting out of my car. I self-consciously brushed off the crumbs from the drive-through burger I had scarfed on my way up. "Is Ethan around?"

Marta's eyebrows shot up but she nodded. "He's in the basement," she said, indicating a sunken set of stairs near the back entrance. She looked over at the Airstream. "Nice rig," she said as she turned to go back inside.

"Thanks," I called after her.

Once the door was shut, I ducked back into my car, searching out some makeup and the rearview mirror. I slapped on some lipstick, blanching when I realized that it was nearly the same color as my still-pink hair.

Okay, I thought as I climbed back out. I sniffed my shirt. It smelled like piña colada air freshener and, more faintly, pot. The legacy of Mei Fang's ownership of the car.

"Billy?"

I snapped my head up, embarrassed to be caught sniffing myself. Ethan stood at the top of the stairs in his chef whites, holding a bin of zucchini.

"Billy! What are you doing here?" He strode toward me with a huge grin on his face. I couldn't help but smile back.

Okay, Sitwell, I thought, *it's showtime.*

"Hey there, Ethan." I met him halfway and tried to lean over to casually kiss his cheek hello, but the bin of vegetables bumped between us.

"Hang on," he said, and put the bin down before reaching over to buss me on the cheek. His lips lingered on my skin a shade longer than was polite.

I felt the heat rush to my face but forced myself to forge on. "I have a business proposition for you," I said.

He cocked his head and smiled even wider. "Oh?"

"Remember when you said you wanted to expand your restaurant?"

His smile faltered a bit. "Yes?"

"And remember the butter sauce? When you said you hate to waste anything?"

"Yes . . ."

"Voilà!" I stepped back, pointing at the Airstream.

He looked at me, mystified. "A . . . trailer?"

"It's not just a trailer, it's an Airstream food truck."

"Oh!" There was a gleam of interest in his eyes as he started to walk toward it. "And you're thinking I could—what? Buy it?"

I shook my head. "No. That's the beauty of it. I don't want you to put any money into it. I just want to partner up and expand your business like you talked about."

He looked back at me, confused. "Do what now?"

"We could call it Leftovers," I said. "It would be a mobile lunch outpost of your restaurant. You know how there's always waste in a kitchen, right? Cooked meat, overripe fruit, the special that didn't sell out, all those odds and ends. And you know how so many things taste better the next day? That feeling when you look into your fridge and realize that last night's dinner is going to make an even better lunch? We could capitalize on that, plus advertise ourselves as a zero-waste kitchen. It would be things like frittatas and soups and sandwiches and salads from whatever is left from the kitchen at the end of every night."

He waved his hands. "Wait, you're going too fast. I'm not really seeing it. And anyway, I don't have time to run a truck."

I grabbed his arm. "But, see, I do."

From the look on his face, I'm pretty sure he thought I was insane. "Um, don't take this the wrong way, Billy, but can you even cook?"

I laughed and tugged on his sleeve. "Let me show you," I said, leading the way.

You would think that when a chef cooks for another chef, they would pull out all the stops. You might imagine that they would unearth their most complicated recipes, use their most expensive ingredients, pile the plate with truffles, foie gras, fugu, and edible gold leaf, and present their creation like it was a fucking Degas, art on a platter. You'd imagine that chefs would want, more than anything, to impress, to compete, to *win*.

But you would be wrong. The chefs I knew, at least the truly great ones, were much more generous than that, and they were wiser, too. They knew that no good cook was going to be fooled by glitz and glitter. They knew that, at their core, every great chef longed for perfect simplicity.

The perfect bowl of soup (we have already discussed mine), the perfect burger, the perfectly prepared dish of pasta (I had already eaten Ethan's), the satisfaction of a great latte with just the right amount of steamy, creamy foam—these were the kinds of things that chefs plunked down in front of other chefs, arms crossed, a little smile playing over their face as if to say, *Go ahead, try it. Your world will never be the same.*

I'd known this moment would come—when I would have to cook for Ethan and prove my mettle. And I'm not going to lie and pretend that I didn't spend half an hour standing in Fairway considering the idea of simply blowing a good chunk of my meager remaining savings on a five-hundred-dollar piece of Wagyu tenderloin and pretending it was left over from my dinner the night before.

But eventually I came to my senses and remembered how we had eaten at all the "family dinners"—the staff meals at the restaurants—in the various places I had worked over the years. Stews and soups, simple salads and roasts, pastas and homey specialties like posole or tripe that were never put on the menu but which we all dipped into greedily, unable to resist the savory warmth and goodness.

Keep it simple, Sitwell, I thought to myself.

So, under Ethan's curious gaze as he leaned against the counter, I pulled out a loaf of crusty white bread; a bulb of garlic; a sweet onion; a mason jar of thick, lemony, homemade mayonnaise; and two heavy, perfect, bloodred beefsteak tomatoes.

I had searched out these tomatoes carefully at the Union Square greenmarket, squeezing and smelling each one like I was an adolescent boy given access to his first pair of breasts. I'd considered more exotic possibilities, Green Zebra or Mortgage Lifters, but when I saw the traditional beefsteaks, I knew I'd found what I wanted.

Ethan's mouth quirked. "Nice tomatoes," he deadpanned.

I started up the grill and peeled the onion, throwing it directly upon the open flame.

"Now, imagine that this was all stuff left over from last night's dinner," I said, as I cut thick slices of the bread and tomato and then placed the bread on the grill to toast. "Say the tomatoes were part of a caprese special, the onion had already been cut, the bread was starting to go stale . . ."

Ethan wrinkled his nose. "I suppose that sometimes happens . . ." He looked around the Airstream. "How long have you had this thing?"

"Oh, awhile," I said vaguely, hoping he wouldn't ask too much more. I retrieved the bread, which was now nicely browned, and rubbed both sides with a piece of halved garlic until it melted into the crumb of the toast. Then I took a slice of the tomato and rubbed again, pressing until the flesh, juice, and seeds were entirely absorbed into the bread and I held only the skin in my hand.

"Ah," he said, watching me intently. "That's a variation I haven't seen before."

I lifted a finger. "Just wait."

I slathered the bread with mayonnaise over the tomato pulp.

Ethan stuck his finger into the jar and sampled the mayo. "Nice," he said, taking another swipe. "Your own, I assume?"

I nodded and then picked up the now blistered and blackened onion off the flame and sliced it thinly, pulling it into soft, ragged ribbons before piling it onto the bread. Then I stacked three thick slices of juicy, ruby-red tomato on top of that, sprinkled the whole thing with salt and pepper, topped it off with the other piece of bread, neatly half wrapped it in a piece of waxed paper, and handed the whole massive and dripping thing over to Ethan.

"Eat it over the sink," I said. "It's the only way."

He considered the sandwich. "I like the presentation," he said, before leaning over the sink and taking an enormous bite.

His eyes slowly closed as he chewed, and a happy grin spread over his face. "Oh my God. Bliss," he said with his mouth full.

I dipped into a little bow. "Et voilà! The perfect tomato sandwich, made from last night's leftovers."

He took another bite, nodding slowly. "Okay, maybe this plan isn't totally crazy . . ."

"This could have been a panzanella or a bread soup, too," I said. "The possibilities are endless."

"Shhh," he mumbled as he continued eating. "Just let me finish the sandwich first."

I watched him eat, aware of the little zings of happiness that darted through me with every bite he took. I fucking loved to feed people. Wait, let me amend that: I fucking loved to feed *hungry* people, and Ethan murdered that sandwich like he was starving. By the time he finished, I honestly didn't know whether I wanted to kiss him or just make the guy some dessert.

He swallowed the last bite, crumpled the waxed paper in his hand, and sighed. "Okay, so I'm pretty sure you can cook. Now, pitch me again. Start over from the beginning, and don't leave anything out."

I climbed into my new bed that night, appreciating the fresh, sweet smell of the sheets ("I hung them out to dry, darlin'," said Portia when she handed over the keys). I smiled, thinking that I hadn't slept in line-dried sheets since I was a little girl.

I should call Lucy, I thought sleepily as I snuggled down into my bed. *She'd appreciate line-dried sheets, too.*

And then I felt a little shock of pain and anger as I remembered that I couldn't actually call her, that we still weren't talking.

I popped my head back up and looked out the window at the moon hanging over the Hudson. It was a half-moon, with smoky and tremulous clouds skating over it. In the distance, I heard the wail of a train.

This is stupid. I should bury the hatchet, I thought. We'd never fought for this long. I reached for my phone on the bedside table.

You up? I wrote. The soft electronic slide and pop indicated that my text had been received.

. . .

. . .

. . .

But then no answer.

chapter 13

Rail trail

Kingston

I'm pretty sure I'm going to die out here," I panted at Lotta through my Bluetooth as I jounced along the trail.

The old red three-speed Schwinn I'd found in the basement of the River House shuddered. It felt like it might fly apart at any moment as I took it up to top speed, trying to get my heart rate up to a decent level.

She laughed up at me from the screen of my phone that I had nestled into the bike basket. "Definitely not SoulCycle, eh, darling?"

My eyes darted around the empty path. Nothing but trees and stone walls and a thicket of wild rose brambles. "There's just . . . no one . . . here," I said. "It's too quiet and peaceful. I'm totally positive some dude wearing a clown mask is going to jump out at any moment and hunt me down with his hatchet."

She rolled her eyes. "It's the country, Bill. I don't think anyone is supposed to be around."

"It's unnatural," I grumbled, standing up in the saddle so I could work my quads a little harder. "If we were in the city, this place would be balls deep in joggers."

"So, anyway," she said, "I thought it was this brilliant idea to do autumn in the Hamptons. The off-season, you know? I feel like Omari and I are so busy in the city. All these parties, these invitations, people who recognize him on the street. I just wanted him to myself for a bit longer."

"Mmm-hmm," I said, distracted by something small and brown sitting in the middle of the path up ahead of me.

"But then, we're here less than two days and who shows up at the door but Sage. She was supposed to be with her mother in Amsterdam, but apparently they had a fight, and so now she's moving back in with us. Oh, Billy, you can't imagine how much this girl hates me."

I nodded, my eyes glued to the little bundle of hair that I was rapidly approaching.

"The first night she was there, she refused to address me directly. I went out of the way to make her a nice dinner and she pretended that I didn't even exist. Just chattered away at her father and ignored everything I had to say."

"Wait," I said, momentarily pulling my eyes away from the path. "*You* cooked?"

"No." She sniffed. "But I ordered out. From a very nice place."

I slowed down. Okay. It was a bunny. There was a cute little brown bunny just sitting in the middle of the path, refusing to budge.

"And Omari was so sweet: he was trying so hard to get her to be polite to me, but she wouldn't have it. And finally, she stood up, dashed her plate into the sink, and stomped off to her bedroom like she was nine instead of nineteen."

I slowed to a stop, planting my feet on either side of the bike.

The bunny peered up at me with its black button eyes. Its nose quivered. "Hello, little bunny," I said.

"What?" said Lotta.

"What are you—GAAAAAH! FUUUUCK!" I screamed as the rabbit suddenly burst into the air and bounded straight at me. I scrambled backward, yanking at the bike, and suddenly I was flat on my back, the bike on top of me, as I watched the rabbit rocketing off into the woods.

"BILLY? BILLY?" yelled Lotta from somewhere on the ground. "IS THERE A CLOWN?"

I stared up into the trees, trying to catch my breath. The bike was sticking up into the air, the front wheel rotating slowly; there was a scrape down my leg; and my ass and hair were coated in mud. I closed my eyes and laughed softly to myself.

Ethan had agreed that I could have a trial run with the Airstream at the coming weekend's Smorgasburg.

He was still a little hesitant. Which was fair. I mean, really, I was basically the crazy woman who'd showed up on his doorstep wearing her wedding dress after just one date. But I could tell he was enchanted by the trailer, and it was an extremely low-stakes proposition. I had promised to pay for any extra needed supplies up front, he'd give me the week's leftovers and a couple of his kitchen staff to help out, and then we'd split whatever profit we earned fifty-fifty.

Smorgasburg was a new northern version of the Brooklyn Flea, its Williamsburg counterpart. About one hundred different food vendors and artisans set up booths on ten acres at the old brickyard factory on the Kingston waterfront. Thousands of visitors came every weekend, spring through fall, to eat and shop. The owners had been after Ethan to contribute, but he hadn't had the time or the manpower, so the Airstream presented an elegant solution.

I only had one day before our launch, so I had decided to spend the time scrubbing down the trailer, with a toothbrush if necessary, making sure I had everything we'd need and really getting to know the space.

Ethan and I had gone over what his kitchen should have available and designed a simple menu to begin with, sticking to the original intent of the truck—sandwiches (I had blushed with pleasure when he had insisted on including my tomato sandwich at the top of the list, although he had also insisted on adding some local bacon to it, which I thought was rather gilding the fucking lily), some salads, and a dessert to be determined by Marta, but which would probably include plums or pears since they were in season and he had more than he wanted in the kitchen.

I'd told him I was going to scrub down the truck today, and he'd said that he would stop by later to drop off the ingredients and maybe even help after the lunch rush, depending on how busy the restaurant got.

I'll admit that knowing he was coming had made me put on a more flattering pair of jeans and replace the dirty sweatshirt I'd been living in for the past two days. I was putting on lipstick using the reflective surface of the stainless-steel cooktop when I heard a knock on the trailer door.

"Come in!" I yelled as I slid the tube of lipstick back into my pocket.

"Hey there," said Ethan as the door popped open. He was carrying a cardboard box full of food and wearing a hoodie, a red plaid shirt underneath, and a pair of skinny jeans. I almost laughed when I saw that the shoelaces on his white Converse were covered in fat red hearts and gold stars. I'd had a pair exactly like that when I was ten.

I told you, taunted Lucy's voice in my head. *He's a child.*

"Hey," I said back, trying not to look too happy to see him. I briefly wondered if I should kiss him hello.

"I can't stay long, but I brought Kai and Marta to help," he said, stepping out of the way.

Kai, carrying another box and wearing a look of faintly disgusted nonchalance, climbed up the stairs, with Marta right behind, her arms full of overflowing paper bags.

"Oh," I said, inwardly rolling my eyes. "Great!"

"This is fucking awesome," said Marta happily as she put her bags down and started poking through all the cabinets. She was wearing baggy overalls and had, I noticed, a gorgeous smile. "Oooh, yeah," she said, tapping the small patch of marble that was inset into the countertop. "Here's my dough spot."

Kai ran a finger over the stovetop and curled her lip. "When was the last time this place was cleaned?"

I shrugged. "It's been a while. I can do it myself."

"And yet," drawled Kai, looking at me with hooded eyes, "here we are."

"Anyway," said Ethan, as he opened the stainless-steel fridge and started loading stuff in, "this is your kitchen crew. Kai is a wiz at prep and salads, and of course Marta is a genius with dessert. I figured it would be good to get you all in the kitchen together before showtime."

"Great," I said again, trying to sound enthusiastic. I knew I should be grateful for the help, but somehow I had imagined all of this with me and Ethan cooking side by side, not me and a couple of his female coworkers.

Whoa, girl, I reminded myself, *this is about the food, not the guy.*

"All right then," said Ethan, as he emptied the box. "I gotta get back to the restaurant. I'll see you guys later." He looked over at me. "Billy? Maybe we can get a drink together soon?"

"Sure," I said, hoping that my face wasn't as pink as it suddenly felt. Then I saw the sharp look that Kai gave him and felt a little less pleased with myself.

"So, where should we start?" said Marta. She was still rooting around in the cabinets. "Hey, how old is this bottle of Malibu? I see a silver lining here."

I looked away from Kai. "Oh, well, I don't know, it's kind of early, isn't it?"

"Pour," said Kai, thrusting a cup into Marta's face. "And don't be stingy."

For the first time in my life, I truly felt like a mother. And not because I was beaming with pride.

"Oh my fucking gaaaawd," giggled Marta as she sat on the floor of the trailer. "Why am I down here again? What am I supposed to be doing? I can't even remember."

"You are supposed to be cleaning the linoleum," said Kai solemnly, "with your butt." And then she collapsed into guffaws.

The girls had gotten progressively more ridiculous with every shot of rum they had bolted down, making terrible jokes, ransacking the cupboards, and not helping with the cleaning at all. I, on the other hand, was as sober as a nun, and ten times as pissed.

"You are supposed to be organizing the spices," I snapped at Marta. "And they are up here, not down there."

She blinked up at me owlishly and hiccupped. "But why am I organizing spices again?"

I barely resisted kicking her. "Because tomorrow is Smorgasburg. And we need to be ready for it."

"Mmm, Smorgasburg," she said, going all the way supine. "I had the best waffle there last weekend. It had roasted pistachios and caramel and cardamom ice cream and candied rosemary." She closed her eyes. "I wish I had a waffle now."

"I hate waffles," pronounced Kai. "And ice cream."

Marta closed her eyes. "You hate everything sweet, hon."

Kai considered this for a moment. "Well. Not everything. I don't hate Ethan, for instance."

Marta giggled. "Yes, that is true. Ethan is sweet."

"Oh my God," I exploded. "You guys are fucking useless. In fact, you're worse than useless because not only are you not helping, you're actually making more of a mess."

"Marta is the messy one," said Kai primly. "I am very neat."

"You literally just dumped an entire jar of oregano all over the floor," I said to her.

"Oooh, right!" piped up Marta. "That's why I'm down here!"

"To clean with your butt," reminded Kai.

"Okay," I said. "That's it. We're done. You two just need to go into my house and sleep this off," I said. "I can't do this anymore."

"I think I'm going to throw up," said Kai, her beautiful face turning a very pale shade of green.

"Not in here you're not!" I roared.

I grabbed Kai by the arm and snatched open the door—only to find myself face-to-face with Brett.

"Billy?" he said, just as Kai stumbled toward him and threw up all over his shirt.

———●

While Brett drove the drunk girls back to whatever Satan's den they had climbed out of, I attempted to clean up the mess they had left behind. So much for scrubbing the place down with a toothbrush. I was going to be lucky if I even managed to get it up to code before we left.

I squatted down to sweep up the oregano and spotted the bottle of rum, now on its side, the cap still on. I shook it, and it was, miraculously, not empty. I unscrewed the cap and took a whiff.

Oof. Coconut rum.

Instantly I was hurtled back to when Lucy and I were in our early twenties, and she had come over to my apartment in a fury because her mother's dog, a super-humpy Boston terrier named Mr. Sprinkles, had found her diaphragm and chewed it to bits.

"That's it!" she declared. "I'm done living with Cheri. She loves that dog more than she loves me." She looked around speculatively at my tiny studio. "What if I moved in here with you?"

I thought that was a brilliant idea (mainly because I didn't know how I was going to make rent that month), and I made Sun Breezes in celebration—Malibu plus grapefruit juice. We spent the night slowly getting toasted and planning our awesome new life together, independent from Cheri and Mr. Sprinkles.

Of course, the next morning she had sheepishly slipped back to her mother's apartment—because even living with a birth-control-stealing dog was better than having to share a pullout futon with me every night—but we'd always looked back on that one night of being roomies with great fondness.

I sniffed the Malibu mournfully and raised the bottle into the air before taking a swig. *Goddamn, do I miss Lucy.*

By the time Brett got back, the oregano was still on the floor, and so was I. I hadn't eaten all day, and apparently Malibu was stronger than I remembered.

"You've got to be fucking kidding me," he muttered to himself as he knelt down to help me up.

I blinked up at him blearily. He was so cute. "You're so cute, Brett," I said. "And so nice. I like you so much. I like your hair and I like your ass."

He gave me a rueful smile. "Ah, yes, drunk Billy—the affectionate, effusive, inappropriate version of normal Billy."

"I miss Lucy," I hiccupped at him as he grabbed my hand.

"So call her," he said, slinging my arm around his shoulders.

"I haaave!" I protested, showing him the digital record of my ten unanswered calls. "She won't answer."

"She will," he soothed. "No one can stay away from you for long."

"I think I need a nap," I told him.

"Yup, honey, that's right where we're going," he said as he led me inside the house and up the stairs to my bedroom.

He helped me get undressed down to my underwear and then tucked me into bed. I closed my eyes, already drifting off, but I felt him sit down next to me and brush the hair from my forehead.

"Mmm," I said, "that's nice. You're so nice, Brett."

He laughed ruefully. "So you keep telling me." He pulled his hand away and sighed. "This was not exactly what I had in mind when I decided to drive up to surprise you, Sitwell. But I'll say one thing: you're never predictable."

I started to say I was sorry, but I fell asleep before I got the words out.

I woke up in a panic later that night, hungover and realizing that I was in no way ready for tomorrow. I stumbled out of bed, pulled on my boots, and headed out to the trailer. The Airstream was gleaming clean from top to bottom. It looked like it had been professionally done. I shook my pounding head as I leaned up against the counter; then I hurried back into the house.

Brett was asleep on the couch in the living room. I hissed his name.

"Did you clean the trailer?" I asked him when he opened his eyes and looked at me.

He blinked, confused. "Um. Yes?"

I felt a surge of anger. "Why? I didn't tell you to do that!"

He sat up, rubbing his eyes. "You weren't in any shape to do it, and you told me it was really important."

"So you just cleaned it yourself?"

He yawned and ran his hand through his hair. "I think the phrase you're looking for here is, 'Thanks, Brett, that was really nice of you.'"

I glared at him. "This is my project. I wanted to do it myself."

His eyes narrowed. "Wait, so you're mad at me because you got drunk and I cleaned up your truck?"

I heard how foolish it sounded. I really did. And I knew I was being a complete bitch. But I also knew that if I thanked him and backed down, I'd have to accept his favor and owe him something— and I just wasn't ready to be in his debt. "No one asked you to help," I said stiffly.

He looked at me for a long moment and then shook his head and stood up. "Okay. I'm going home," he said. "Good luck with the truck tomorrow."

I almost said something as he gathered up his stuff. I almost apologized as he put on his shoes and then headed for the door, but I just couldn't bring myself to do it.

You are an idiot, said the Lucy in my head as I watched him drive away, *and you do not deserve that man. And if you ever see him again, you should immediately sink to your knees and give him the world's best blow job as an apology and a thank-you present, both.*

Okay, the last bit about the blow job was more Lotta's voice than Lucy's—but I pretty much agreed with them both.

Marta and Kai were waiting when I pulled up to our designated spot at Smorgasburg early the next morning. Apparently, they had continued to drink once they had been dumped off last night, and looked and smelled like a hungover version of Satan's handmaidens. They brought in more supplies that Ethan had sent over, and got to work doing prep, but they were moving at about half the pace I needed them to, and Marta kept stopping to take hits off her vape.

"What is that?" I asked, wrinkling my nose. "Flavored tobacco?"

She shook her head, holding in the smoke. "It's pot," she wheezed.

I blinked rapidly, quelling the urge to snatch it out of her hands and throw it into the river. "What? Why?"

"It's that or I hurl all over the hand pies," she said, taking another hit. "Trust." She looked sheepish for a moment. "By the way, I'm really sorry about yesterday, Billy," she said. "I guess that rum was a little more potent than we thought."

"Looks like you managed to get the truck cleaned up, though," chimed in Kai, who was chopping kale into ribbons at a funereal pace that made me want to scream. "Guess you didn't need us after all."

"Yes," I agreed quickly, "amazing how that happened."

"That Brett guy was super cute," added Marta as she got back to slicing her pears.

"He was super old but he was okay." Kai shrugged. "He was pretty cool about me puking all over his shirt, I guess."

"Is he your boyfriend?"

I paused for a moment, and then: "No. Kai, can you please move a little faster? We need to open in less than thirty minutes."

She rolled her eyes and increased her pace by a smidge.

Marta speared a slice of pear from the bowl she was preparing and passed it over to me on the tip of her knife. "What do you think?"

I bit into it. It was red Anjou sprinkled with sugar, cinnamon, and cardamom.

"Good," I said, "but I would add a little pepper, too, maybe?"

Marta opened up her mouth in what looked like protest, but then snapped it shut. "Fuck you," she said. "You're right." She reached for the pepper mill.

"Um, ladies," said Kai. She was standing in front of the refrigerator. "We've got a problem."

I turned to look at her and squinted. She was holding up a wrapped piece of cheese that was dripping with condensation.

I shook my head. "Wait, why—?" And then I sprinted over to the fridge and stuck my hand inside. "Nooooo," I groaned. It was warm.

"Someone must have tripped the plug yesterday," said Kai.

"No, no, no," I wailed, pulling out Tupperware container after Tupperware container of meats and cheeses and cooked vegetables and sauces—all undoubtedly absolutely teeming with bacteria at this point.

"Fuck," said Marta. "Oh, man. Fuck."

I dug through everything desperately. "There must be something salvageable. At least one thing, right?" But it was all slick and warm and soft and completely unsafe. Ruined.

I sunk my head against the counter. I didn't even know who to blame. It could have been either of these two, wriggling around in their drunken stupidity. It could have been me, equally idiotically drunk. Or it could have even been Brett, with all his good intentions. All I knew was that all of our leftovers were down the tubes, we were supposed to open in less than twenty minutes, and we had absolutely nothing to serve our customers.

"We could just do drinks?" suggested Marta. "Like, lemonade and coffee?"

I shook my head. "No ice. No dairy."

Kai stared at me blank-faced. "Bummer," she said, shrugging indifferently.

"We could shop? I could run to Adams," said Marta.

"No time. By the time you got there and back, and then we did prep, half the day would be gone." I put my head back up, feeling sick to my stomach. "We can't do it. We'll have to take the loss and pack it in."

Marta blinked unhappily. Kai looked out the window and hummed.

"Fuck, fuck, fuck!" I swore loudly and kicked the refrigerator door.

The girls looked at each other. "Who's going to tell Ethan?" squeaked Marta.

chapter 14

Manhattan

Knicks game

So," said Sarah, as we hurried up Seventh Avenue, "who told him?"

"I did," I said. "I almost let Marta do it, but I sucked it up at the last second. I figured I had to clean up my own mess."

After the whole debacle, I had wanted to call Lucy, of course, but that wasn't an option. Then I had tried to text Lotta, but she was apparently in the middle of something with her stepdaughter and said she'd get back to me later. I didn't call Brett, for obvious reasons. So I finally broke down and called Sarah.

Sarah and I were probably the least close of all four of us. I had met her through Lucy after Sarah's first husband had purchased a small painting from Titus. Sarah and Lucy had hit it off right away—and I will admit, back in those days, Sarah wasn't quite the extension-wearing, fame-chasing, mildly manic woman she had turned into lately. She was just a bored, slightly insecure, ex–gossip girl type with a wicked sense of humor and great style.

And to be fair, she had totally come through for me. She sat there on the phone, listening to me blubber about what a fuckup I was, without offering any unnecessary commentary, until I finally calmed down. Then she told me to get on the bus and come back to the city. She was going to take me out for a night on the town.

"So, how'd the baby chef take it?" she asked, turning off the street toward a white metal door with the words THE FLOATING FIRE emblazoned across it.

"He was less than impressed, to say the least. But at least he didn't lose any money. Most of the stuff was leftovers, anyway, and I paid for any extra new stuff." We started walking up an echoing stairway. "Sarah, where the hell are we? What is this?"

She turned to me, grinning. "Surprise! I thought we could get colonics together before we go to the Knicks game!"

I stopped walking. "Colonics? What? Like, when they shoot water up your butt?"

She grabbed my arm and started tugging me back up the stairs. "Oh, but it's so much more! It's awesome. I mean, the actual butt part isn't that great—but the way you feel after? All cleaned out and fresh! And the fact that you can basically eat anything you want for, like, a week, without gaining a thing?"

"But isn't that because everything you eat for a week just comes shooting out the other end five minutes after you put it into your mouth?"

"No, I mean, yes, kind of, but it's more than that. You get all the bad bacteria out of your gut."

"But I thought gut bacteria was supposed to be good."

She yanked me through the door. "You'll love it."

A smiling blond woman met us at the entrance. "Welcome to the Floating Fire," she said in singsong voice.

"We have an appointment for two," said Sarah.

"Nope," I corrected. "Just one. I am happy to hang out in the waiting room or whatever while you get to experience the 'floating fire,' but none for me."

"It's very safe," wheedled the blonde. "We simply insert a small plastic tube into your anus and gently fill the cavity with warm water until it flushes back out again. It's such a healthful way of releasing toxins."

"Yeah, I'll keep my toxins, thanks."

"Billy," whined Sarah.

"No." I held firm.

"Fine," she said. "But you don't know what you're missing. Seriously."

The place, appropriately enough, looked like a giant pink-tiled bathroom. The woman led Sarah into a separate room, where I glimpsed a very medical-looking bed, and handed Sarah a paper gown before shutting the door.

After a few moments, the blond woman reemerged and gestured me over. "She'd like you to keep her company," she whispered.

I wrinkled my nose. "Really? I mean, while she's actually getting it?"

"She's covered up. You won't see a thing."

I heard Lucy's voice. *This is what you get for trying to replace me with Sarah.*

Sarah was lying on her side under a fuzzy green blanket when I came in. I noticed a long, clear plastic tube snaking out from under the sheets but I quickly looked away before I could ascertain where it led.

I sat down on the far side of the tube.

"Don't worry," Sarah said cheerfully. "I'll send you out before anything serious starts happening."

I grimaced, trying not to imagine what "anything" might be.

"So, how's the pregnancy chase going?" I asked, desperate for a change of subject.

She frowned. "Not great so far. I mean, I'm sure I'd totally be pregnant by now, but Brian is working so late almost every night that we hardly even see each other. And then when he gets home, he's so exhausted that he basically falls asleep at the dinner table. It's almost like he doesn't want me to get knocked up."

"Hmm," I said, not meeting her eyes.

"It's driving the producers on the show crazy. I mean, the whole point of the baby plotline is all the sex that happens before it, right?"

"Huh," I hedged. "I guess?"

Sarah looked at me, suddenly serious. "So, do you miss her?"

"Who?" I asked, relieved that she had changed the subject, but not sure I wanted to talk about this, either.

She shook her head. "Don't play coy."

I sighed. "Have you seen her?"

"Not really. I mean, a coffee here, a text there. She seems really busy, but I'm not sure why."

I shrugged. "Fucking her besotted husband. And probably that article for *Grub Street* or whatever."

She shook her head. "No, I think there might be something else. Something just seems like—" Suddenly, her eyes widened. "Oh. Okay. Time for you to go now."

I bolted out of there as fast as I humanly could.

Forty-five minutes later, the door slammed open and Sarah raced out across the room, her bare ass hanging out of her paper gown, into what I could only imagine was the bathroom.

Fifteen minutes after that, she reemerged, pale, but with a bright smile on her face. "Okay, I'm ready. Let me just get dressed and we can go."

I raised an eyebrow. She looked a little shaky to me. "Are you sure?" I said. "We can skip the game."

"No, no, no. I always feel so energized after a good flush. Why waste it?"

I shook my head. "Whatever works for you, sister."

"Remember," the blond woman called after us as we walked out the door, "no dairy for forty-eight hours!"

I sometimes forgot that Sarah was a quasi-celebrity. I mean, I've known famous people before. Titus was ridiculously famous. You didn't run around with him and Lucy without meeting a bunch of the illuminati. And, of course, Omari basically *was* the illuminati, but Sarah was actually on TV, even if it was just cable, and thus she was treated differently. Which is how we found ourselves signing autographs in a Starbucks in Midtown before we went to the Knicks game.

"You know," I told the overly excited elderly lady who had spotted Sarah dusting her flat white with cinnamon, asked for her autograph, and then demanded that I sign her napkin as well, "I'm not anyone famous."

The lady thrust her pen into my hand. "But you know her," she said, pointing back at Sarah, "so maybe someday you will be."

I couldn't argue with that logic, so I signed her napkin and followed Sarah out the door.

I looked at her paper cup as she greedily sipped the coffee. "I thought no dairy?"

Sarah waved her little green plastic stopper around. "Oh, this is fine. Hardly any. I've done it a million times before."

We took a cab to the Knicks special entrance for celebrities and their hangers-on, and a whole line of paparazzi started flashing their cameras at us before we even had a foot out the door. Once we were all the way out, a few of them seemed to recognize Sarah and kept shooting, but when she passed through ahead of me, they put their cameras back down, instinctively knowing that I wasn't anyone, and not nearly as democratic as the lady in the Starbucks.

Security checked our bags, and then we took the elevator up to Suite 200, the skybox where all the rich and famous met and dined before being strategically released among the general public.

I liked basketball, and since Sarah had somehow ended up with seats in Celebrity Row, I was excited that we were going to see the game up close, but what I was *really* excited about was the insanely extravagant buffet that Jean-Georges had created for the suite. It was the stuff of legend, and I couldn't wait to get my chance at it.

A-list celebrities clustered around the long banquet table, nearly blocking it from my view. I was a little intimidated, but then I caught a flash of the sushi bar, and I figured that if I could just squish myself between Hugh Jackman and someone who looked a lot like Khloé Kardashian from behind, I could get at the gigantic snow crab legs that I had spied when we first walked through the door.

"I see a whole pile of tuna tartare I plan to plunge my face directly into," I whispered to Sarah and started forward, but she clutched my arm.

"Oh, Billy, I don't feel very well."

I looked back at her. She was even paler than before and was weaving a little.

"I need a bathroom, but I'm feeling a little light-headed, could you—?"

I grabbed her round the shoulders and marched her back to the bathroom, where she hurriedly entered a stall.

"Are you okay, hon?" I said through the door.

"Yes," she called weakly. "Just the remains of my treatment."

I took a quick step backward. "Um, okay, do you mind if I go back to the—"

"Can you wait for me?" she interrupted. "I won't be long."

"Sure," I said, leaning up against the bank of sinks and taking my phone out of my purse.

Sarah had a colonic and wasn't supposed to have dairy but she had dairy (OF COURSE) and now she's shitting her brains out in the Suite 200 bathroom and won't let me leave, I tapped out. Then I looked up at the woman washing her hands next to me and calmly added, And Liza fucking Minnelli is washing her hands RIGHT NEXT TO ME RIGHT NOW. Then I sent the whole message to Lucy before I remembered that I probably shouldn't.

But still, maybe this was all weird and funny enough to jog a response.

. . .

. . .

. . .

Nothing.

Sarah staggered out. "Billy, I'm so sorry but I think I have to go home."

I nodded, trying not to look annoyed.

"But you can still totally stay for the game if you like." Her legs actually wobbled as she uttered these words.

I sighed and patted her arm. "No, it's fine. Let me help you home, S."

Sarah's apartment was only a few blocks from Brett's place. I thought about what a bitch I'd been the last time I'd seen him.

What the hell. No time like the present.

"Can I use your bathroom real quick?" I said after I settled her into bed with a cup of chamomile tea. "And can I borrow your trench coat? The coat I brought isn't warm enough."

"Sure." She waved at me, already absorbed in her cell phone. "Whatever you need."

It's a cliché, but it's a cliché for a reason, I thought as I buttoned up the trench over my naked body and slipped my heels back on.

"Sarah, I'm going to leave now." I poked my head through her bedroom door. "You all good?"

I let the door block my body as she waved me out: I didn't want her to notice my bare legs where my jeans used to be.

It was cold outside, and I briefly considered hailing a cab for the three-block distance, but I figured if I walked fast, or even ran, I'd warm up soon enough.

I slipped into his building with a tenant, took the elevator up, and knocked at his apartment door.

I smiled, imagining the way he'd look at me when he opened the door. I figured if we went straight to bed he would understand this as the apology I meant it to be, and not think to ask me about how things had gone with the maiden voyage of the leftovers truck. Or mention what a pathetic, drunken cunt I'd been the last time he'd seen me. In fact, my basic plan was just to surprise him, have some I'm really-really-sorry sex, and get out before we had to talk about anything at all.

He answered the door in pajama bottoms and a ragged T-shirt. His eyes were puffy, his nose was red, and he was carrying a box of tissues and a twenty-dollar bill.

"Oh," he said. His voice was hoarse. "You're not Thai takeout."

"You're sick?" I asked.

"Sick enough that I'm not entirely sure you're not a hallucination," he said.

I pushed past him. "I'm not a hallucination."

He followed me inside, shutting the door behind us. "Billy, it's not that I'm not happy to see you, but you don't want to catch this. It's total misery."

I felt his forehead. He was burning up. "Are you taking anything?" I asked him.

He shook his head. "I ordered from the drugstore but that seems like a very long time ago."

"Okay, cowboy," I said. "Let's get you to bed."

He squinted at me, finally seeming to notice what I was wearing. "Oh my God," he said. "Are you actually naked under that coat? Are you actually fulfilling the fantasy I've had since I was fourteen years old?"

"Maybe," I said.

"Wait, is this because you were such an asshole the last time I saw you?"

"Yes," I said shortly.

He grinned goofily. "This is the best apology I've ever received."

"Alas," I said, steering him to his bedroom, "you, my friend, are way, way too sick to do anything about it."

"Fuck that," he said, leaning toward me and tugging at my top button. "I would have to be dying not to take advantage of this."

He fumbled for a moment and then groaned and closed his eyes. "Actually," he said, "I'm pretty sure I'm dying."

"Yup, okay," I said, and guided him to his bed.

After I settled him down, I put my clothes back on and went out for Advil and NyQuil and Vicks VapoRub. I stopped at Whole Foods and bought some groceries, and then popped into Saiguette—a Vietnamese restaurant we liked—and bought a container of spicy bún bò Huê so he could have some immediate sustenance.

He was asleep when I got back in, but I woke him long enough to spoon some soup into his mouth.

His eyes flew open. "Spicy!" he coughed.

I gave him another spoonful. "It'll help clear your sinuses."

After he finished the soup, I gave him a glass of water and a small cup of NyQuil.

"Tastes awful," he groaned.

"Don't be a baby," I said, and rubbed some Vicks on his feet and chest.

"Thank you," he said meekly, and then promptly fell back asleep.

I filled a stockpot with water and then threw in a whole chicken along with some extra thighs and wings, a few carrots, an unpeeled onion, and a split head of garlic still in its skin. I added peppercorns and a small handful of fresh thyme and a couple of bay leaves. I wanted this to cook faster than the average chicken soup, so I measured out a few tablespoons of chicken bouillon as well. I brought it all to a boil, skimmed off the scum that had risen to the top, and then turned it down to a simmer.

He slept and I kept myself busy reading his one cookbook—a signed copy of Marcus Samuelsson's *New American Table*, that, as far as I could tell, he had never actually cracked open.

After a couple of hours, I strained the chicken broth and then picked the meat off the bones. Then I threw out the bones and used-up vegetables, poured all the soup back into the pot, and added the meat and some new slices of carrots and celery, and tasted for seasoning.

I heard a sound from his bedroom, so I went to check on him. "You awake?" I whispered.

He cracked his eyes open. "You're actually here. I thought maybe you were a dream. Were you really wearing nothing but a trench coat and heels?"

"Nope," I said. "That definitely never happened." I walked over and felt his forehead again. "That's better," I said. "I think we're over the worst of it. How do you feel?"

He considered this for a moment. "Better, actually. Hungry."

I brought him some soup, crackers, and orange juice on a tray. He sat up and fed himself and then looked at me, a little smile playing over his face.

"Are you staying the night, then?"

I nodded. "I'll stay until you don't need me anymore."

He scooted over. "Can you stand to share my sickbed?"

I laughed and climbed in next to him. "No point in getting persnickety about it now."

We lay together for a moment, my head on his shoulder. "So," he said, "you gonna put your trench coat back on anytime soon?" he said.

I laughed. "It's Sarah's, actually."

"Remind me to buy you your own, then."

"How about some more NyQuil instead?"

He sighed and closed his eyes. "Hardly seems a fair fucking trade, but I guess I'll take what I can get."

I measured out some more medicine for him and he swallowed it, grimacing, and then pulled me closer.

"See, Sitwell," he said, his voice already drowsy. "I knew you weren't all bad."

He was better by morning. A little groggy, but he got up out of bed to eat the toast and tea I made for him. By noon, I was looking up the bus schedule and getting ready to leave.

He took my hand across the kitchen table. "Thanks again for saving my life. When will I see you again, buddy?"

I shrugged. "Soon, I'm sure."

He slowly let my hand go. "Okay then. Soon. And next time maybe I won't be such a writhing heap of fever, germs, and snot."

I laughed. "One can only hope."

I caught the one o'clock bus back up to Kingston. As we lurched into the Lincoln Tunnel, I took out my phone. For a moment, my finger hovered over Brett's number, but then, feeling guilty and a little furtive, I sent Ethan a text instead.

I have a funny story to tell about nearly eating at a Jean-Georges buffet.

He answered right away. Oh? Want to come over tonight and tell it in person?

I considered this for a moment.

Kai made a cheesecake, he added. And texted me a picture of the round white cake dripping with blackberries.

I curled my lip. Pfft. Kai.

Looks good. But that's okay. I'm not that hungry.

We don't have to eat cheesecake, he returned. Why don't I come to your place?

I smiled and sent him a thumbs-up emoji. That was more like it.

chapter 15

The River House

Kingston

I lit a fire in the kitchen fireplace. It was one of the things that I loved the most about this house. The view, of course, but also the fact that there were three separate fireplaces.

One of my earliest memories was of watching my mom build a fire in our little beehive fireplace. I must have been four, maybe even three, and I was fresh out of the bath. I knelt on the hearth, waiting for her to get the flames started so I could drop my towel and enjoy the crackling warmth on my bare skin as she changed me into my cozy pajamas.

I don't think anyone would have called my mother beautiful. She was short and plump, with dark circles under her eyes and rough, straight hair that she kept in a sensible bob. But when she was "on"—in those brief, flickering moments when she wasn't being sucked under by her tide of sadness—I thought she was the most extraordinary thing. She was wickedly funny and warm, and when she turned her attention on me, I felt almost desperate, I was so grateful for that temporary thaw.

The fire caught and flared.

I opened a bottle of Manzanilla sherry and poured myself a tiny glass; then I rummaged through the fridge until I found a small round of Brillat-Savarin cheese and a bag of Marcona almonds I had been hoarding. Add a few handfuls of dried cherries and a scattering of butter crackers, and I had a decent cheese plate.

There was a knock on the kitchen door and I turned to see Ethan's face peering in from the dark. "Come in," I called, and he opened the door, bringing in a cool sweep of night air as well as half of Kai's cheesecake on a platter.

"Hey," he said. He looked as if he had freshly showered. His dark hair was brushed back from his face and his forehead was exposed.

He seemed achingly young.

"Does Kai know you stole her cheesecake?" I asked him as he put the plate on the counter.

He shrugged. "She never eats what she bakes anyway." He examined the fireplace appreciatively. "Wow, this is something. Do you have a spit? I bet I could roast a suckling pig in there."

I nodded. "I was thinking about setting up a couple of racks for sure."

He stretched. "I'm so glad it's September. I'm sick of grilling and cold salads. I can't wait to braise and roast and bake. Everyone eats more in cold weather."

I nodded. "Fall is my favorite, too. You want a glass of sherry?"

"Sure." He sat down on one of the tall metal stools that flanked the kitchen island.

I pushed the cheese plate closer to him. "Help yourself."

"Nice," he said, cutting into the Savarin.

Nice, sneered Lucy's voice. *Have fun with the scintillating conversation.*

I noticed a large angry burn on the back of his hand. "New one?" I said, pointing it out.

He rolled his eyes. "So stupid. I was pulling out a rack of lamb and Davey, my line cook, came up from behind and goosed me."

"What? Why the fuck would he do that?"

He took a sip of the sherry and shook his head. "Prank war. It's been going on for like two months now."

I laughed disbelievingly. "But you're the chef. They should know better than to fuck around with you like that. I would have fired someone who pulled that shit on me."

He smiled uncomfortably. "They're also my friends."

I shook my head. "You're making it harder than it needs to be. What do you do when you actually have to fire someone?"

He didn't meet my eyes. "I don't."

"Wait, so you've never fired anyone?"

He suddenly reached out and turned over my hand. "How about this one?" he said, touching a large jagged scar on my thumb. "Where'd you get that?"

I laughed. "Oh, are we changing the subject now?"

"I'm a good chef, Billy."

"You're a great one," I said sincerely.

"So where'd you get that scar?"

"Fine. Okay. So we're going to play this game, huh?"

Everyone who worked in a kitchen knew this game. The history of scars and burns.

He nodded. "Humor me."

"Okay." I took a deep breath. "Funnily enough, that one is actually a dog bite. Nothing to do with cooking. My high school boyfriend and I were making out in his basement and apparently it got his Springer spaniel all worked up, because suddenly he sank his fangs into my thumb."

"Wow. Talk about ruining the mood." He laughed.

"Yeah. We broke up after that. I fucking hated that dog. Okay, your turn," I said. "What about this one?" I pointed to a faint white line across his palm.

"Stale bagel. Total rookie mistake." He touched a burn at the tip of my right index finger. "And this one?"

"Tasting caramel. I was stupid and greedy." I started cataloguing, then, skipping from scar to scar. "Cutting butternut squash. Slicing a baguette. That one was three stitches. Frying donuts. Frying oysters. Oh, God, that one was making taffy. It was so gnarly. That stuff just sticks, and when you peel it off it takes all the skin with it. It hurt like a motherfucker."

He laughed, his long fingers lighting from place to place on his hands and lower arms. "Filleting a salmon, breaking down a pig. I thought I might be a butcher at one point. Deep-frying Twinkies—"

"Wait, what?"

"I worked at the county fair for a while. But don't turn up your nose, they're super good. Caramel. I guess everyone's got a caramel scar, right? Oh, and feel this one."

He took my hand and guided it to a raised white spot on his wrist. I brushed the tips of my fingers over it and wrinkled my nose. There was something round and smooth and jutting out from under the scar. He pushed my fingers and I could actually feel a ball roll underneath the skin.

"Yikes. What is that?"

He grinned. "A BB. Doesn't count, but still cool, right? My brother shot me when I was ten."

I laughed, trying not to think too hard about the way I was still touching his wrist, the way that his hand was still on mine.

Lucy's voice.

Dammit, Billy, don't.

I took my hand away. "Do you want to go for a walk? The river is pretty amazing at night."

He nodded. "Sure, sounds nice." He quickly drained his glass of sherry before wiping his mouth on the back of his hand.

We went out the back way and took the path down to the river. It was breezy and a little cold and the moon was bright, bathing us in a fluttery silver light that filtered through the swaying tree branches. I led the way, skidding on my heels in the spots that were steep, and trying very hard not to fall on my ass. We reached a set of rickety stairs down to the dock. Ethan peered down suspiciously.

"Those steps look pretty fucked up. Think they're safe?"

I shrugged. "Probably not. Save me if I fall through." I started down.

"No fear at all, huh?" he called as he followed me.

"Not of this particular thing, anyway," I called back.

The dock was small and swayed alarmingly when I stepped onto it, and even more so when Ethan joined me, but we made our way to the water and sat down, not quite trusting the wood enough to stand.

We looked out at the river, which was streaked black and silver and making a soft, hushing, tidal sound as it spread out before us. On the other side were the twinkling red lights of the railroad, and above those, the golden glow of lights from a scattering of stately old mansions that made up the Dutchess County side of the river.

"The Hudson might be my favorite river," said Ethan. "I know it's dirty and you probably can't swim in it, and you sure as hell don't want to eat out of it. But there's just something so . . . alive about it, you know? It's seems almost sentient to me."

I nodded. "Yeah," I said. "Tidal rivers are weird. Not quite river, not quite ocean. A lot of mojo going on."

Ethan leaned back on his elbows. "The greatest date I ever had was overlooking the Hudson."

"Oh?" I said.

Shut up. I am not jealous.

"Yeah, you know Bard College? In Annandale-on-Hudson? They have all these incredible old mansions that they've converted into dorms and classroom spaces, and it's really easy to sneak onto their campus. So, there's this one building—Blithewood. I think it's, like, an economic institute or something now—but it looks like some crazy Southern plantation house or something. And next to the mansion is this sunken, walled garden, all planted with roses and herbs and those soft, silvery-green plants. What are they called?"

"Lamb's ears?" I said.

"Yeah. Lamb's ears. Anyway. This girl—I had been trying to get her to go out with me for so long—agreed to meet me there for a night picnic. And I just thought it would be, you know, some beers and sandwiches or whatever, and maybe, if I was lucky, we'd finally make out. But she had packed a basket with stuff that she must have taken all day to make—"

"Which is what happens when you go to culinary school," I pointed out.

"For sure." He sighed. "I'll never forget these little fritters she made. They were salt cod and cassava, and she'd managed to keep them warm, all wrapped up in a linen napkin, and we just sat there, side by side, in this crazy gorgeous garden, looking out over the river, eating these delicious fritters that just sort of melted in my mouth, and talking about . . . everything, right? Like, when one thing just leads to the next and there's no end to all the things you have in common and you know you could probably talk all night?"

I nodded.

"And so we did talk all night. Then, when it was nearly dawn, we shared one perfect kiss—like a ridiculous, movie version of a kiss— and then she remembered that she had a sauce test in, like, two hours, and that was that. End of date."

I was silent for a moment, listening to the water lap at the shore. "So then what?" I said. "Did you guys keep dating?"

"I wanted to," he said. "I tried. But she almost flunked her sauce test and it freaked her out so much that she said she needed to con- centrate on school—we were graduating that year—and after that, we were working together, so . . ."

Kai, I thought.

I looked over at him. He was gazing at me with this sincere, sweet look that made him look about fifteen.

I was way too old for this shit. I stood up.

"Oh, wanna go back?" he said.

"Yeah, I had a long day, so . . ."

Suddenly, the puppy-dog look was gone, and he looked like a man again. A man who knew he had blown it. "Sure, yeah. Cool. This was fun. Thanks. We should probably get together again soon, though, and talk about where we can take the truck next."

I nodded. "Absolutely."

He smiled slyly and punched me softly in the arm. "And maybe this time you won't unplug the fridge."

"Shut up. Fuck off."

We walked back up the hill side by side.

chapter 16

"Please say you'll do it, Bill. Please, pretty please."

I walked through my kitchen, heading for the back door. "It's a really long drive, Lotta," I said into the phone. "I don't know if the Kia will even make it that far."

"If it doesn't, I will buy you a new car. A better one."

I rolled my eyes as I walked out onto the porch. "Why don't you just hire someone there?"

"Because I want you. I need your food, but mostly I need your support. Omari is going to leave for Germany and I just want to do something special before he's gone, because after that, it's just going to be me and terrible Sage and the empty fucking Hamptons, and God only knows what I will do then."

I sighed. "Okay, let me talk to Ethan about taking a couple of the kitchen staff for help . . ."

She squealed. "Oh, thank you! Thank you! Now, let's talk about the menu! I was thinking—"

All of a sudden I wasn't listening to her, because, out of the corner of my eye, I noticed a small white flash hurtle across the lawn. I craned my neck. *Another rabbit?*

No. It was a dog. A tiny, ugly, matted, shivering dog sitting in the cove of the lawn and staring up at me.

"Lotta?" I said. "I'm going to have to call you back."

I hung up before she could answer.

"Hey," I said to the dog.

It flinched but stayed put, still staring up at me.

"Where did you come from?"

It blinked. Its bulging, runny eyes made up like three-quarters of its face.

I slowly started to walk down the stairs, not breaking its gaze. "Hey there, puppy," I said.

A quiver ran through its body as I reached the last step. It barked sharply but remained glued to the ground.

I took a step toward it. Then another. It held firm.

Then, once I was close enough to stretch out my hand and almost touch it, it let out a howl of anguish and bolted, disappearing into a little shed at the edge of the yard.

"Goddammit," I swore, running after it. I poked my head into the shadowy building and waited for my eyes to adjust. There it was—shaking in the corner and softly growling.

"Come here, baby," I said, slowly stretching out my hand. "Come here . . ."

The dog struggled to its feet and snarled at me, peeling its lips back to bare its little white teeth. I yanked my hand back.

"Okay. Fine," I said, slamming the door shut behind me. "Stay in here then."

I stood outside the shed for a moment, wondering what to do

next. It was a gorgeous fall day. The sky was bright blue, the leaves were starting to turn red and yellow, and the light was starting to take on that slanted and golden autumn cast.

Maybe if I crack the door, it will just go away. Be someone else's problem.

I reached over to open the door but paused. Inside, I heard it whimpering.

Fuck.

"Fine. Fuck! Fine!" I yelled, and marched back up to my house.

Growing up, I had a cat. It had been the one thing I had ever heard my parents argue about. Normally my father, afraid of the way my mother was slowly disappearing into herself and constantly searching for ways to make her happy and bring her back, capitulated to anything my mother ever bothered wanting. He was willing to let her call any and all shots in the hope that it might help lift her cloud.

But then a kitten had shown up on our back porch when I was four years old. It was scrawny and tiny and mewling and my mother didn't want it. I'm sure she looked at it and merely saw one more thing she couldn't care for, one more burden to add to her already almost impossibly heavy walk through life. But I looked at that kitten and I saw . . . a kitten. And if there is anything more appealing to a semi-neglected four-year-old girl than a fucking kitten, I'll eat a roach.

I saw it first. I was lying on my stomach in the living room coloring when I heard the little mewl from outside, and my heart just about leapt from my chest. I knew *exactly* what that sound was. I ran to the window, and there it sat. All ruffled gray fur, pointy oversize ears, and big blue eyes. Just sitting on the porch and looking right at me.

I called to my mother, happy hysteria in my voice, and she came running. But once she saw what it was, she shook her head and backed away. No, she said. It would find another home. It was not our responsibility. She didn't even want to open the door and look at the little thing.

But my dad happened to be home that day, and he always had a soft spot for animals, so as soon as my mother went back to the kitchen, I snuck into the garage and whispered to him, telling him about the little beast who was waiting for us out front.

Within minutes, that tiny ball of fur was nestled in my lap and happily purring and making biscuits on my belly. I was dizzy with joy.

My parents argued for an hour. It seemed to go on and on. Up until then, I had never even heard my father raise his voice at my mother, but he just kept at her. I was freaked out as hell, and half of me wanted to march in there and tell them never mind, but the other, stronger, and perhaps more self-protective half just clung to that little animal like it might kill me to lose it.

I'll never forget the words that won the argument. I'll never forget, because they were absolutely cruel, absolutely devastating, and absolutely true.

"Dammit, Caroline," my father had finally shouted, "she needs something she can love that will actually bother to love her back!"

A shiver ran up my spine at the silence that followed that pronouncement. And then I heard my father's murmured, broken apology, but my mother wasn't having it.

"You're right," was all she said as she marched out of the kitchen.

She looked at me, but past me, blindly, not really seeing me at all. "You can keep the cat."

Which is a long story explaining why, exactly, I was standing back outside the shed with half a chicken, a wedge of Brie, and a roast beef sandwich I had been about to eat for lunch before Lotta called.

I eased the door open again. The dog whimpered.

"Hey, baby," I called in a soft voice. "Hey, little guy, are you hungry?"

I waved a chicken leg through the air, hoping it would pick up the scent.

The dog stopped whimpering. I could see its protruding black eyes fix on me.

"Hey, little guy, you want this? You want a bite of this?"

The dog lifted its nose and scooted forward a bit, snuffling. I pinched off some of the meat and threw it so that it landed halfway between myself and the hungry dog.

After a moment's hesitation, the dog flashed forward and scooped up the chicken and then backed up again, smacking loudly as it bolted it down.

"You liked that, huh?" I said, breaking off another piece and throwing it a little closer to my feet this time. "You want more?"

This time the dog didn't even hesitate—just ran for the food and stayed over it, not even bothering to back its way into the corner again. I took a step back then, leaving the shed, and took the rest of the meat and skin off the bone and laid it just outside the threshold.

In a moment, the little dog was at my feet, happily scarfing down the chicken and then looking up at me hopefully for more. I smiled at it and tossed it a piece of thigh this time.

Then it wagged its tail.

I wasn't surprised. The fucking chicken was free-range and local and cost seventeen dollars a pound. I had slow-roasted it with cipollini onions and about a stick of truffle butter.

I named that kitten Mittens, by the way (what do you fucking want? I was four). And less than a year after it showed up on my porch, my mother was dead.

But Mittens lived to be nineteen.

chapter 17

En route to the Hamptons

Why. Whyyyyy did we have to bring the stupid dog?" whined Kai as she sat in the backseat of the car, wedged as far away as she could be from the shrilly yapping (and newly christened) Chicken. Apparently, he had seen something he didn't like out the window as we trundled toward East Hampton and was letting us all know about it.

"Okay, okay," I said. "Enough now, Chicken. We're good."

My soothing voice had exactly zero effect, so I threw him a Brazil nut that I fished out of the gorp I had sitting in the cupholder.

Marta, who was riding shotgun, looked doubtful. "Nuts? Is that even good for a dog?"

"If it poisons him, at least he'll be quiet," said Kai.

We had been driving almost five hours, with frequent stops for doggy potty breaks (I was in the midst of housebreaking Chicken, who seemed to have exactly zero familiarity with the concept).

On the way down, we had eaten at two different drive-throughs (Kai refused to go with Burger King and made us pull over again for Wendy's), refined the entire menu for Lotta's house party, and argued incessantly about the name of the food truck.

Kai said that the name ought to be Huma as well, that we weren't even sticking with the theme this weekend (Lotta was paying us a pile of cash to do a riff on food-truck fish and chips), and that it was supposed to be publicizing Ethan's restaurant, so why wouldn't it have the same name?

She curled her lip. "The idea of leftovers is totally gross, anyway," she said. "It makes me think of being a kid and of all the congealed, nasty things growing mold in the back of the fridge that you're forced to eat when there's nothing else left."

I huffed in disbelief. "What are you talking about? Why was your mother feeding you moldy food?"

"I didn't have a mother," she answered casually. "She died when I was three."

I was quiet for a beat, unsettled to have something so visceral in common with this girl.

"My mother once made this thing she called compost soup," interjected Marta in a high voice, obviously trying to break the tension. "It was the end of the month and we were broke, so she took everything left in the refrigerator and poured it together into a saucepan. Cottage cheese and milk and cut-up carrots and lemon juice, and the worst part was that she had a can of beets—so the whole thing turned pink."

"That's disgusting," said Kai.

"It tasted like puke," agreed Marta. "But we also had a package of Oreos for dessert. No cookie until I ate the soup. So I ate the soup." She laughed. "That's probably why I'm a pastry chef. Fucking Oreos."

"It's called Leftovers," I said forcefully. "That's the name."

Kai rolled her eyes. "Fine," she said. "Just don't come bitching to me when all the rich, middle-aged Hamptonites won't eat what we serve because they think it's past its freshness date."

Chicken started barking all over again. Not even a cashew would shut him up.

"Oh, thank fucking God!" said Lotta as she rushed out to greet us in front of her beach cottage.

She looked, as always, better than 99 percent of the populace, and I could see Marta's and Kai's eyes widen as they took in her six feet of curves draped in a casual, off–the-shoulder black caftan, but I also thought I could sense some tension around her mouth and eyes. She seemed tired.

She folded me into a hug and I felt a little tremor run through her. I pulled back. "Lotta? You okay?"

"I'm just so happy to see you," she said in her smoky voice. She wrapped me back into her arms and laughed. "I've missed you, Billy. I've missed all the girls."

I laughed back at her, and then, over her shoulder, I saw Omari, in jeans and a formfitting red tee, followed by his daughter, Sage, wearing a tight yellow minidress, come down the steps.

"Hello, ladies," said Omari. His voice was deep and warm and he beamed at all of us like we were his favorite people on earth. "I'm so glad you could make it."

Kai and Marta tittered. They had met Omari and Lotta before, of course, because they had helped Ethan cater their wedding, but they were going to be dealing with them much more closely this time, and I could see that Omari's celebrity was throwing them off a bit. I gently disengaged myself from a still-clinging Lotta.

"Hey, Omari," I said, and he leaned over to kiss my cheek. "You remember Kai and Marta?"

"Of course," he said, and leaned over to kiss them, too. They both blushed and I thought Marta might actually burst into tears.

"And you all remember Sage?" said Lotta.

Sage's eyes skipped right past me and on to Kai and Marta. She sucked on her lower lip as she sized them up. "You guys party?" she finally said.

Marta had the grace to shoot me a worried look, but Kai just met Sage's gaze straight-on. "Sure," she said.

"Cool," said Sage. "Follow me."

I sighed as the three young women wandered into the house, but didn't say anything. They weren't children, after all, and we didn't need the full two days to prepare.

Lotta watched them go, a look of annoyance in her eyes. "Sorry," she murmured to me.

I shrugged. "Hey, as long as they're ready to prep when the time comes, I don't care. They're not my kids."

Omari shook his head. "Unfortunately, I can't say the same of Sage."

Lotta took me out to Pierre's that night, just the two of us. She said she had a big day planned for me and the girls the next day and she wanted a chance to catch up before the party. Omari promised to take care of Chicken (who instantly seemed to take on the role of yet another of Omari's dedicated fans and had been following him around since we had arrived) and "the girls," as he called them, but judging from the funky smell emanating from Sage's room, I didn't think we'd be seeing those three until morning—unless it was to raid the fridge.

Pierre's was a French café in Bridgehampton. Even in the off-season, it was never empty. Lotta and I snuggled into a red leather booth and we both ordered "La Mer"—steamed mussels with French fries and housemade mayonnaise.

"You mind if I have a glass of wine?" I said to Lotta, trying to be respectful of her sobriety.

She sighed. "I would join you, but I already allowed myself a little helper this morning."

I raised an eyebrow.

"Just half an Ativan," she said, her eyes widening innocently. "Trust me when I tell you that I needed that baby."

"Lotta," I said, "what is going on?"

"Oh, Billy." She took a sip of her water. "Where to begin?"

"Everything okay with you and Omari?"

"Oh," she said, smiling, "yes. I mean, aside from the fact that he has to go to Germany for this recording thing. But otherwise, we are great. I mean, he's just . . . he's such a good guy, Billy. I never knew someone could be so good."

My mind flashed guiltily to Brett. We had barely communicated since I had seen him in the city. I knew he was waiting on me to make the next move, but I was too distracted to know, exactly, what that next move should be.

"But I have to confess to something," said Lotta, dragging a French fry through the garlicky mayo. "Part of the reason I decided to come out here was that I felt like it was too hard keeping sober in the city."

"Oh?" I guiltily eyed the glass of rosé the waiter had just plunked down in front of me.

She shook her head. "That glass of wine is not the problem. It was just—well, Omari is very in demand, and he has to keep up a certain profile, you know? He has to promote his artists and the label, and he likes us to go to these things together. He is proud of me. Wants to show me off a little."

I picked up a mussel and nodded.

"And so between all that, plus seeing you guys . . ."

I looked up at her. "So it was us?"

She shrugged. "That last time—in Brooklyn. It was out of control, Billy. You and that stupid ex, and then you and Lucy . . . Have you talked to her yet, by the way?"

"She won't accept my calls," I said. "I'm trying, Lotta."

She frowned. "Yes, actually, I'm finding it very hard to get hold of her lately, too. It's odd . . ." She played with her engagement ring, flipping the giant sapphire round and round. "But anyway, so we came out here—easier for Omari to only go to the most necessary events then, you know? And less pressure for me to attend. And it was just wonderful at first. You know how it just clears out here after the summer. So quiet and peaceful."

"Pretty much dead," I offered.

"Yes, but I need that right now. Or I thought I needed that, anyway. But then Sage shows up. And ugh, Billy."

"Is she that bad?"

She laughed. "She is me. I mean, she is me twenty years ago, or ten years ago, or I guess even two years ago. She is smart and beautiful and absolutely lost. She has everything—money and connections and talent—but can't sit still in her own skin for more than a minute at a time." She shook her head. "She is so familiar. And I could help her. That's the crazy thing. I actually could help her. But"—she waved a French fry in the air—"she hates me. She won't listen to a word that comes out of my mouth."

I sipped my wine. "What does Omari say?"

She shook her head again. "Oh, he feels guilty. Says that she worked too hard when she was little. That his ex was unstable, and that maybe Sage shouldn't have been left alone with her so much. He feels he made mistakes. So he's easy on her. Indulges her, you know? And honestly, I don't know that him being any more strict would make a difference. I mean, my father threw me out of the house when I was a fuckup teen and it took me another thirty years before I found some peace." She sighed. "Maybe it's simply out of our control. I just worry so much."

I smirked at her.

"What?" she said.

"I just can't believe you're being such a mom. I mean, who would have thought?"

She laughed and flapped her hand at me. "Okay. Enough. So, tell me how you ended up with that wretched little dog."

We had breakfast on the terrace the next morning. It was a cool autumn day, and there was a brisk breeze coming off the ocean, but we bundled up and warmed our hands with giant foamy bowls of latte and hot croissants. There was also steel-cut Irish oatmeal and stewed berries and a pile of glistening, maple-brushed bacon for those of us who needed more sustenance.

Kai and Sage picked at their food, looking wan and hungover, but Marta cheerfully polished off her plate.

"Oh, I can always eat," she said, when she caught me looking at her.

"End of the world will come and you'll probably find me making a peanut butter sandwich."

Omari excused himself, saying he needed to get to work but that he'd see us for dinner, and then Lotta clapped her hands together.

"So," she said, beaming around the table, "I have a plan. We are going to go see my horse."

I choked on my croissant. "Your what?"

Sage rolled her eyes. "Lotta bought a horse. She can't ride, like, at all, but she bought a two-hundred-thousand-dollar horse."

I coughed harder. "What? You did what?"

"I am taking lessons!" insisted Lotta, who did not look embarrassed at all. "And I have always heard that the rider is only as good as her horse, so I bought a good one."

"But why?" I said. "Why not just use, like, the one they have at the barn?"

"Because I don't have to," said Lotta firmly. Then she stood up. "I'm going to go get dressed for riding. I want you all ready to leave in twenty minutes."

OMG, OMG, I frantically texted from the back of the Range Rover as Lotta drove us out to the barn where she kept her horse. She seemed pretty sane at first, but then I just found out that Lotta bought a $200,000 horse even though she doesn't know how to ride and we're going to see it and she's wearing, like, formal riding wear—like a velvet jacket and jodhpurs and these shiny, knee-high boots like she's going to a show—remember when the 4-H kids used to compete in English riding? God, I wish you could see this. I wish you were here . . . I miss you.

I sent it. I had been doing this a lot lately. Just sending Lucy messages even though I knew she wouldn't answer. I didn't understand it. I knew that our fight had been bad, but I had apologized and apologized—sent texts, left phone messages both drunk and sober, and not a word back.

After we pulled up to the farm and got out of the car, I surreptitiously snapped a picture of Lotta as she headed out to the field to meet her trainer. Of course, I sent that, too.

"It's like watching a giant toddler get led around on her party pony," said Sage as we sat in the viewing room and watched Lotta out in the ring.

I tried not to laugh, but it was hard. Sage was right. Lotta, who I had never seen look anything but sexy and at ease in pretty much any situation, looked like an oversize kid, desperately jouncing around and clinging to the grab strap of a ridiculously beautiful black Friesian, who seemed insulted to have this amateur upon his back.

Her trainer, casually dressed in a T-shirt, riding pants, and ankle boots as if in direct rebuke to Lotta's crazy, formal getup, kept a tight hold of the lead as they slowly walked the perimeter. I wondered how much Lotta paid her not to laugh.

As they came round to where we were standing, Lotta cheerfully lifted one hand to wave at us through the glass, but then quickly dropped it again and frantically grabbed at her horse's mane as he walked on, shifting and jouncing her like a sad little boat on a stormy ocean.

"Two. Hundred. Thousand. Dollars," said Sage.

"Maybe she'll get better?" said Marta.

"More likely she'll get bored," suggested Kai.

I didn't think this was doing much for Lotta's prospects in getting Sage to listen to her.

The millennials are making merciless fucking fun of her, I texted Lucy. I wish you were here.

We had lunch at World Pie in Bridgehampton. In the summer, this place was teeming with the young, hot, and scantily clad, all sitting out in the courtyard, eating enormous wood-fired pizzas and drinking wine. But it was dead out of season. Just a few stalwart year-round residents quietly enjoying the warmth and coziness of the indoor dining room.

We ordered antipasto, fried calamari, and three pizzas—fresh clam, duck, and *carciofi*, for the table, plus two bottles of Malbec. When the food arrived, I watched Sage fill her wineglass to the brim, but then she picked and poked at her plate, not actually eating anything.

This didn't get past Marta or Kai, either.

"Why aren't you eating?" asked Kai bluntly. "It's good."

"And expensive," added Marta, popping some calamari into her mouth.

"I'm intolerant of lots of stuff," said Sage airily. "And anyway"—she shot a pissy look at Lotta—"I don't like pizza."

"Who doesn't like pizza?" said Marta. "That's cray."

Kai narrowed her eyes. "When you say 'intolerant,' do you mean allergic? Like, an actual medically proven allergy?"

Sage shrugged. "Kind of."

"Or do you mean you're the type of person who orders well-done burgers at every restaurant and then doesn't eat the bun?"

"I'm on a restricted diet," said Sage defensively. "And I can't do gluten."

"If you say that to most chefs, they'll spit in your food, you know," said Marta cheerfully. "And add, like, handfuls of flour to all your sauces." She batted her long lashes. "I mean, *we* wouldn't do that, of course. But *some* chefs."

Kai leaned closer to Sage. "You're the kind of customer chefs hate."

"Now, now, girls," said Lotta hurriedly, "Sage really does have sensitivities. I've seen her get hives, myself."

Sage darted a look at Lotta that was almost grateful. "Yeah, I break out all over if I eat the wrong thing," she said.

Lotta, quick to take an opportunity, put her hand on Sage's shoulder and shook her head sympathetically. "Big, itchy welts. It's really quite terrible."

Sage violently shrugged her off. "It's not that bad," she hissed. "God."

Before the look of disappointed resignation had left Lotta's face, a tall, bearded blond guy with casually torn jeans and paint on his hands approached the table.

"Lolo!" he said to Lotta in a plummy English accent. "You don't know how excited I am to see you. I thought all the interesting people had left for the season."

"Ah, Martin. Billy, do you know Martin?"

I shook my head. "I don't think so."

"Everyone, this is Martin DiSantorino. He's an excellent painter. He just had an exhibition at the Keszler."

He didn't bother to tear his gaze away from Lotta. "When are you going to model for me again, my lady? I'd love to paint you, just like this, in your riding clothes. Or how about that nude we always talked about?"

Lotta laughed. "I'm an old married woman now, Martin. I'm afraid my nude modeling days are over."

"I'll do it," piped up Sage.

Martin looked over at her curiously, and a smile bloomed behind his shaggy beard as he took in the stunning young woman. Sage was wearing a deep-red V-neck sweater and a short denim skirt with knee-length boots—all designed to show off her lithe curves. Her hair was in long, intricate braids and a glossy lip stain made her full lips appear as if she had just eaten a particularly delicious plum.

"My, what a lovely idea. And who are you, exactly?" he said. His eyes practically gleamed with greed.

Lotta shook her head. "You are not painting my daughter, Martin," she said.

"Stepdaughter," corrected Sage. "And by the way, who the fuck are you to tell me what I can or can't do, Lotta?"

Lotta looked at her coolly. "Fine. The last time I modeled for Martin he spent half the time with his dick out and the other half chasing me around the studio, trying to stuff his hands down my pants. So if that interests you, I guess you're welcome to it."

Martin went purple. "I most certainly did not! I don't know what—"

"Oh, shut the fuck up, Martin. You're a predatory shit-weasel and you know it. I wouldn't let you get within spitting distance of Sage. And trust me when I tell you that you'll be lucky to escape with your soft little cock still between your legs once I tell her father about this conversation."

Martin gaped for a moment, struggling to respond, and then he seemed to notice that everyone within earshot had gone still and silent, listening in. He opened and shut his mouth like a gasping fish, gave one last grunt of protest, and then turned on his heel and stiffly marched out of the restaurant. The younger girls at the table, even

Sage, all turned wide, round eyes back to Lotta, who calmly took a sip of her water.

"He's fucking disgusting," she said to Sage, "and I was lying when I said he's a great artist. If you truly want to model nude, I'll find you a real painter—someone who actually knows what he's doing and can keep his dick in his pants unless he is expressly invited to do otherwise."

At dinner that night, something seemed to have thawed between Lotta and Sage. They sat next to each other and even though Sage mainly ignored Lotta to talk to Marta and Kai, her indifference seemed markedly more benign and less openly hostile. They now looked and acted like a slightly estranged parent and child, not comic-book archenemies.

At first, Omari seemed puzzled by this turn of events, darting nervous looks between the two women as if he couldn't quite believe what he was seeing—as if he expected a blowup at any moment. Then Lotta asked Sage to pass her the jug of water and Sage calmly complied, even saying, "You're welcome," to Lotta's polite thank-you.

Omari grabbed my arm in an excited grip.

"Did you see that?" he whispered. His voice was choked with emotion, his eyes shining.

I patted his hand. "I sure did," I affirmed.

He released my arm and sat back in his chair with a happy sigh. He looked like a man who had just experienced a significant weight being lifted from his shoulders.

"This salad is the bomb," whispered Marta in my other ear, oblivious to the family drama swirling around her. "I wouldn't have thought that beets go so well with plums. I'm going to text Ethan all about it."

I was probably one of the few people in the world who did not find the sound of the ocean particularly soothing. The sound of the Hudson River was okay, because I had to actively listen to hear it and could easily tune it out when I wanted to, but the ocean was like a giant fucking mouth breather panting directly in my ear.

The guest room I was staying in was, of course, exquisite, with every possible comfort and convenience. And I'm sure that if I had poked around long enough, I would have found the requisite white-noise machine along with a satin sleep mask, a lavender sachet, and a giant bottle of temazepam all there to help facilitate the sweet dreams of the über-wealthy, but I rolled out of bed and went down to the kitchen instead.

There was a light on and the sound of John Coltrane's *My Favorite Things* playing softly, and I found Omari sitting at the kitchen table, pen in hand, papers and a packet of Entenmann's chocolate donuts spread out around him.

"Oh, sorry," I said. "You're working. I can go back upstairs."

He smiled at me and shoved his papers over, clearing a space at the table. "You found out my dirty little secret," he said, indicating the donuts. "Might as well have one, then."

I sat down and took a donut. "It's the coating that gets me," I admitted, taking a bite. "It's like they mixed wax and chocolate, but in a good kind of way."

He laughed. "Want some warm milk to go with your wax?"

I nodded. "That was my dad's solution to everything. Warm milk. He said there was nothing it couldn't cure."

He got up, lifting a copper pan from the pot rack. "Sounds like wishful-single-dad thinking to me. No need to talk to your teen girl about birth control if there's warm milk, right?"

I laughed. "How long were you a single dad?"

He poured some milk into the pot and then added some honey. "Seven years. Sage was twelve when her mom and I broke up. Those were some tough times. I was on the road a lot, trying to get my career in place. Sage's mom wasn't really well enough to take care of her properly. And oof, my girl was wild. I can't tell you how good it feels to have Lotta around for a second parenting opinion these days."

I took another donut. "You know, she's surprisingly good with kids. I remember once when Sarah had her six-year-old niece staying with her for the weekend and she ran out of things to do with her in, like, an hour. Lotta swept in and took that girl to FAO Schwarz and Serendipity and the natural-history museum. And she actually seemed to enjoy it."

Omari stirred the milk with a whisk. "Have you ever had that frozen hot chocolate? What's not to enjoy?"

"Maybe Lotta can just take Sage to Serendipity," I said, laughing.

He chuckled. "Oh, man, can you imagine? That would not go well."

He poured the milk into two mugs and placed a cup in front of me. I sipped it and closed my eyes. Warm. Creamy. Sweet.

"Just like my dad's," I said.

He shook his head. "At least I can do something right."

The party was on the beach and the day was cold and windy, but Lotta arranged for a huge bonfire and made sure that all her guests had access to cashmere shawls and scarves ("Oh, just keep it, dar-ling," I heard her say to more than one person. "What am I going to do with fifty pashminas?").

We drove the Airstream down onto the sand and set up shop. I was a bit disappointed not to be trying out our leftovers theme on our inaugural launch, but of course we didn't have access to Ethan's kitchen leavings here. And Lotta, as usual, had a very specific vision in mind. She wanted über-fancy versions of Hamptons beach food, and I planned on delivering it by simply upping the wattage on tra-ditional things like lobster rolls (in this case, heavily seeded with uni and caviar) and fish and chips (we were deep-frying tuna and Chi-nook salmon instead of the more homely cod and pollock). The girls had complained a bit—lobster mac and cheese wasn't exactly the cutting-edge cuisine they'd grown used to cooking with Ethan—but Lotta had been thrilled with my ideas.

I tried to work up some excitement about finally launching the Airstream (the refrigerator was definitely working—I had checked at least half a dozen fucking times), but as I looked at the expensive ingredients and the elite crowd, I worried that it felt a little too close to my old supper clubs for me to be particularly happy about it.

Here you are again, whispered Lucy's voice in my ear as I began to scoop out shooters of blue-crab bisque, garnishing them with a sprinkling of chive flowers and then handing them off to Kai to give out through the Airstream window.

And she was right, I thought. I might be in my own truck rather than someone's West Village kitchen, but it was all too familiar. I was not doing anything new. I peeked out the window. This crowd was a little different than the one at Lucy and Titus's had been. It was younger, hipper, more diverse and casual, but it was still all money and power and excess. I watched Lotta dance by, looking effortlessly cool in her Acne jeans and Yeezy bomber jacket, and my heart sank. All the hope and excitement I had been feeling about my work since I had arrived in Kingston seemed to melt away.

I watched the people all around us. The wind was whipping everyone's hair into a mess, and all the women were wrapped in their party-favor pashminas, leaning in toward the men, gesturing and laughing. And practically everyone held my food: the small glass cylinders of crab soup; the crisp, hot, little shrimp cakes; the expensive fish and chips in a clever cradle of folded-up newspaper. They were laughing and talking and dancing and flirting . . . and eating on automatic. The food was an absolute afterthought.

"Looks like fun," said Marta, going up on tiptoe to peer over my shoulder. She sounded a bit wistful.

"It looks like a bunch of rich morons who would eat dog shit on a cedar plank if we served it to them," reported Kai from her station at the window. "I just watched an old dude choke down an entire lobster tail in, like, thirty seconds. It was like he just unhinged his jaw and inhaled it whole."

I sighed. "It's not their fault. It's mine. It's the food."

The girls looked at me, stricken, and I hastened to add, "I mean, it's all good. It's fine. But it's not because they're a bunch of rich morons. We just aren't offering anything new."

"Don't go," wheedled Lotta as I hugged her good-bye. "You can stay and be our personal chef."

"You already have a personal chef," I pointed out as I disengaged myself from her tight grip. "His name is José and he's very good."

"Fine, then he can cook for you and you can cook for us."

I knew she was joking, but she kind of sounded like she wasn't.

"Hey," I said, "at least things seem a little better with Sage, right?"

She laughed and shook her head mournfully. "Oh, yes, that détente lasted about thirty seconds. Then this morning she remembered how much she hates me and called me a cunt because I asked her to take her flip-flops off the dining room table."

I raised my eyebrows. "Maybe you should have let Martin DiSantorino have her."

She laughed again. "I obviously missed my golden opportunity."

"Billy!" shouted Kai from inside the car. "Ethan needs us back for the dinner rush. We gotta fucking go!"

I smiled apologetically. "Thanks for the amazing time, sweetie. And for the job."

Lotta frowned. "Watch out for that Kai girl, Bill. She's all sharp edges and rusty nails."

I laughed. "Ya think?" I turned to Omari, who was waving us off from the front porch. "Thanks again, O! Come on, Chicken!"

My dog hesitated for a moment, looking up pleadingly at Omari, who was now, apparently, his new favorite person.

"Go on, boy." Omari laughed, and after another moment of desperately trying to eye-hump his true beloved, the dog reluctantly walked down the steps and climbed through the car door that Marta held open.

"Traitor," I said as I followed him into the car. "Omari didn't rescue you from the shed."

"Yeah, but you didn't produce Rihanna's last album," pointed out Marta as we drove away.

chapter 18

New Paltz, NY

K ingston isn't just Kingston, you know," said Ethan. "I mean, it's the biggest town around here, but it's really just part of a whole chain of little towns and villages that form the wider community."

We were heading to a butcher in New Paltz, a little college town about fifteen minutes from Kingston, because Ethan wanted to source some ethically raised veal.

"All these little villages have their own thing," he said as we bumped over the bridge that spanned Rondout Creek. "There's Woodstock, of course—I mean, everyone knows about Woodstock. Old hippies, artists, tourists, and celebrities who keep weekend homes up here instead of the Hamptons. Then there's Rosendale— four or five blocks of Victorian houses, some cute little shops, and a bunch of eccentric artists and political types. Ulster Park somehow missed the tourist boom—it's kind of blue collar and depressed, but it has this gorgeous waterside park that practically no one knows about. High Falls has a great food co-op and an amazing florist, and strangely, Marc Chagall lived there in the 1940s. Stone Ridge is big, expensive historic houses, serious farms, and a pretty good independent grocery store. And New Paltz has college students, more bars than it needs, a whole tourist industry based on rock climbing and leaf peeping, and some really great restaurants and shops that were doing local and seasonal before it was even a thing."

I leaned back in my seat and watched the landscape fly by as he continued describing the towns across the Hudson as well. He was right when he said that the villages were strung together like beads on a chain—spaced out by farmland and forest and the Shawangunk Mountains and more rivers and creeks than I'd ever seen. I swear, every time I turned a corner, there was a babbling brook, a picturesquely dilapidated barn, a swath of trees showing off their fall colors, and another farm stand selling heirloom apples and jars of locally harvested honey.

We parked along Main Street and walked over to a meat market called Jack's. It looked like your basic convenience store from the outside, but when we walked in, I was hit by a strong, tangy, mineral scent. We wound our way past the newspapers and dry goods and postcard stands, and in the back was a long glass case filled with glorious, glistening local meat. There were thick, red-and-white marbled slabs of rib eye and porterhouse; small, plump little chickens nestled next to each other, their legs jutting out like a line of avian chorus girls. There was brisket and short ribs and spare ribs and roasts, hulking pork shoulders and cylindrical rolls of belly. My eyes lingered over the tenderloins, all neatly tied up and just begging to be taken home, sprinkled with rosemary and thyme, and roasted over a bed of apples, onions, carrots, and fennel. Each piece of meat was carefully labeled not only by type and price, but according to the farm of its origin. Thunderhill and Veritas and Four Winds and Movable Beast, Fox Hill and Full Moon and Brookside . . .

"Everyone always talked about Fleishers meat market," said Ethan, peering into the case, "and don't get me wrong, they were great. But Jack's was here first and he outlasted them all. Am I right, Abdul?"

The guy behind the counter flicked his eyes at Ethan. "By many years, my friend. But just so you know, flattering me isn't going to change my prices."

Ethan laughed and held up his hands. "I'm just here for some veal, man. What you got?"

After Ethan and Abdul discussed the relative differences between two different beef farms and the way they raised their veal, Ethan put in an order to be picked up the next day and guided me back out of the store.

"You hungry?" he asked.

"Always," I answered.

He led me across the street to the Village Tea Room. It was a snug, red two-story cottage set back from the road, encircled by a white picket fence that spilled over with late-blooming roses. Inside it looked like a European inn—all deep windowsills and a display case full of gorgeous pastry—which was not surprising, since Ethan told me it was owned and run by an Irish expatriate named Agnes.

"She's been here over a decade now," he said, after we ordered the ploughman's lunch for two and a couple of bottles of Mother's Milk stout. "Doing locavore since the beginning. She's got it all figured out. The food, the service, the atmosphere . . . Before I opened Huma, I would come here and order the turkey pot pie and just sit and watch how the place was run. And now that I have a place of my own, whenever I have trouble trying to source something, I just ask Agnes. She knows all the best places."

Our lunch arrived and I gazed approvingly at the generous hunks of crumbling farmhouse cheddar, the thick slices of good brown bread, the wedges of apples and plums, the golden hand pies stuffed with ground lamb, the earthenware pot of hot, seedy mustard, and the petite pile of tiny green cornichons. I slashed a knife full of mustard across the bread, applied a slice of the crumbly white cheese, added a chunk of rosy apple, and then took a laden bite.

"Oh, man. So good," I groaned. "Now see, this is where I went wrong in the Hamptons. If I was going to make simple beach food, I should have just done the most beachy-beach food that was ever made. I didn't need $150-a-pound tuna—I needed to find the best, freshest cod so people would feel like they were eating cod for the first time. I mean, this is just cheese and apples and bread—but everything tastes like more, right? The apple tastes like the best version of an apple ever. The cheese is amazing. The bread is the bread I want for toast every morning of my life."

"Yeah," agreed Ethan, tearing into a dingle pie. "She knows what she's doing. It's all so natural. It just feels like we're sitting in her kitchen."

I washed the food down with a gulp of the creamy, bitter stout, savoring the silky way it slid down my throat.

This wasn't a particularly fancy restaurant. People were wearing jeans and sweaters. There was a guy eating alone while he read a book in the corner. The food was simple and hearty—no froths or deconstructions or things that tricked you into thinking you were going to eat one thing when it was really something altogether different. The staff were young and warm and friendly but not particularly fussy. But every bite was contentment. Every need felt met.

I could do this forever, I thought to myself. *This food. This town. This man . . .*

"So," said Ethan, "how come you don't have kids?"

I blinked, the food turning ashy in my mouth. "What?"

He ate another bite of his pie. "I just mean, most of the women I know who are, like, your age already have kids. I think it's kind of cool that you held out or whatever, but are you doing the whole child-free thing for good? Do you just not want any?"

I put my beer down. "Um. I'm just trying to launch my business. I'm not really thinking about it, honestly."

Liar! hissed Lucy's voice in my ear.

It was one of the strange things about the four of us, and one of the things that bonded us the most—four women, all in their forties, and none of us had children. Lucy didn't have any because she always claimed that managing Titus took all of her attention and energy, and she didn't have room for a child with all his demands. After her divorce, Lotta had been as adverse to serious relationships as she had been enthusiastic about drugs and partying. She was sober and married now, but she was also forty-eight. Her window was closed. And of course, Sarah had frozen her eggs long ago and felt she had all the time in the world.

And me? How could I think of children when I was always living hand-to-mouth? When my own life had been such a spectacularly shitty mess? How could I think of children when I thought of my own mother and the smothered, panicked look she so often wore on her face when she had actually bothered to look at me?

"Do you want kids?" I said, turning the question around.

Ethan took a swig of his beer and considered this for a moment.

"I don't know. The chefs I know who have children seem to work for different reasons than I do. I mean, right now, I don't have to answer to anyone. I can spend all my time working or researching. I can sleep through my whole day off if I want and not feel shitty about it. The guys I know with kids always feel torn between work and home. Their heart isn't really in either place. For me, Huma is home. They have to work because they have kids to support. I work because I love my work. Period."

I shrugged. "I don't think it's necessarily mutually exclusive."

He nodded. "Yeah, I know. And I mean, I like the idea of kids running around the restaurant, teaching them the basics in the kitchen, taking them to the farms and showing them how everything grows. But I'm really far off from that. I need to meet the right woman, of course. And get further along with the restaurant. And those things kind of cancel each other out. I don't really date seriously because the restaurant takes up all my time. Not many women are too excited about being with a guy who is never available in the evening, sleeps half the day, and smells like garlic and wine twenty-four-seven."

That sounds delicious.

I went for a nonchalant shrug. "You gotta date someone who works the same hours as you. Who gets it. You gotta stay within the industry."

"Yeah, but if I do that, then it gets complicated. I'm everyone's boss, you know?"

You're not my boss.

I almost said it out loud. Instead I turned my eyes away from his earnest gaze and lifted a piece of plum and took another bite, willing myself to think of the dark, sweet juice that filled my mouth and stung the back of my throat, forcing my mind to turn to texture, firmness, flavor . . .

Good girl, said Lucy.

Oh, fuck off and leave me alone, I thought back in return, wondering for a split second what would happen if I just leaned across the table and kissed this man, giving him a taste of the wild, honey-sweet fruit in my mouth.

But instead I swallowed the plum and resigned myself to listening to Lucy.

"So, let's talk about the Halloween festival," I said. "What do you think you can give me for the truck?"

I called Brett that night.

I hadn't planned on it. But I was alone in my big, empty house, and it was raining. The steady sound of the rain hitting the metal roof, and the way the river sort of disappeared into the darkness when I looked out the window, and Chicken's insistence on refusing to come out from the blanket on the couch that he had burrowed under, and yes, okay, maybe the three-quarters of a bottle of amarone I had consumed on my own, all combined to make me reckless and lonely enough to pick up the phone.

He answered on the first ring. "Hey, stranger," he said.

His voice was deep and smoky and comforting. I curled into the couch and immediately felt better.

"Hi," I said. "I'm a little drunk."

He laughed. "Me too."

I smiled. "What are you doing?"

"Just sitting here, watching the rain on my window."

"It's raining here, too. What are you drinking?"

"Macallan, neat. Finally finishing up that bottle you gave me."

I flushed, remembering the time he had once spilled that same whisky onto my naked skin and then slowly lapped it back up again. "I thought we killed that bottle," I said. My voice came out a little breathless.

He chuckled. "There was a bit left. We got distracted, as I recall."

I closed my eyes for a moment, letting my mind slide around in that memory.

"You still there, Sitwell?"

"Yes. I'm here."

"Good."

"Brett, can I ask you something?"

"Anything."

"Do you want children?"

There was a pause, and then, "Huh. That's not exactly the direction I was expecting this conversation to go."

I shook my head. "Sorry. It's just—it's just on my mind."

"I would love to have kids with you, Sitwell."

I sat up straight, almost spilling my wine. "Oh. Oh. That's not what I was asking. I mean, I was just curious. I didn't mean—"

"Calm down. I'm not going to run up there and impregnate you. You asked. I answered."

I bit my lip. I couldn't think of what to say.

"Billy?"

"Yes?" I squeaked.

"Why do I fucking scare you so much?"

I bristled. "You—you don't fucking scare me."

"I think I do. And I think you know I do."

"Don't be ridiculous."

"I like you, Sitwell. I really, really like you. I might even love you. And I am willing to put up with all sorts of shit from you because I know that you're kind of fucked up, but I also know that, deep down, you probably love me, too. And I have this idea that someday, if I'm patient enough, you'll drop all this bullshit and stop holding me at arm's length and we will take this thing between us and let it become what it's meant to be. But man, Billy, you make it so fucking hard sometimes."

I swallowed. "But I—I never said I loved you."

He laughed, and this time the laugh sounded bitter and tired. "I never said you did."

And then he hung up the phone and I was left listening to dead air and the raindrops drumming on the roof and, underneath it all, the gentle lapping of the river, which was still there, out in the darkness of the rainy night.

chapter 19

Violet Hill Estate
Kingston

We were harvesting black walnuts in Ethan's yard. Ethan and Kai, Marta and myself, gathering the fragrant, bright green orbs from the ground.

"They smell like tea-tree oil," I said, inhaling the pungent, medicinal smell of the husk.

"Or bergamot," said Marta.

"And they stain like fuck," said Kai, wiping at a smear of purple-black ooze on her hands.

Ethan lived in a converted teahouse on an old Ulster County estate. The house looked like an iced gingerbread cottage on the outside, and it was cozy and sweet inside—just two small loft bedrooms, a bathroom, and an open space where the kitchen, dining room, and living room all came together as one. The house was filled with clever built-ins and ornate cornices and trim, more a piece of folk art than an actual home. The last dregs of the original family—an elderly grand dame and her sister—still lived in the crumbling manor house on the other side of the property. I knew that Ethan's eventual plan was to have a farm of his own—one where he could grow and tend to any foodstuff his restaurant might need. But in the meantime, the ladies of the manor were more than happy to let their handsome young tenant cultivate his own little garden and have the use of their old-fashioned and somewhat dilapidated greenhouse in exchange for a weekly basket of his fresh produce.

"You can actually make a really incredible dye out of the husks if you boil them down," said Ethan, digging his thumbnail into the flesh of the nut and bringing a teardrop of dark liquid to the surface. "Also, did you know that the black walnut tree secretes a substance called juglone that basically poisons any nonnative plant that grows within its root range?"

"Nerd," taunted Kai.

"So," I said, looking doubtfully at the knobbly green ball in my hand, "how do we get to the actual nut? Just tear the husk off?"

"First you put them in a bag and run them over with your car to get rid of the husks," said Marta. "Then we have to wait for the shells to dry. Then we have to hand-crack every single nut with a vise grip. He makes us do this crap every year."

"For fuck's sake," I said. "I mean, I like black walnuts as much as anyone, but is it really worth it?"

"Absolutely," said Ethan, bending to pick up another nut and giving me a view of his ass that made me feel like a dirty old woman. "A fresh black walnut tastes like nothing else, and then I'll pickle the rest and put them in the ajil I make for the restaurant."

"Ajil?" I asked, momentarily distracted from his butt.

"It's an Iranian thing. A dried-fruit-and-nut mix that basically every Persian family offers their guests when they first arrive in their home. I do a spin on it for an amuse-bouche. Pickled walnuts and dried mulberries and chickpeas and sour cherries."

"It's fabulous," said Marta. "Like nothing you've ever tasted."

"And I have a new idea for black walnuts, too. I have this amazing Ceenowa red rice that I sourced from this farm just around the corner from here—"

"Wait," I said, "someone is growing *rice* up here?"

"Yes, there's this family from Gambia who grow and harvest rice in the traditional Gambian way. It's totally fascinating. I volunteered at their farm over the summer."

"Of course you did," muttered Kai.

"They're growing everything in the Hudson Valley now," continued Ethan. "Rice and wheat and every vegetable and fruit you can imagine. The farmers around here are brilliant. They're breeding for flavor and nutrition and heritage—not just big, shiny soulless produce. It's a revolution."

"Anyway," said Marta, "I think we got all the nuts."

I peered around. We were standing under a grove of black walnut trees that had to be over a century old. They were tall and twisted, and their fluttering, feather-like leaves shone bright yellow against the soft blue sky. When we had walked out here an hour ago, there were hundreds of tennis-ball-size nuts littering the ground. Now, except for a few already rotting black husks, the grass was picked clean.

"So we did," I said.

Ethan's phone buzzed.

"Aw, fuck," he said. "That's the third server out tonight. This stupid flu that's going around. We're going to be criminally short-handed." He looked at me. "Unless?"

Serving is not like riding a bike. You don't stop for years at a time and then put up your hair, tie on your apron, and just pick up where you left off. There are literal muscles that need to be exercised every night. Muscles that, no matter how often you might work out, don't get used properly if you're not stacking three plates up your arm and skidding across a wet kitchen floor at top speed.

We were only an hour past opening, and I was already in the weeds. We were short two other waitstaff and I was learning as I worked. My back was aching, my shoes were all wrong, and I had spilled a carafe of red wine across a table of six in an epic gush that left no one unstained. Plus, I wasn't using my reading glasses, so even if I wrote something down, I had trouble reading my own writing by the time I got to the kitchen.

The staff was being tolerant of my mistakes since I was just filling in, but I caught more than a few raised eyebrows and rolled eyes as I struggled to recite the specials and grew more and more behind on my orders.

"Four guinea hens for table two on a rail!" I said, squinting at my order pad. "Shit! No, I mean, two guinea hens for table four! Shit. Sorry!"

Ethan gave me a look of saintly patience. "So which is it?" he said. "Two for four or four for two?"

"Four for two—no, two for four! Two for four!"

Ethan laughed. "I thought you said you'd done this before."

"Oh, fuck off, Chef," I said. "You're lucky I'm even here. I should quit and go home."

"He'd be in better shape if you did," called out Kai from her station.

"Be nice, Kai," said Marta as she crisped a crème brûlée with a small blowtorch. "Otherwise you're going to end up out there sling-ing plates in her place."

"Fire up two guinea hens," shouted Ethan. Then he looked at me. "Um, pickup for table seven, Billy? Remember?"

"Oh, right! On it, Chef!" I said as I grabbed my next plates and headed back to the front.

No fear, I thought again. There was no fear in Ethan's kitchen. He never lost his patience, he never seemed to blow up, and for all the crap they gave him, his staff seemed to genuinely like and re-spect the guy. I had never encountered that in a restaurant. Most of the chefs I knew—especially the great ones—were brutal and ugly with their staff, demanding nothing less than perfection, and making their people feel like shit when they screwed up. So many of the places I had worked in claimed that they were like "family." And per-haps they were—if family meant an incestuous, dysfunctional group of people who were all terrified of the same strutting, puffed-up daddy figure—but Ethan didn't treat his staff like his children: he treated them like his peers.

My shoulder pinged dangerously as I reached across the table to take away a proffered menu, and I froze, terrified that my whole back would seize up. After a moment, the pain passed and I relaxed again. I shook my head ruefully. My waitressing days were obviously num-bered.

"Staff drink, Billy!" yelped Marta as she raced for the bar. "It's staff drink time!"

I raised my eyebrows. I doubted that Ethan could afford to let his staff drink for free, but apparently that hadn't stopped him from

making it a tradition. Every night, after cleanup, the staff was allowed one free drink each before they all headed home. Wine. A
shot. Mixed drinks. Beer. They crowded around the bar and demanded whatever they wanted. I had known a few other restaurants
that observed this tradition—but they had all been top level, making
money hand over fist. They could afford it.

Drinking with people half my age was a mistake I should have
known not to make. I probably should have just downed a shot and
headed home, but, I'll admit it, I was lonely as of late. Brett had been
absolutely silent since that drunken, rainy night—and I was doing
everything I could not to think about him. Lucy continued to be
missing in action. Lotta was pining away for Omari, who had left for
Germany, and the only things she could talk about were how much
she missed him and what a hard time Sage was giving her. And
whenever I got Sarah on the phone, she sounded more and more
frantic.

"I think Brian is having an affair," she had breathed to me the
last time we had spoken. "He's been working late almost every night
and he just told me he has to go in this weekend. I mean, don't you
think that's suspicious?"

"Doesn't he always work long hours?"

She paused for a moment. "Yeah. I guess. But my producers are
going nuts. I mean, he's never around, and there are only so many
times they can film me freaking out over the phone, you know? It's
getting boring."

"Sarah, sometimes I wonder if you should worry less about your
show and more about your life."

She sighed, exasperated. "The show *is* my life. Haven't you been
listening at all?"

So there I was, foraging, working, and then drinking with a

bunch of twenty-somethings, which made me feel both young again and incredibly, incredibly old.

Ethan was dancing. Someone had had the bright idea to hook up their iPhone to the restaurant's sound system, and a few other people had pushed the tables back, and now Ethan was standing in the middle of the room, obviously a little drunk, with his arms raised and his eyes closed, his fingers snapping and a look on his face that made me realize I either had to finish my drink and leave, or maybe get up and join him on the dance floor.

I knocked back the rest of my gin and juice, wondering where I had left my coat, but before my glass hit the counter, Kai was behind the bar, leaning toward me. "Should I start a tab?"

I looked around. Nobody was stopping at one drink. And apparently, they were all paying.

Ah. Maybe the kid isn't such a fool after all . . .

"Yeah, okay," I said. "Give me another."

Beyoncé's "Blow" came on. Her teasing voice, her sly innuendos.

Ethan licked his lips and smiled—a slow, wide grin—and then looked right at me and crooked his finger.

"Come on, Billy," he said, laughing. "I can tell you love this song."

Fuck it, I thought. And I slammed back my drink and got up to join him.

I've danced with a lot of people in my life, and I'm no slouch, but fuck, when Ethan wrapped his arms around me and started moving across the floor, I was shocked. I was expecting some goofy, clowning version of a dance—not to be literally swept off my feet.

"Where the hell did you learn to dance like this?" I asked when I got my breath back.

He spun me around. "Ten years of ballet lessons."

I laughed. "Seriously?"

"Yup. My parents tried sports first. Soccer, baseball, basket-ball . . . but I hated the competition. I hated feeling like I was always trying to best someone. That blood-hungry thing. I quit every team. Just refused to go. So one day my mom decided she was enrolling me in ballet, just so I'd get off my ass and stop playing video games all day. I fought it tooth and nail, of course. I mean, I was an eight-year-old boy. But then, in that first class, when I realized that there was a team but no competition, that we were actually working in unison, I liked that. And of course, it didn't hurt that I was one of the very few boys in the class, so I got all kinds of awesome attention from the teachers and all the dancer girls."

"Were you good?"

He shrugged. "I mean, I was never going to be a professional. I wasn't dedicated enough. But I guess I did my share of *Nutcracker*s."

I laughed, imagining him as a dark-haired little boy, those big, slanted eyes, dressed in tights and ballet slippers . . . It made me smile and move closer to him.

Then I felt a light shove at my back.

"All right you two," said Kai's voice. "Knock it off."

I turned my head and looked at her glowering face. She was standing, arms akimbo. "No one else is dancing," she said. "You're making a spectacle of yourselves."

I started to step away, but Ethan pulled me closer. He was surprisingly strong. "Fuck off, Kai," he said. He was being good-natured, but there was steel in his voice.

Her mouth twisted. "You look fucking ridiculous. Everyone is watching."

Ethan went still but didn't loosen his grip on me. "What are you doing?" he said to her. There was an angry glint in his eyes.

Marta hurried over. "Hey, hey, I've got more drinks for all of you!" She shoved a tumbler of something lurid and green into Kai's hand. "What were you drinking, Ethan?"

He relaxed and I quickly stepped away from him. Marta took him by the hand and pulled him toward the bar. "You were drinking tequila, right? The Milagro?"

Kai and I stood on the dance floor, facing each other. She looked at me. Her pale eyes were practically glowing.

"Stay away from him," she muttered.

"Jesus, Kai, what is your problem?"

She stepped toward me and I felt the beginning of a headache bloom in my temple. I was pretty sure I could take her, but it had been a really long time since I had stared down a bar fight.

"You don't know what you're getting mixed up in," she said.

"You sound insane," I told her. "We were just dancing. Are you two together or something?"

Her mouth twisted into a sneering smile, but before she could answer, Marta had hurried back over. "Everyone's playing Kill, Fuck, Marry at the bar," she said breathlessly. "It's so funny! You guys should come!"

"No thanks," I said. "We're not drunk enough for that."

"Sure we are," said Kai. She drained her glass. "Or we will be in a minute."

The crowd at the bar was laughing raucously as we rejoined them. Marta quickly handed me another gin and juice and I made sure to stand far away from both Kai and Ethan. I would have just left, but the second drink that I had slammed down was stronger than I'd expected and I knew I was already too fucked up to drive.

"Kill Bieber, fuck Gosling, marry Clooney," said Anissa, the pretty hostess with the enormous ear gauges.

"That's insane!" said Freddie, one of the dishwashers. "I mean, yes, you obviously kill Bieber, but you definitely fuck Clooney and marry Gosling."

"No, because Clooney is old and has a bad back. He's just going to lie there and hope a disc doesn't slip. He'd be a waste of a fuck," said Anissa. "Plus he's richer than Gosling, so you want to nail down that villa in Lake Como, amirite?"

"Let's only play with people we know personally," said Kai, grinning wickedly. "I'll go first."

There was a hoot of approval from the staff, but I glanced over at Ethan and Marta and they both looked worried.

"Okay, Kai," said Anissa, obviously happy to stir the shit. "Marta, Ethan, and Billy. Kill. Fuck. Marry."

Kai grinned even wider. "Easy," she said. "Kill Ethan. Fuck Billy. Marry Marta."

I blinked in confusion.

"Explain yourself," commanded Anissa.

Kai took a sip of her drink and then slowly put it back down. "Well, fuck Billy for obvious reasons." She glanced at me and sneered. "I mean, seriously, fuck Billy."

I held up my drink to her and smiled sarcastically in return.

Kai took another drink. "Marry Marta because I love her and she's awesome, and maybe I can turn her into a proper lesbian, and—sorry, E—but kill Ethan because what the hell do I want with a penis?"

The crowd laughed and I took a breath. *Wait. Kai was gay? Then what the fuck had just happened between us?*

"Okay, Marta," said Kai. "You're next."

Marta blushed so hard that her brown skin turned red. "I have to go to the bathroom," she announced, and hurried out of the room.

I put my drink down and followed her.

"Marta," I said as she disappeared into the stall.

"I don't want to play, Billy!" she called back.

"I don't fucking want to play, either. Now tell me what the hell is going on with you three."

She sighed and opened the stall door. Her blue fauxhawk was drooping to one side and her eyes were bloodshot.

"I'm sorry you got dragged into it," she said. "It's a mess. It's always been a mess."

"I don't understand," I said.

She bit her lip. "Kai and Ethan and I have always been super close—since school, you know?"

I nodded. "He said something about that to me."

"Kai and I used to be roommates, and the three of us basically hung out all the time and we always planned on doing the restaurant together. Ethan was the chef, I was the pastry chef, and Kai was going to be our sommelier. We had it all figured out."

"Okay," I said.

"Except, that last month of school, everything went haywire. I had a huge a crush on Ethan—like, I'd had it since I met him."

"Oh."

"I don't have it anymore, though!" she hurried to say. "I mean, it was kid stuff."

I raised my eyebrows. "All right."

"And then, just before school ended, during finals week, I don't know why, but Ethan asked me out."

"To a picnic," I said, suddenly remembering Ethan on the dock, telling me about the salt-cod-and-cassava fritters. "At Blithewood."

She looked surprised. "He told you about that?"

I nodded. "Yeah. A little. But go ahead."

"And we had this amazing time. Like, spectacular. At least, I thought it was. But then, after, he didn't call. He didn't come by. So, I thought that maybe he didn't like me after all. That I had misunderstood."

I bit my tongue. This was not, of course, what Ethan had told me at all, but I had no desire to get into the middle of this mess, so I stayed silent.

"I tried to just shrug it off," she said. "I mean, no big deal, right? Boys do stupid things all the time, but then Kai came in and caught me crying and she was so, so sweet—and so then . . . well, we ended up sleeping together."

I suppressed a smile. *God. I am so fucking glad I'm not twenty anymore.*

"Ah," I said. "So she wasn't kidding when she said she was in love with you."

She nodded, nervously turning the tap on and off. "Anyway, then, practically just after, Ethan came around and told me that he'd had an amazing time on our date, but I had just seemed so upset about almost failing my sauce class that he thought maybe I needed some space. So he had been waiting for me to call him. But I had already— done what I had done with Kai, you know?"

I nodded. "Right."

"And you know, it was really, really nice with Kai and she's totally beautiful and everything, and I absolutely believe in a fluid sexuality, and I don't think anyone is just gay or straight, right? But I just—"

"Didn't feel the same way about Kai that you did about Ethan."

She nodded, her big brown eyes wide and guileless. "Has that ever happened to you?"

I laughed. "I went through an experimental stage. Lots of girls do."

"So I didn't want to tell Ethan that I had slept with Kai right after I had, you know, made out with him, so I just said that I thought maybe we should cool things off until graduation? And then I told Kai that maybe what we had done was a mistake, and I guess I kind of hurt both of them. Kai especially. She went away to Europe after we graduated. Said she didn't want to be around me or Ethan anymore. And so Ethan and I went ahead and opened the restaurant, but—you know, with all the work and the money we were putting into it, it didn't seem smart to get involved again, and so that all just kind of faded away. And then Kai came back. And she said that she still loved me but she knew that I loved Ethan and she could live with that—she just missed us both and wanted back in our lives. But then you showed up and obviously Ethan is interested in you and that's totally, totally okay, because I'm not in love with him anymore, but Kai thinks I am and she's totally sure that Ethan loves me, too. So she doesn't like you, or rather, she doesn't like you to be around Ethan because she's afraid I'll get hurt again and it's just so stupid, but anyway, that's what just happened."

She took a deep breath, still on the verge of tears.

I looked at her. At her messed-up hair, and her red eyes, and her impossibly young, sincere, and confused face, and suddenly my pinging back and aching feet and stupid, squinty, weak-ass eyes all seemed like a small price to pay.

Okay, said Lucy, *are we done with this shit yet?*

There is nothing, I thought in reply, *absolutely nothing you could give me to be that fucking young and stupid again.*

chapter 20

I swear," said Sarah, eyeing the tanned, muscle-bound bartender with a man bun mixing our drinks, "the Australians have taken over everything. Look at all these hipsters from Down Under."

Lotta shrugged. "And what's so wrong with that?"

"They all need a major hair update, for one," said James. "Who the fuck wears man buns anymore?"

"Jesus, James, how can you be so straight and yet so very, very gay at the same time?" I asked him.

Sick of millennial drama, I had hopped the bus down to the city to meet Sarah and Lotta for drinks at a new bar on the Lower East Side called the Flower Shop. It was Midwestern-rec-room chic—with wood paneling and faux-family portraits and multiple pool tables. We were drinking vodka and cranberries (except for Lotta, who was having soda and lime) and scooping up several orders of steak tartare with potato chips.

Lotta was in the city because Omari was still in Germany. I was in the city because I was tired of feeling like the only grown-up in the room, plus I still hadn't heard from Lucy, and I was starting to get really worried and hoping that someone knew what was going on with her.

But it seemed she was no longer really talking to any of us. She had simply gone silent.

It had been Sarah's idea to invite James—figuring that Lucy had never missed a hair appointment, and that maybe he'd have some insight into why, exactly, our girl had dropped off the face of the earth. But so far, he wasn't giving up any useful information.

"She didn't even come in to be colored this week," he said. "I have no idea what's going on with her." He craned his neck around. "Jesus, why are there no women in this place? It's, like, a million fucking Chris Hemsworth clones. And why are they all wearing gigantic key rings on their pants? Who needs that many keys? When did this become a thing?" He turned back to us. "Okay, well, looks like you three are my only shot at having any fun tonight. Who's taking the bullet?"

I rolled my eyes but had to admit that inwardly, I thought about how Lucy had once told me that James kissed like he cut hair—with genius and precision (how Lucy knew this was a long story)—and for a moment, I almost considered missing the last bus back upstate.

But James was already giving Lotta his best head-to-toe eye sweep. "What about you, Eklund, what are you doing later?"

Lotta demurely sipped her drink. "Married woman now, James. Or have you forgotten so soon?"

He frowned. "Well, maybe if I had been invited to the wedding . . ."

Lotta shrugged. "Omari and I made a deal—no one we'd slept with on the guest list."

Sarah and I shot stunned glances at each other. This was news. But then, I thought back to the worst period of Lotta's addiction—she and James had run in the same crowd—and it was entirely possible that they'd had a little fling or two.

James actually flushed. "Oh, so we're talking about that now?" he said. "No more deep, dark secrets, Lotta?"

She graced him with a beatific grin and spread her hands wide. "I'm an open book, darling."

James snorted. "I liked you better when you were an addict. At least you were fun."

"James!" cried Sarah. "That's a terrible thing to say!"

Lotta's smile only crumpled a tiny bit. "I'm sure many people would agree with him."

"Okay," I said, "cut it out, you two. I thought we were here to talk about Lucy."

"All right," said James, rising, "I'm out. I have nothing more to contribute to this conversation. She hasn't had her hair done in a month. Someone let me know when you hear from her."

"But James!" sputtered Sarah as he threw down a fistful of cash and exited.

Lotta waved her hand dismissively. "Good riddance."

"Anyway, maybe he's right. Maybe there's nothing to be said about Lucy," said Sarah. "She and Titus are probably just having a second honeymoon. She'll turn up soon enough."

"The longest second honeymoon fucking ever," I muttered.

"What if he's got her locked up?" said Lotta. "What if she's chained to a radiator somewhere?"

"Stop it," said Sarah.

"I just hope she's okay." I tore at a paper napkin until it was shreds in my hand. "This is really fucking weird."

"She's fine!" chirped Sarah. "Now, can we talk about my show for a moment?"

Lotta and I glared at her in unison.

"What?" she cried. "I have some real problems!" And she immediately plunged into a long explanation about her producers and how they didn't want to do anything she wanted to do.

I thought about Lucy as Sarah babbled, wondering whether she'd even tell me if something really bad was going on. Once there would have been no question—we told each other everything—but not now. Now I wondered if I really knew her at all.

I waved over our waitress and asked for another round. "Actually," I said as Sarah showed no sign of slowing down, "better double that order."

chapter 21

The River House
Kingston

I was baking.

Not particularly well, I might add. As any chef knows, there is a huge difference between baking and cooking. Cooking is improvisational and subject to ingredients and whim. A small mistake when you cook could actually end up as inspirational, but make even the slightest wrong turn while baking, and your bread won't rise, your cake will taste like salt and soda, your cookies will end up a sloppy, melted mess in the middle of the pan. Baking is pretty much chemistry and just as precise and volatile.

I hated to admit this, but great bakers are smarter than great cooks. Because in order to improvise while baking, you have to be a master of the craft. You have to know your shit so well that you can guess exactly what will happen when you change up even the smallest things. A cook can play around like a sloppy toddler with their ingredients and still probably end up with a perfectly edible dish. A baker has to know what's what or it will all end in ruin.

I was, obviously, much more a cook than a baker. But the house had been shockingly cold when I'd rolled out from under my down comforter that morning. No more glorious golden days of Indian summer—it was truly fall. Chicken snuffled at my ankles, leaning against me for heat, and I shivered as I pulled all the windows shut. The billowing gray fog that drifted in over the river made me crave something sweet and warm to savor with the pot of hot Assam I planned to brew.

So I laid a fire in the kitchen, wrapped a soft plaid shawl over my pajamas, and rummaged through my larder until I found some dried apricots and a small, stained paper bag of the shelled black walnuts that Ethan had insisted on pressing upon me the last time I had seen him.

I had been avoiding Huma since the disastrous night I had wait-ressed, but I couldn't altogether avoid Ethan, since we were plan-ning on the Airstream coming out for a big Halloween festival they did at the Rondout in Kingston. It was only a week away.

This would mean that I would eventually have to deal with Marta and Kai, too. They were, after all, my crew for the truck, and actually, since Halloween fell on a Monday this year, and Huma was closed on Mondays, Ethan planned on joining us as well.

The idea of the four of us all crammed into my truck together made me queasy if I thought about it too much, so I pushed it from my mind as I gathered up the ingredients I needed.

Muffins, I thought. But then, remembering that I had some cream I needed to use in the fridge . . . *No, wait. Scones.*

I searched my mother's now-tattered copy of *Joy of Cooking* for the recipe—it was rich and simple and stood up well to additions. When I reached the page, I ran my finger over it, wondering which smears and butter stains were hers and which were mine.

My mother hadn't cooked that often, of course. Many days, she didn't even make it out of bed, but sometimes, on her better days, she would get up before me and light candles and the antique oil lamp on the table. She'd put soft classical music on the stereo, and then she'd bake.

Anytime my father and I woke up to the sound of Mozart or Puccini and the smell of butter and sugar caramelizing, the warm smell of yeast, or the fatty, saturated scent of dough frying, we would take a deep, happy breath of relief because we knew we were guaranteed at least one day where my mother would be whole and okay.

I was just pulling the scones out of the oven, fragrant and golden brown, when the doorbell rang and Chicken went into a paroxysm of barking. I froze. First of all, people rarely dropped in without warning. My landlady, Portia, would call ahead of time if she needed access to the house, and Ethan always texted before he showed up. And even if someone did come, no one used my front door. Everyone knew to come to the kitchen.

I placed the pan of scones on top of the stove. "Calm down," I said to the little dog as he bounced around the floor like a crazed squirrel.

The doorbell rang again—a long, harsh buzz.

"Hang on!" I shouted, annoyed.

Before I opened the door, I tugged my shawl tighter over my shoulders, suddenly aware of my faded and worn pajamas, clunky leopard-print faux Uggs, and the way my (still pink) hair was caught up in a plastic banana clip.

Fuck it. It's probably the UPS guy or a Mormon or something . . .

But it wasn't the UPS guy, or anyone trying to convert me. It was Titus. On my front porch. Carrying a package wrapped in brown paper.

"Hello, Billy," he said.

He looked like shit. Pale and tired, his usually immaculate hair rumpled and fuzzed. Chicken rushed at his ankles, all bark and bluster, but he didn't even flinch.

Suddenly I went cold with fear. "Is Lucy okay?" I demanded.

He half smiled. "May I come in?"

I grabbed Chicken, who was still rushing Titus's ankles, and then stepped aside. "Sure. Okay. Yes. Of course."

I led him down the hall to the kitchen, trying to control my need to turn and grab him by the shoulders and shake him until he told me what was going on.

"Lovely house," he said, examining the kitchen. He drifted to the window. "Spectacular view. I could paint that."

"Titus," I said, way too anxious to be polite, "what the fuck are you doing here?"

He chuckled and sat down at the kitchen island, carefully laying his package on the counter and then pushing it toward me. "I brought you something."

I stared at the package for a moment, my lip curled in question. "What? Why?"

"Just open it, Billy."

I tore at the paper, impatient to get it out of the way.

But then I went still.

You see, maybe I haven't made this totally clear, but Titus was a very famous painter. Like, very. Picasso-level famous. He was famous in a genius sort of way, in a best-of-the-best kind of way. And sometimes I forgot that. Because usually, to me, he was just a dude who had made my best friend happy and fucking miserable in equal measures over the years. He was the guy who had swept her away from me into a world of rarefied glamour and money and fame and left me scrambling to catch up. I honestly didn't even *like* Titus that much, but that didn't matter, because Lucy loved him, so he was part of my life if I wanted to be part of hers.

But sometimes, in moments like these, I remembered what he really was: not just my best friend's sometimes badly behaving husband whom I merely tolerated for her sake, but a world-class, once-in-a-lifetime, breathtaking, heartbreaking artist of the first fucking order.

He had given me a painting. A painting of myself and Lucy as young girls together. I knew what photo he had based it upon—it was one I kept framed on my bureau, and I knew that Lucy had a matching copy that she kept on her dressing table.

The original picture had been taken when we were at a pool party. It was the summer we both turned thirteen. Lucy was posing in a gingham bikini, all legs and white teeth and golden skin, with a plume of long, perfectly straight, platinum-blond hair that reached her tiny, perky ass. She looked like a miniature Farrah Fawcett. I was sitting off to the side, wearing an oversize dark green T-shirt that I'd snatched from my dad to hide my utilitarian navy one-piece. My hair was an insane orange halo around my chubby face, a huge piece of luridly blue cake was sitting on a plate in my lap, and I had the most lemon-sucking, pissed-off expression anyone has ever seen.

I loved that photo. It made me laugh every time I looked at it—which was almost every day. I fucking adored that photo. But this painting was so, so much more than the original.

This painting was us—best friends on the cusp of puberty—but instead of a funny little vignette of two adolescent girls in the '80s, it was now us to an über degree. It was us on acid, us times a billion. It was our very souls marked out in oil paint and canvas. Titus had made my childhood misery gigantic—as gigantic as that fucking piece of blue cake, which now spread to cover my entire lap and dripped down my fat little white thighs. My face was mine, but instead of the funny, sour look I'd had before, it was now twisted to reflect the anguish and enormous burden of the loss I had been carrying. My hands were clenched in a way that explained just how angry and disappointed I already was with this world, but they were also balled up like I was ready to fight.

Lucy, in all her beauty and budding sexuality, on the other hand, was both angelic and dangerous, knowing and completely innocent, and trembling on a terrifying precipice between child and adult. Titus had perfectly encapsulated the enormous gift that she was about to grow into and consider both a blessing and a curse for the rest of her life.

It was *us*, it was completely us. It hurt to look at it, it was so true.

A sob ripped out of me as I gazed down at it.

Titus patted my hand. "She misses you, too," he said.

I started to cry so violently I couldn't even answer him. I turned away, the tears pouring down my face, embarrassed by my emotion, embarrassed by the snot snaking its way out of my nose and the way I couldn't stop myself from making the most horrible choking sounds. I continued to cry as I plated a scone, poured him a cup of tea, and put out sugar and cream. I shoved the whole mess at him, and then I managed to gasp out, "I—I just need a minute," before I ran upstairs to get myself back under control.

I stood at my bedroom window, my whole body shaking. I wanted nothing so much as I wanted to call Lucy at that moment and demand to know that she was okay, but Titus had just given me an enormously valuable gift, one that he had obviously spent a great deal of time on, and I felt that I should at least allow him to say his piece before I took things into my own hands.

So I washed my face and took my hair out of the banana clip and patted on some powder to cover up my red nose and puffy eyes. I exchanged my pajamas for jeans and a sweater, but I kept my plaid shawl. I needed that extra layer.

Titus had taken a bite of the scone and then left the rest. He had let his tea cool in the cup, untouched, but I didn't say anything about it.

"Thank you for the painting," I said instead. "I think I just vividly demonstrated how much it moved me."

He smiled a handsome half smile. "I don't believe my art has driven anyone to tears before."

I shook my head. "I'm pretty sure that's not true. But maybe I'm the first to have a nervous breakdown right there in front of the actual artist."

He smiled again.

"Now, tell me what's going on with Lucy."

He nodded, pushing the scone around on the plate with his long, elegant fingers, but not picking it up. "Honestly? I'm worried about her. She told me about the fight you two had, of course." He focused his bright gaze on me. "What you said."

"I didn't mean it," I protested. "And I've apologized about a thousand times now."

He nodded. "I know." His voice was soothing. "And I was surprised that she would take things so hard. But you know Lucy—she feels things very deeply. You hurt her."

I felt that I would start crying again. "I don't know what I'm supposed to do to fix it. She won't answer my calls or texts. I would show up in person, but I'm pretty sure she'd just slam the door in my face."

"Well, Billy," he said gently, "you left her. I mean, think of it.

You're like sisters. You two have never really been separated before, and when you announced you were leaving Manhattan—"

"Only an hour and a half away!" I cried. "She could visit any-time!"

He shook his head. "In any case, I think she has just needed time to heal a bit, to lick her wounds, as it were. But I also know that you two need each other."

"Of course we do," I answered. "I miss her horribly."

He picked up the scone for a moment and then put it back down.

"There's another reason she has been out of touch lately, Billy. And I am embarrassed to be part of the reason. I know it's been ter-ribly hard on you both. You see"—he shoved the plate away—"we're having a bit of trouble in our marriage again."

I glowered at him, all defensive self-pity suddenly erased in a surge of protective anger. "What the fuck did you do now?"

"I have not . . ." He paused a moment, as if searching for words. "I have not behaved fairly toward her. And I've been selfish. And, of course, it's been particularly hard because she hasn't had you to lean on while she was going through all this. But I think that we are get-ting better. Or, at least, we're working on it. And I think that things will be much better soon. And when they are, I'm certain she will come back to you. Perhaps to us both, really."

I shook my head. "Titus, you're such a fucking idiot. You are married to one of the most beautiful women in the world. I mean, that's not even an exaggeration. I've never met anyone else as beau-tiful as Lucy is—inside and out. And she adores you. She has built her life around you for years now. Why do you need to fuck around? What more could you possibly get from another woman?"

A shadow crossed his face, and for a moment, Titus just . . . kind of caved. He looked old and sad and regretful. He looked like he honestly felt shame. Then he laid his hands palms-up on the table and smiled a twisted smile.

"I wish I knew," he said. "She's more than I deserve."

"Well, that's the fucking truth," I said. But I softened a little, looking at his miserable expression. "It's an amazing painting, though, Titus. What did she think of it?"

He smiled again—that smile that didn't really look like him. "She hasn't seen it yet, actually. You'll have to let me know what she says after you show it to her."

chapter 22

Stone Ridge, NY
Halloween

I was lost in a fucking corn maze. And even worse, I was lost in a fucking corn maze and I had spilled my coffee.

I could hear Ethan's voice—he was shouting and laughing with Kai and Marta, but at some point they had run ahead of me and taken a turn that I'd apparently missed.

I felt like I had been trudging through this thing for hours (though it was probably no more than fifteen minutes) and I was beginning to feel prickles of claustrophobia. Still, it was already embarrassing enough to be lost—I wasn't about to compound my humiliation by calling out for help.

We were in the fucking corn maze to begin with because Ethan had sent out a group text last night:

Hey Leftovers crew!

Let's start Hween right! Mt me at Saunderskill Farms in Stone Ridge at 8 a.m. I know the baker. Hot cider dnuts fresh out of the grease! ☺ ☺ ☺

Fuck it, I thought. I hadn't seen the girls since the night I wait-ressed. Maybe donuts would help.

But donuts had not helped, as good as they were (and they were really, really good), nor had the pretty, sprawled-out farm with its gigantic piles of pumpkins, its hay ride with a matched pair of white Clydesdale horses, the overflowing baskets and pots of purple asters and autumn-colored chrysanthemums . . . Nothing was making any difference. Everyone except for Ethan (who seemed to be running on pure, unfettered determination to make everyone happy) was ex-hausted. Eight a.m. might as well have been four in the morning to a bunch of restaurant workers (and I had been up all night prepping for the festival). Kai was completely icing me out, Marta was bab-bling nervously, and Ethan couldn't seem to stand the idea that his people weren't getting along. That was when he suggested the corn maze.

"It'll be fun!" he cried as he bounded toward it. "Come on!"

Marta ran after him with a happy squeal. Kai and I exchanged sour glances but then trudged behind, our cups of coffee firmly in hand.

I spilled my coffee within minutes, tripping over a root in the muddy ground. Kai didn't even stop, just turned briefly to see that I was back on my feet and then disappeared around a corner.

I stopped for a moment, pulling out my phone.

It's 8 a.m. and I'm in a fucking corn maze covered in mud with no coffee, I wrote in a group text. Where the fuck are all of you?

I'm in bed, of course, darling, wrote Lotta in return. As any decent person should be.

I'm on my way to SoulCycle, answered Sarah. It makes me miss you guys soooo much!! Then I'm filming later today. We're considering thawing my frozen eggs!!!!

I waited a moment, hoping against hope, before I put my phone back in my pocket and trudged on. I hadn't really expected an answer from Lucy, but since Titus's visit, I had thought that maybe things would change soon. Or at least eventually.

Within a minute, I hit a dead end. Then I turned around and hit another one.

Aren't these things for children? taunted Lucy in my head. *How complicated can this possibly be?*

I rounded a corner and encountered a scarecrow I was positive I had already seen. *Fuck.*

I couldn't hear anyone anymore, either. And look, logically I knew that I was not going to be trapped in this fucking corn maze forever. I knew that at some point, probably soon, I would find the exit and be free, but that didn't help the surging panic I was beginning to feel.

I came to a fork in the path. I was completely turned around and couldn't tell east from west anymore, so I randomly chose the left path, which led me in a circle right back to where I had just been.

Fuck it. I sat down on the ground, no longer caring about the mud, and texted Ethan:

Lost in this motherfucking corn maze. Come find me. Preferably alone.

Ten minutes later, I heard him crashing through the stalks before I saw him. "Billy?" he called.

I didn't get up. "Here," I said.

He came round the same path I'd taken earlier. He was carrying a cup of coffee.

"Oh, come on!" I spluttered. "How is that even possible? I was just down that path. It led absolutely nowhere! This thing is ridiculous!"

He looked down at me and handed me the coffee. "I heard you spilled yours."

"Thank you." I pouted. "I am now going to drink the whole thing before I get up."

He plunked down beside me. "Ugh," he said, examining his dirty hands. "This is way muddier than I thought."

I shrugged, chugging the hot, bitter drink.

"So," he said. "You going to tell me what's going on with you and Kai and Marta? Because they won't tell me anything, but obviously, things are not exactly cool between you all."

I shook my head. "Not really my story to tell."

He raised his eyebrows. "So there's a story?"

I looked at him. The sun was slanting through the cornstalks and shadows were playing over his face and shoulders. His golden skin was poreless. His blue-black hair was literally gleaming, and his eyelashes were longer than mine, even after three applications of mascara.

Goddamn.

I could smell him, too. He must not have showered since he came home from the restaurant the night before, because he smelled salty and herbal and a tiny bit sweet and musky.

I sniffed. "Were you working with Concord grapes last night?"

He blinked, surprised. "How did you know that?"

I sniffed again, a little closer this time. "You smell like them. You smell . . . purple."

His face flushed. "Fuck. You are so sexy, Billy."

I laughed. "Because I can recognize the smell of Concord grapes?"

"Yes," he said, leaning toward me. "Yes, that and, like, a million other reasons."

And then he was kissing me. And for a moment, I thought about everyone—Marta and Kai and Brett. I thought about what Sarah and Lotta and most especially Lucy would say.

But then I closed my eyes and thought about absolutely nothing except the way his lips felt on mine, the way his front teeth clinked against my front teeth, the way our breaths wove together.

I let myself enjoy this for another moment and then:

"Um, guys?"

It was Marta and Kai. Standing there. Watching us make out like teenagers in the mud.

I sprang away from Ethan and scrambled up.

Marta looked absolutely stricken. Kai was stone-faced, but her eyes were glittering and there were red spots of color on each cheekbone. But Ethan sprang up behind me, a big grin on his face.

"Caught us," he said cheerfully. "Now, who remembers the way out?"

When I was a kid, I loved Halloween. Christmas in my childhood home was, of course, like walking on the thinnest ice that just happened to have a World War I–level minefield floating underneath. After my mom died, Thanksgiving always meant a visit to my great-aunt's very depressing nursing home. Easter and New Year's Eve were nonexistent jokes. But Halloween was all mine. I didn't need to depend on the adults in my life to slap on a fifty-cent eye patch, tie my hair in a scarf, and call myself a pirate, and I was living in the Midwest in the '80s. I could just join the hordes of other kids rampaging through my neighborhood, no adult supervision necessary.

And it didn't hurt, of course, to be able to be someone else for the night, to hide behind a mask. There was intense, joyous relief in imagining a different version of life, a different version of me.

Plus, candy.

There was a costume shop in Kingston—Columbia Costumes. Unlike all those cheap, pop-up costume shops that opened in September and closed on November 1, this place was open year-round. It was a town landmark, had been in existence for nearly fifty years. It sold a huge collection of wigs and cosmetics, and if anyone needed to rent a full-body gorilla costume or be the Queen of Hearts or a flying blue monkey from *The Wizard of Oz* for any reason whatsoever, Columbia was there to accommodate them.

I had found the place on my own when I had first moved up. I was wandering uptown, trying to get my bearings, when I'd walked past a window display full of mannequins dressed as zombies that were arranged as if lurching toward a sleeping child.

I was delighted when I walked in. It was a sprawling, two-story space, absolutely crammed with every possible kind of disguise anyone could want. I could be a hundred different people here. Maybe even a thousand.

I spent an hour in the place, just sifting through the possibilities, until, finally, I found some devil horns. Small and realistic, they looked as if they'd been carved out of rough black bone and were attached with a thin, transparent headband that disappeared perfectly into my curly hair. I bought the devil horns and a sharp, metal pitchfork to go with them, and a springy, forked red tail that promised to attach to almost any fabric.

So that's what I was wearing that evening at the festival. My chef whites with the tail attached and hanging out from under my jacket. My chef cap, the little horns just peeking out nonchalantly from under the brim, and my pitchfork tossed to the side, because, well, I needed both of my hands, of course.

We were making pho and borscht. Ethan had provided me with the week's beef bones and trimmings, which I threw into two baking trays—each with half a dozen cut onions, plus the week's collection of onion tops and outer peels that Ethan had saved for me. And then, to one tray I added some generous knobs of ginger, and on the other I placed heads of garlic, tops lopped off and drenched in oil, and a scattering of bay leaves. It all roasted until my house was so deliciously fragrant that Chicken had lifted his little snout and howled in despair, driven wild by the smell.

While that was cooking, I toasted handfuls of star anise, cinnamon sticks, cloves, and whole cardamom pods in a cast-iron skillet on top of the stove, closing my eyes and inhaling the sweet, powerful, comforting scent. Then I grated beets (Ethan had been tearing his hair out trying to figure out what to do with the surfeit of beets he had in the kitchen) and carrots, chopped potatoes, and sliced cabbage.

After they were ready, I'd divided the pans of roasted bones and meat into two giant stockpots, added water, and let them both simmer for hours until they were reduced into rich, flavorful, and bubbling liquids. I strained them both and flavored one with yellow rock sugar, salt, and fish sauce, and the other with just salt and pepper. Then I carefully delivered the enormous pots to Huma (it was closed for the night, but Ethan had left a key), wedging them into the oversize walk-in.

Halloween was supposed to be cold that year, and hot, fragrant, simple, and comforting soups seemed just the thing to be selling to groups of drunken college students and tired parents who had just spent the evening walking in the Halloween parade and tailing their children as they ran door to door collecting their candy.

Marta, who was dressed in a fur hood and fluffy tail over her whites (squirrel chef), refused to look at me, quietly fussing over little round potato rolls with clever bats and pumpkin faces pressed into each piece of bread and meant to be given out with the borscht. She'd also prepared a choice of tiny pumpkin or apple tarts—the farmers' market was overflowing with autumnal produce at the moment, and Ethan had over-ordered.

Kai (an extremely grumpy-looking Hermione Granger: Hogwarts robe, frizzy hair, wand) tended to the toppings for the pho—lime and sprouts and thinly sliced raw beef. Ethan (amazingly, endearingly, jaw-droppingly kitted out as the Prince in *The Nutcracker*—gilt-edged red coat, tights, and all. "Our conversation the other night inspired me," he'd said, grinning) had shown me how to make those melting, gelatinous squares of herbs that I had first tasted in his melon soup at Lotta's wedding, except this time they were made of basil and cilantro for the pho, and dill and parsley for the borscht.

"It's not all local," Ethan had pointed out a few days before when I had presented him with the menu.

"I know," I said. "But it's using up so much stuff from Huma, and aside from the lime and some of the spices and the fish sauce—"

"And the rice noodles," he added.

"No," I said, excited to tell him, "I'm going to make the noodles myself! I got rice flour from that Gambian family you told me about. They will be totally local."

He smiled.

But he wasn't smiling now. We were all in the Airstream, crammed in on top of each other, and whatever good feelings we'd been wrapped up in earlier in the corn maze had vanished. I had spent the afternoon prepping for the truck and listening to Lucy castigate me in my head. And I imagined that Kai—or maybe even Marta—had gotten to Ethan after I had gone home to change my clothes. But whatever had happened had left everyone grim, sour, and bordering on mean.

Out on the street, children and adults alike were parading down the street dressed as clowns and monsters, bats and wolves, fairies and goblins. There was a motley group of horns and percussion leading the parade, playing the theme to *The Addams Family*. On the sides, people were watching and waving and laughing and shouting. The storefronts were decorated with hay bales and cornstalks and flickering jack-o'-lanterns. Kids were scampering from door to door, collecting their treats. We hadn't even opened yet, but there was a small crowd already queued up in front of the truck, eager to temper all the candy and chocolate with something more substantial.

"We really should have done a better job of coordinating costumes," ventured Ethan. "We don't make any sense together."

"You can fucking say that again," said Kai as she violently chopped some cilantro.

I was veering between worrying about the truck—overtending the food, micromanaging each little ingredient—and reliving the kiss and its aftermath.

It wasn't the best kiss I had ever had. It might not have even been top five. Ethan was young and a tad bit tentative. He was intimidated by me, I could tell. But there had been a sweetness to it, and a certain promise, as if he might grow into greatness.

I could teach him, I thought dreamily while mixing the cabbage, beets, and carrots into the soup. *That would be fun.*

But all that faded when I thought about the look on Marta's face when she saw us. She was not over him. Of course she was not over him, I had known that before I had let him kiss me. And Kai, standing behind a sad-eyed Marta—the absolute fury that had shone from her eyes . . .

I shook my head. As overdramatic and riddled with silliness as I found their story to be—I had been twenty-five once, too. And I had been just as foolish, if not more so. And I remembered the intensity of that time, the overwhelming need and emotion, the way I had obliviously let men screw me and use me, and then turned around and done the same things to them. The stupid fucking mistakes I had blithely made over and over and over again.

I had crushed Marta. I could see that. And Kai—now that I knew that most of her bitchery came from a fierce desire to protect her beloved friends—I couldn't even dislike her anymore. She was *right*. I was a threat to Marta's happiness.

And potentially Ethan's, too, I thought as I watched him adeptly turn from one task to the next. The truck was hot, and he had stripped off his ornate coat and was just wearing the dance tights, high leather boots, a black T-shirt, and an apron. His face was flushed, and his hair was pushed back from his forehead. He looked ridiculously handsome.

But what if I actually wanted him? What if I pursued this to see where it went? How could it be anything more than a fling?

I thought of Lucy and Titus—even with their much more conventional older man/younger woman match-up, she in her forties and he in his late sixties—I could see the holes that were springing up between them. I was sure that one of the main reasons Titus felt it necessary to go out and fuck other women was to prove to himself—and her—that he was still strong and virile, that he wasn't slowing down in any way. And yet, anyone who had known him over the years could see that he was getting softer, weaker, slower. He drank too much and didn't exercise enough. He worked too hard, and ate based on pleasure and desire. He was a glutton of sorts. Lucy had once told me that he refused to see a doctor, seemed terrified of them, actually, so who knew what his health was really like?

Lucy had been a muse who had turned into a caretaker. She had been caring for him for years—clearing all the day-to-day stuff out of the way for him so he could create, making sure that everything ran like clockwork in deference to his genius. But the kind of life that was staring her in the face lately was something altogether different. The next ten to twenty years with him were probably not going to be about passion or partnership: they were probably going to be about the hands-on work of tending to a faltering body and mind.

And the shelf life was even shorter between an older woman and a younger man. I mean, I couldn't even admit that I needed reading glasses: how could I go through menopause with a boyfriend who was just hitting thirty? I imagined being sixty and him being in his prime at forty. I shook my head. Wasn't one of the benefits of pairing off supposed to be finding someone to grow old with together? Not having someone stand by and just *watch* you get old.

Well, Brett is only two years older than you, said Lucy's voice.

"Billy?" asked Ethan. "Billy, the parade is over. Are we ready to go?"

I shook myself out of my reverie. "Right. Yes. Everyone ready?"

"Yes, Chef," they answered as one.

"Then open it on up."

Whatever else was going on, we were all professionals. We had all been trained. We opened up our window, smiled at our customers, and started our careful choreography.

Ethan took the front, warmly greeting each person in line, answering questions, taking enough time to explain the menu and concept of the truck, and then taking their order. Kai manned the soups—making sure they were staying at temperature, that each recyclable paper cup was filled with the right amount of noodles and broth for the pho, the correct split of vegetable and meat for the borscht. I was doing the finishing—garnishing the pho with meat and vegetables, splashing the borscht with a drizzle of crème fraîche I had made from some cream that was about to hit its sell-by date, and then adding the correct square of herbs to each. And Marta followed up by tucking in her fresh, hot rolls and clever little tarts—each no bigger than the palm of her hand.

There was a crowd, and we had to work fast, but I wanted to make sure that each order was treated thoughtfully, that the soup looked pretty, that it was just hot enough, that the rolls had nice pats of butter, that it was all handed out with a warm smile. I wanted everything, humble as it all was, to be perfect.

I eagerly peered out the back window, looking for people who were carrying their cups of soup back into the crowd, and I spotted a middle-aged mom wearing a crooked witch's hat, herding her two young children who were dressed as fat little ghosts. She grasped a red paper cup of borscht in one hand (I knew it was borscht because we had color-coded the cups to avoid mistakes) and was trying to direct her children—both of whom seemed to want to go in opposite directions—safely across the street with the other.

I watched her thoughtlessly lift the cup to her mouth, hands not even free enough to use the bamboo spoon we had provided, taking a gulp of its contents as she jostled her way through the crowd.

And then, suddenly, she stopped and paused, glancing down at the contents of her cup with a look of surprise on her face.

Then I watched her take another sip, close her eyes, and smile.

It was a split second, a blink in time. She had turned away and hurried after her children before I could even react, really. And it wasn't my father crying over the chocolate pudding, or even Ethan eating the tomato sandwich—but it was a start. It was the sweetness of feeding someone who really tasted what you had made for them; it was the pleasure of knowing you had just changed someone's day, even just a little bit, for the better.

"They like it," I said softly.

"Of course they like it," snapped Marta. "Why wouldn't they like it? What choice did they have?"

I turned to her, surprised by her tone. It was the first time she had spoken directly to me all night. "What?" I said.

She looked at me, her chin tilted high, her normally cheerful face lit up with anger. "I mean, it's good soup. It's really good, almost irresistible, soup. It's soup that's new and mysterious and just showed up out of nowhere and fucking changed everything without asking anyone. It's awesome, cool, exciting soup that looks amazing in short skirts and just takes what it wants and doesn't give a shit about anyone else! I mean, of course they like it!"

"We're not talking about the soup," I said.

"Fucking duh," said Kai from my other side.

"Of course we're not talking about the soup," spluttered Marta.

My phone buzzed in my pocket, but I ignored it. "Marta—" I began.

"Everything okay?" said Ethan from the front.

"No, everything is not okay, Chef!" called back Marta. "You fucking kissed Billy in the corn maze!"

"What?" said Ethan. He sounded genuinely bewildered. "So?"

"You're such a cunt, Ethan," said Kai. "Don't act like you don't know what she's upset about."

"But I don't," said Ethan. "I really don't!"

My phone buzzed again. I ignored it again, and put my serving spoon down. "Oh, for fuck's sake," I said. "Ethan, Marta is still in love with you. She always has been, but you didn't call her soon enough after your date, so she slept with Kai and she was embarrassed, so she told you she didn't want to see you anymore because she was worried about her sauce class. But the thing with Kai was just gay for play and never really meant anything."

"Gee, thanks," said Kai.

"Hey!" said Marta. "I told you that in private!"

"Wait, what?" said Ethan. "What?"

"And Marta, Ethan is still completely, ridiculously gone over you. He spent like two hours lovingly describing your bacalao fritters and talking to me about how you were the one who got away. He thinks he's interested in me, but I'm just a totally inappropriate distraction to keep his mind off the fact that he's working day in and day out with a woman he's madly in love with but thinks he can't have."

"You are?" said Marta. "You do?"

"I am?" said Ethan.

"And Kai," I said, turning toward her, "your loyalty to your friends is admirable but you have got to fucking move on. Get out and meet some people. Get a girlfriend. Take up a hobby. It is not your fucking job to fix all this. You don't need to spend your life protecting Marta. And you don't need to be such a royal bitch all the time."

"Fuck you, Billy," said Kai.

"She's not wrong," said Marta.

"Fuck you, Marta," Kai returned.

"I'm sorry I kissed Ethan," I said. "It was neither professional nor wise. Ethan is an amazing chef—"

"Thank you," said Ethan.

"But," I said, ignoring him, "I do not want to get hot flashes and vaginal dryness while Ethan is hitting his sexual prime. I have a friend who says that I self-sabotage and I think she might be right. There is another man—a man that I might even—"

The phone buzzed again. Insistently.

"Fuck, fuck, fuck! Who keeps calling?" I said, snatching it out of my pocket.

I looked at the screen.

Lucy.

"Hello?" I said. "Lucy? Hello?"

"Billy?" Her voice sounded weak and soft and so far away. "Billy? I need you. It's Titus. He's gone."

chapter 23

Manhattan

Lotta and Sarah were already there when I arrived. They had come straight from Heidi Klum's annual Halloween party, and, like me, they were still in costume.

Lotta was dressed as Pippi Longstocking, eyeliner freckles scattered across her nose and two long braids incongruously held up by red balloons floating at each end of her plaits. She was bent over Lucy, one hand on her shoulder as she sat at her kitchen table with her head in her hands.

Sarah, wearing a pink satin Playboy Bunny one-piece and fishnet stockings, her fluffy little tail and ears on full display, was turned toward the stove, tending the teapot.

I paused for a moment on the threshold of the kitchen, unsure of my welcome. It felt like it had been years since our fight in Brooklyn. I briefly wondered if Lucy really wanted me there. Lotta and Sarah seemed to have things well in hand.

But then Lucy looked up, and our eyes locked, and she was up out of her chair, and then in my arms, clinging to me like a lost child, sobbing into my neck. "He's dead, Billy," she choked out. "He's dead. He's dead."

"Prostate cancer," explained Lotta. "Apparently he was diagnosed three months ago. Advanced, but treatable."

"Except that he refused treatment," said Sarah.

We were sitting around the kitchen table, drinking tea. Lucy had been inconsolable, so we had dosed her with a couple of Xanax and tucked her into bed, waiting for her to drift off before returning to the kitchen.

"But why?" I said. "Why would he refuse treatment?"

Lotta shrugged. "Side effects. Incontinence. Impotence. You know what a macho fuck he was. His pride could never take it."

"He was also terrified of doctors," said Sarah.

"But why didn't she tell us? I mean, you guys didn't know, did you?"

Lotta shook her head. "We found out when you called us tonight."

"And so, what? She helped him kill himself?"

"No," said Sarah. "I think she was taken by surprise by that part. She said she found him in his studio, and he was already gone. Empty pill bottle. Note on the table. I don't think she was expecting it at all."

"What an asshole," I said. "I can't believe he'd do that to her."

"I can," said Sarah. "He always was a selfish bastard."

Lotta bit her lip. "I don't know. He made it easy in a way, didn't he? Over before the worst of it came."

"Lotta?" I said. "Will you take the motherfucking balloons out of your hair already? They're really distracting."

Lotta smiled grimly and untied the balloons, her long braids dropping back to her shoulders. We were quiet for a moment, watching the red orbs as they drifted slowly up and away from us, bouncing against the ceiling with soft little bumps.

"Well," said Sarah finally, "what now? She can't be alone."

"I'll stay," I said quickly. "I can stay."

I laid down on the enormous leather couch in the living room, but I couldn't get comfortable. There was a guest room, but I wanted to be sure that I wouldn't miss Lucy if she got up. Lotta had taken her car and driver and gone back to the Hamptons that night. She was worried about leaving Sage alone in the cottage for too long. Sarah had gone home to her apartment. She had to film in the morning. Both women had promised to come back as soon as they could.

I thought about Titus. About the painting he had brought me. The last few words we had exchanged. He had been tying up loose ends. Making sure that I would be there for Lucy when the time came.

My mother had not planned things out so elegantly. Certainly, there had been nothing like a final, glorious masterpiece of a painting, or even a simple note explaining herself. She probably felt that my father and I wouldn't need a note to understand. We had lived with her long enough.

She had done it in the garage. Gone out after everyone was asleep one night, stuffed a rag in the car's tailpipe, and left the engine running until my father found her in the morning. I had wandered downstairs, rubbing my eyes and wondering why no one had woken me up, and I'd interrupted him on the phone, dully repeating our address to the emergency dispatcher on the other end.

He looked up at me, his eyes cloudy and confused. "Stay here. Don't go into the garage, Cricket." And then he left the kitchen.

I knew in my gut that something bad had happened. I could see it in my father's face. But I wasn't sure I wanted to know what it was. And so I carefully made myself a bowl of cereal. Cornflakes. Milk. Two heaping tablespoons of white sugar that immediately turned translucent, wet, gray, and saturated, coating the flakes. I sat down at the kitchen table and slowly ate one bite and then another, dragging my spoon at the bottom of the bowl, scraping up all the gritty sweetness, hoping to put off whatever was coming next.

I woke up with a start the next morning, momentarily disoriented, unable to remember where I was, and then I heard a crash on the floor above. I jumped off the couch and raced up the stairs, only to find Lucy's empty bed.

Another crash, still above me.

Lucy was standing in the middle of Titus's studio on the third floor, wearing nothing but a scant white nightgown, her long blond hair loose and flying. There were pots of oil paints broken and splashed in a multicolored swirl at her feet. A large easel had been knocked over and she was wordlessly kicking at it, her face red with rage.

"Luce?" I said. I had never seen her so upset.

She whirled on me, panting, her eyes wild.

"Lucy," I said quietly. "Hey, let's go downstairs, okay?"

"Just a moment," she said, her voice eerily calm. Then she turned back and kicked at the easel again and again, and then one last time, putting her foot through the half-finished canvas.

She turned back. "Okay." And then she docilely followed me downstairs and sat down at her kitchen table.

"Are you hungry?" I asked.

She laughed. "Most people would ask if I was okay, but you ask if I'm hungry. Oh my God, I've missed you."

"Are you okay?"

She laughed again. "What do you think?"

"Is your foot bleeding?" I asked. "Or is it just paint?"

She bent and examined it curiously. "Both, I think."

I wet a clean dishcloth. "Put this on it."

She pressed the cloth against her instep and then looked up and met my eyes. "He made me promise not to tell anyone," she said. "He told me about it a few months ago, and he said that we could handle it ourselves. That he could get treatment, and that he would get better, and no one would have to know."

"Except he didn't get treatment."

She shook her head. "He was scared. And stupid. He started researching all these alternative therapies. Herbal remedies and dietary supplements." She rolled her eyes, blinking away tears. "We flew all the way to Brazil last month to search out this shaman who supposedly could just chant the cancer away . . ."

"You were in Brazil and you didn't tell me?"

She shrugged. "I was terrified, but I made a promise to him to keep it secret. I knew that if I told you anything, I'd have to tell you everything."

I filled the kettle at the sink. Took out a frying pan.

"I'm not hungry, Billy," she said quickly.

I shrugged. "Just a cup of tea, then. Maybe some toast."

She shook her head. "I can't eat."

I put the kettle on anyway.

"We had a deal," she continued. "He would have another scan, and if it had grown at all, he would get the surgery. He had the scan last week."

I looked at her. "And?"

"It had spread. But the doctor said it was still operable. So we set up the surgery date, made all our plans, and then . . ." She trailed off. She looked up at me, her face flushed, her eyes shining with tears. Her voice was a hiss. "I'm just so furious at him, Billy. I'm so fucking angry."

"You should be," I said. "You have every right to be." I retrieved two mugs from the cabinets, dug out two chamomile tea bags from a drawer.

"He spent the last half of our marriage walled off with work, with other women, with his own grandiose ambition. Then he said . . . he said he wanted to come back to me, to make it up to me. He played such games. He made such a pageant of it all. But I wonder . . . I think he must have known that he was sick even before he told me about it. I mean, maybe it was just a sixth sense, maybe he just suspected it was coming, but I feel like maybe he just wanted to come back to me because he knew he would need the help. Maybe he just wanted me back so I could—"

She broke off again and stared at the steaming cup of tea I put in front of her.

"I got all your texts. All your messages," she said. "I missed you so much."

"Me too," I said.

She laughed suddenly, looking up at me. "Did Lotta really buy a two-hundred-thousand-dollar horse?"

The funeral was small and private. Lucy sat through it silently, pale and watchful, as various friends stood and testified to Titus's genius and generosity. He was cremated. There was a brief and succinct press release that left the art world gasping in shock. The calls and e-mails started to flood in. There was a demand for a more public service, but Lucy told Titus's agent that they could do a bigger memorial later in the year, after she'd had some time to sort things through.

As soon as she'd heard the news, Lucy's mom, Cheri, had flown back from Spain, where she had been vacationing with a boyfriend, but she had claimed exhaustion after the funeral and headed back to her own place.

"She doesn't like thinking about death," said Lucy wryly as she watched her mother, pleading a terrible headache, practically run out of the room. "Titus was actually only a little bit younger than her, you know."

I had seen Brett at the funeral. He had stopped and hugged Lucy, whispering his condolences, and then turned to me.

I had leaned into his arms, breathing his scent, feeling momentarily safer, better, happier than I had for days.

"If you need anything, Billy," he'd said. "You or Lucy. Just call. Anytime."

Stay. The word almost popped out of my mouth. *Please. Stay.* But there was a roomful of other people waiting to talk to Lucy. It hadn't been the time.

We were all in the living room. Me, Lotta, and Sarah. Omari was still in Germany, and Brian had left for work again right after the funeral.

Lucy walked into the room, a blank look on her face, and sat down next to me on the couch. "Guess what?" she said. Her voice was shaking. "I just got off the phone with Titus's lawyer and it turns out I'm pretty much completely broke."

"What? How is that possible?" said Sarah.

"But his paintings have been selling for top prices for years!" exclaimed Lotta.

Lucy shrugged hopelessly. "He didn't like to keep his own work. Once he was done, he always said he wanted the painting gone, that he couldn't move on to the next piece without banishing the last, so I never thought it was strange that everything he did was sold practically before he even finished."

But his wealth was illusory. Apparently, more often than not, hoping to avoid taxes, he had worked in trade. A painting for a high-end restaurant, where they told him he could always eat for free. A painting promised to his assistant, in lieu of her salary. When he needed cash, he had mortgaged and then remortgaged the town house without telling Lucy. He had taken out multiple credit cards and opened up several lines of credit at various banks. Her jewelry, her clothes, the furniture in their home—all bought with plastic.

All she had was a bit of money she had made on her own as a model many years ago and put in an account in her name only. That was still there. But it was nothing she could live off of for long.

She looked around, her eyes glittering, her face pale. "I need to get out of here," she said. "I can't stand it. He's everywhere here, and it turns out that this place isn't even mine. I need to leave."

chapter 24

L ucy was not eating.

She seemed basically intact, otherwise. I mean, of course, she was dark and sad and still in shock, and she wandered around my house like a fucking river wraith, but she was still recognizably Lucy. She was still smart and funny and annoyed by Chicken, who continued his faithless streak and immediately attached himself to her as if he was still a starving stray and she was carrying around an extra steak in her pocket.

But I put dish after dish in front of her—all the things I knew she liked. Carefully cooked eggs every morning, artfully composed salads with poached salmon at lunch, clams and pasta or a roasted chicken, at dinner . . . And she always smiled politely and said thank you sincerely, and maybe even took a symbolic bite or two. But then she would just sit there, watching me eat, until whatever was in front of her was cold and congealed and tasteless, and I finally gave up and took it away again.

She drank. She drank the wine I gave her and the endless cups of tea and sometimes even a weak cocktail or something as wholesome as a glass of milk. But she would not eat.

I tried other things. She claimed she was still too raw to be out in public much, so I couldn't take her to Huma or show her around town, but, reasoning that exercise would make her hungry, I made her strap on her sneakers and walk the rail trail with me every day.

It was always empty. Most people had given it up as too cold and too muddy this time of year. The best colors of fall were over, the asters and goldenrod long gone. The tall grass on each side of the path was now brown and brittle, no longer a deep green. But the pale, late-autumn light still streamed down through the bare branches, the rock walls and cliffs still towered above us, and an occasional deer or fat gray squirrel still scampered out to cross our path.

"Isn't it hunting season now?" asked Lucy as she picked her way around a puddle. "Shouldn't we be wearing, like, red or bright orange or something?"

I shrugged. "Maybe?" I let Chicken off his leash, and he ran joyfully ahead of us, bounding through the mud. "They'll probably get Chicken first, though."

Lucy laughed. "He can be our warning shot. At least he's good for something."

Sometimes Lucy wanted to talk. Sometimes she was the woman with a complicated, decades-long marriage behind her. Sometimes she was bitter and furious. Sometimes she wanted to vent and process or just curse Titus's name. We would walk side by side and she would spit out every wrong he had ever done her, every hurt he had ever inflicted. Sometimes she inhabited the young girl who first met him. She would talk about how handsome he had been, how charming. The way he had opened up the world to her. What he had taught her. A funny thing he had said.

Mostly, though, we walked in silence on those hikes, listening to birds and insects and the wind in the trees. Sometimes I would look over at her and there would be tears coursing down her face, but I quickly learned that she didn't necessarily want or need my comfort when that happened. It was okay, and perhaps even necessary, to just let her cry.

We spent a lot of time on the dock at my house, too. We would wrap up in layers (I gave Lucy my plaid shawl—I figured she needed it more than me), grab a bottle of wine, and pick our way down to the river. I had placed two small folding chairs at the end of the dock now that it was too cold to sit on the ground, and we would sit and share the wine, passing the bottle back and forth and swigging directly from it. The river seemed to compel Lucy. She said she could watch it for hours. She especially liked the way it looked on gray, cloudy days, like undulating, dimpled, molten steel, she said. And she loved it when the train would come past across the water.

"There is no sound more lovely or lonely," she said as the low whistle bounced back and forth between the banks.

She drifted. She walked from window to window in the house, staring out at the river in front, the forest in back. She took long walks down at the river's edge, coming back with her pockets laden with bits of jewel-bright sea glass and odd little horn-shaped, primeval-looking black seedpods that were so dangerously sharp that they could bite through the sole of your shoe.

She slept. She went to bed early and got up late. She took long, deep naps that I could barely shake her from. She was always tired, she said.

She said she couldn't read or write or watch television—she didn't have enough concentration. She couldn't follow a story.

"It's like I'm underwater," she said one day as we sat in the kitchen, in front of the fire.

It was too cold to go down to the dock, so we were watching a blue heron through the window. He was standing at the waterside, one long, prehistoric leg raised, his crested head pointed out at the waves, as still and silent as the rocks and sand around him.

I'd made her an open-faced sandwich—dark brown bread, a slick of good, salted butter, slices of smoked salmon interspersed with thin rounds of cucumber, all drizzled with crème fraîche, and topped with a scattering of dill.

She was ignoring it, as usual.

"Or there's a sheet of ice between me and the world. It's like I can see this fire, but I can't feel its warmth. I can touch the wood on this counter, but I can't really feel the grain. And when I look at this food"—she waved in the direction of the sandwich—"I know I should be hungry, but I'm just . . . not."

I sighed and removed the plate.

"It's like living with an anorexic fucking teenager," I complained to Kai, Marta, and Ethan.

Ethan had asked me to tag along on their weekly trips to the local greenmarket, so that if I saw something that inspired me for the truck, he could be sure to include it in his purchases.

"Sounds like rich-lady disease. My mom would just force me to eat," said Marta. "I wasn't allowed to leave the table until I had a clean plate."

"No one gave a shit about what I did or didn't eat," said Kai. "Uncaring servants. Busy father. Dead mom, remember?"

"Both my parents were amazing cooks and I was always hungry. I can't remember ever *not* wanting to eat," said Ethan.

Despite, or maybe because of, all my truth-telling on Halloween, Ethan and Marta were still acting careful and skittish around each other, and Kai was as much of a surly cunt as she had always been.

I had taken Ethan aside early, determined to make sure our kiss was not going to poison our professional relationship.

"I guess I should thank you," he'd said before I could spit out my patented let-him-down-easy speech.

I knit my eyebrows. "What for?"

"For clearing the air between me and Marta. I just thought she wasn't into me that way, you know?"

"Well, apparently she is," I said. "So are you going to do anything about it?"

He bit his lip. "Yeah. I will. Or maybe she will. I don't know. We're talking. It's complicated. Good, but complicated. Anyway, I just wanted to tell you thanks, and also, I wanted you to know, that kiss wasn't nothing to me."

I looked at him, nervous.

"Don't worry." He grinned. "I'm not going to try for another one. I know you like to do the lone-wolf thing. That you're not looking for anything more. And you know, now there's Marta, so . . . But I just needed you to know that I didn't kiss you just for the hell of it. I kissed you because I really, really wanted to."

"Uh." I gulped. "Okay. Good to know."

He slapped a hand on my shoulder. "Good. We're good, then." And he lumbered back to his station in the kitchen, oblivious to my baffled stare.

Still, good or not, things were moving forward. The Airstream was getting booked at more and more places, and we were starting to get some press attention as well. Ethan had done an interview with the local NPR station, where he had explained our no-waste concept, and a Hudson Valley magazine, *Chronogram*, had done a long article on various food trucks in the area that singled out Left-overs as being particularly good.

"Well, what are you feeding her?" asked Ethan as he examined a stalk of brussels sprouts at one of the greenmarket booths.

I shrugged. "Things she likes. Things I know she ate regularly in the city."

He raised his eyebrows. "Maybe that's the problem. You know, people have memory palates. Everything we've ever eaten is tied to emotion and context. Maybe the things you're serving her remind her too much of her husband."

I stopped for a moment. This was why it was so hard to completely dismiss Ethan as a callow young thing. Every time I would decide that he was twenty-five, and that's all there was to him, he would pop out with something brilliant like this.

"Jesus," I said. "You could be right." I got excited. "Like, I keep trying to feed her eggs every morning, because I know that's what she and Titus ate every day. She always claimed that the only thing she could really cook was eggs, and Titus always insisted on having them. But maybe you're right—maybe it just makes her think about him. Of course it's ruining her appetite!"

Ethan smiled and put down the brussels sprouts. "Maybe she needs something altogether new."

I looked at him, and then at Marta and Kai, who were poking around a pile of hydroponic lettuce. "You guys," I said, "will you cook for her?"

Afraid we'd spook her into hiding, I decided not to warn Lucy that we were coming back to the house, and so when we all trooped into the kitchen, carrying bags of food from the market, she was sitting at the kitchen island, dressed only in a pair of panties, an oversize sweatshirt, and scrunched-up knee socks.

"Oops," she said, leaping up and tugging frantically at the hem of her sweatshirt. "I'll meet everyone in a second, just give me a chance, to, uh, put on some pants." And she scampered down the hall toward the stairs.

"Damn," said Marta as all three of them watched her go. "Why do all your friends look like supermodels?"

I snorted. "Because she actually was a supermodel."

Kai rolled her eyes. "Of course she was."

"Well, even supermodels gotta eat," said Ethan as he started unloading the bags.

Lucy returned a few moments later. She had added jeans and subtracted the sweatshirt, replacing it with a sleeker tee. I noticed that she had also smoothed out her hair and smeared on a little lipstick, which I took to be a good sign.

"Lucy," I said, "this is Marta, Kai, and Ethan. They are some of the best cooks I know, and they are going to make you lunch."

Lucy's polite smile of welcome turned into a frown. "Oh, wow. Thank you, but I couldn't put you to the trouble. That's really not necessary."

"Billy says you haven't eaten in days," said Marta. "So actually, maybe it is necessary."

"I eat," protested Lucy. "I just don't eat much."

Kai looked her up and down, her lips pursed. "You obviously could eat more."

Lucy blushed and sat down. "I'll try, you guys," she said. "I'll do my best, but—"

"How about some wine?" said Kai.

"Or how about something stronger?" said Marta, pulling out her vape. "A little appetite enhancer?"

Lucy shook her head. "No, I don't think I can handle getting stoned right now. Too—"

"Raw," provided Kai. And Lucy nodded.

"Billy?" offered Marta.

"No thanks," I said. "I'm good."

"Well, you guys don't mind if we do, do you?" said Ethan.

I shrugged. "Knock yourself out. Anything I can do to help?"

Ethan pointed at the empty chair next to Lucy at the kitchen island. "Just sit down and relax. We got this."

"So, wine?" said Kai.

I pointed over to the pantry. "There's a little rack at the bottom of the shelves."

While Ethan and Marta traded the vape back and forth, Kai wandered over to the pantry, squatting down to examine the bottles I had hoarded. "Nice selection," she finally said.

My eyebrows shot up. "I think that's the first compliment I've ever received from her," I whispered to Lucy.

"Oh, gross, except for this Pinotage. What fucking idiot would buy that?"

I laughed. "And there she is."

Kai came back carrying an Australian Shiraz. "This one is good," she said. "It's comforting."

She opened the bottle and then retrieved two glass tumblers from my cabinets, pouring a couple inches for each of us.

Lucy bit her lip. "Thank you," she said.

"We are having lamb," announced Ethan. "My father used to make a Persian herb stew called ghormeh sabzi, but that would take all day. So this is my deconstructed version."

"Ethan's father is Iranian," I said to Lucy.

"Straight outta Isfahan," he said, throwing lamb chops into a smoking pan.

"And warm rice pudding for dessert," said Marta. "With pistachios. And maybe some nice rosewater madeleines to go with it."

"Nice! Keeping with the Persian theme," enthused Ethan and offered her a high five.

Marta's hand landed against his in response, but before she could take it away again, he closed his fingers over hers, holding her skin to skin for a brief, poignant moment until she flushed and pulled away.

I'll admit, I felt a small ping of jealousy in my heart, watching what was obviously blossoming between them again.

And as if she could read my mind, Lucy said to me, "Have you heard from Brett lately?"

I shook my head.

"Ooh, Brett!" said Marta. She sounded happy to have a new subject. "He was dreamy. Wasn't he hot, Kai?"

Kai shrugged. "Obviously not my type."

"Who's Brett?" said Ethan.

"Billy's perfect boyfriend," said Lucy.

"He's not my boyfriend," I said quickly.

"He should be," said Lucy. "He could be. He wants to be."

"Wait," said Kai. "So Billy has a perfect boyfriend but she still made out with Ethan?"

Lucy's eyes went wide. "You made out with Ethan? You didn't text me about that."

"We didn't make out," I said. "It was more like one kiss."

"Well," said Ethan, "I wouldn't say just one."

"But," piped in Marta, "it didn't mean anything because Ethan is in love with me." She stared defiantly at him. "Right, Ethan?"

Ethan blinked for a moment and then smiled. "Yes," he said softly. "Yes, I guess I am." He reached over and kissed her on the forehead as she beamed at him.

"Jesus Christ," said Kai. "Make the fucking lamb."

"What is happening here?" Lucy whispered to me, completely bewildered. "What am I missing?"

I shook my head. "Later," I said.

The lamb was exquisite. Tender little chops caramelized on the outside and pink, sweet, and juicy on the inside. Ethan had made a tangle of crisp shredded potatoes to nestle them into and then drizzled the whole thing with a green sauce made with reconstituted dried herbs and a little lamb stock.

"Lime," I said, smelling it. "There is definitely lime in this. That's not local, Chef."

Ethan shook his head. "It's preserved lime that the pickle guy does at the greenmarket—so it pretty much counts as local."

We all turned to look at Lucy. She was staring at the beautiful plate in front of her with absolute dread in her eyes.

"Luce?" I said.

"I'm so sorry, you guys," she whispered. "Ethan, I'm sure it's amazing, but I just can't—" She scraped her chair back and lurched up, practically running out onto the front porch.

I sighed as I looked at my plate, but then pushed away from the table. "You guys go ahead," I said, and followed her out the door.

She was around the corner, curled up in a wicker chair, her hands tucked into her armpits.

"I'm sorry, Billy," she said. "That was so sweet of them, but I look at the food and I know I should be hungry, but I just can't eat. It's like there's a big, bitter tangle of sadness in my gut. I feel like I swallowed my sorrow."

"No," I said. "I'm sorry. I shouldn't have sprung them on you like that. I just had this dumb idea that maybe you needed something different to eat. Something I didn't make."

She looked surprised. "You know I love your cooking."

I sighed and collapsed into the chair next to her. "I know. I'm just worried about you."

She nodded.

We stared out at the river for a moment.

"Luce," I said. "You should have told me. I mean, I know he was your husband. But you shouldn't have had to go it alone. I never would have left the city if I'd known you were going through all that."

She bit her lip. "He could be so selfish," she said.

"I didn't know why you wouldn't talk to me. He told me it was because of our fight. I thought that maybe you weren't ever going to—"

"I know." She cut me off. "I'm sorry," she said. "I missed you so much."

"And you know that I know you worked hard, right? That you weren't just handed everything because you're beautiful?"

"Yes." She sighed. "Though I sure as hell don't feel very beautiful these days."

I laughed. "I think Kai might beg to differ."

She glanced at me. "Your friends make me feel really old," she admitted.

"I've been wearing reading glasses for a year," I blurted out. "But only in private."

She laughed. "My pubic hair is going gray."

I looked at her, eyebrows raised. "Since when do you have pubic hair?"

She waved her hand. "Getting waxed hasn't exactly been my first priority lately."

"Fair enough."

She looked down at her lap. "What am I going to do now, Billy?" she said in a tiny voice. "I feel like my life is over."

I grabbed her hand and squeezed. "First, you're going to eat. Then we can decide the rest."

She squeezed back.

That night, I lay in bed, thinking about what Ethan had said about every meal being part of our collective taste memory.

My mother had cooked a pot of chili before she died. I will never know if this was a coincidental act on her part, or if she felt that the very least she could do was leave us with a couple of nights' worth of dinners before she made her permanent exit.

After the funeral, after all the neighbors and coworkers and family had left, my father bypassed all the hot dishes and casseroles that had been carefully deposited in our refrigerator by well-meaning friends and churchgoers, and he had warmed up the chili.

I was young, but I wasn't stupid. I stared at the steaming bowl he put in front of me, remembering that the last time I had tasted it, my mother had served it to me herself.

"But," I said, pushing the bowl away, "but she's *dead*, Daddy. This is dead-person food!"

He had stared at me sadly, shaking his head. "This," he said, gently pushing the bowl back toward me, "is the last time you will ever taste anything that your mother cooked for you, baby. She made this for you. She cooked it because she knew you liked it." He pushed it even closer. "She would want you to eat it."

I stared at him for a moment and then looked down at the chili. My father had swirled in a spoonful of sour cream and then added orange shredded cheddar that melted into a gooey crust over the top.

I took a trembling bite. It was rich with soft kidney beans and chunks of simmered beef; there were bright, sunny-tasting chunks of tomato that burst in my mouth. It had a little spice, but the sour cream was cool and creamy, so it wasn't too hot for my young palate.

"It's good," I told my father.

He nodded, taking his own bite.

We sat across from each other, eating in silence. Each bite I swallowed felt like a small bit of warm comfort, a little piece of her.

But then my bowl was empty, and that was it.

No more.

That was the first time I cried after she was gone.

I lay in the darkness for a moment and then got up and pulled on my clothes. It was well past midnight, and I assumed that Lucy had been asleep for some time already, but I left a note saying I'd be right back just in case she woke up.

Hannaford was basically deserted when I got there. A big, bright empty supermarket with just a couple of sleepy checkout clerks slumping at their registers. My cart had a squeaky wheel and loudly announced itself as I pushed it up and down the aisles. I had a list of what I needed, much of which was in the frozen-food section.

I bought things I hadn't eaten or cooked with in years. Campbell's cream of mushroom soup, slices of American cheese. A box of frozen mixed vegetables (a sudden memory—my mother had called this particular combination of corn, green beans, cubed carrots, and lima beans "magic vegetables" when she served it to me), a pound of ground beef, and a bag of frozen tater tots.

There was nothing seasonal or local or, frankly, particularly edible, in what I was buying. And though I'm sure the checkout girl could have cared less, I gave her my best "don't you fucking fuck with me" stare as she rang me up. I would brook no comments on my philistine, cheap-ass purchases.

The house was quiet and dark when I got back home. Chicken, who had taken to sleeping on Lucy's bed, didn't even bark when I let myself back in.

Humming softly to myself, I took off my coat, emptied my grocery bag, poured myself a glass of pinot gris, and took out my trusty cast-iron frying pan. I chopped an onion as a couple tablespoons of butter slowly melted, and then threw it in to soften and brown a bit. After the onion was done, I added the ground beef and stirred until it smelled like my father's taco night.

I poured the beef and onions into a baking dish, and then spread the now-thawed "magic vegetables" over that. I topped that with two cans of undiluted mushroom soup, then ten slices of American cheese, then the entire bag of frozen tater tots.

It all came back to me with no Googling or leafing through a cookbook, as if it was in my Midwestern bones.

In the oven at 350° for an hour. While I waited for it to cook, I downloaded *Say Anything*, *Bull Durham*, and *Heartburn*.

Finally, everything was ready, and I stuck my laptop under my arm, put on a pair of oven mitts, and carried the casserole dish, complete with two forks stuck into it, up to Lucy's room.

"Lucy," I whispered.

In the darkness I could just make out Chicken sitting up, his little nose twitching.

"Luuuuucy," I said again, turning on the light by her bed. "Wake up."

She rolled over and her eyes fluttered open. "What the hell, Billy?" She yawned. "What time is it?"

"Time to get up," I said. "It's midnight-movies-and-treats time."

She sat up, and her eyes got wider as she took in the dish in my hand. "Is that what I think it is?"

I nodded happily. It had been one of our most beloved childhood rituals. Lucy's mother, Cheri, had, let's just say, a casual way of parenting and a very active social life. Meaning, from the time Lucy was ten years old, Cheri would hand her daughter twenty bucks and then leave her alone in the house for weekends at a time while she went off with her various paramours.

Lucy hated it at first. She would lock all the doors, double- and triple-checking to make sure no one could get in. She would keep the TV and the radio on at night, trying to block out any scary noises, and she never left the house, pocketing the twenty and living off cold cereal and milk until her mother finally got back home.

But once she and I became friends, her mother's bad parenting became our greatest joy. I would simply tell my dad that I was spending the weekend at Lucy's house, and because he was a distracted and trusting parent, it never occurred to him to ask if Lucy's mother *would actually be there.*

We started out small. Sips out of the bottle of Cheri's rum. Prank calls to boys we liked. The thrill of ordering a pizza for delivery . . . And we took that twenty bucks and bought ingredients for all sorts of things I wanted to try cooking. Lucy was my guinea pig. As we got older, we became more daring. Keggers, and bongs, clumsy dinner parties with boys, naked hot-tubbing in Cheri's Sundance Spa 1000, and one ill-advised acid trip that left me convinced that I had somehow figured out a way to mind-meld with my cat.

But no matter what we did, no matter how hungover or wiped out or fucked up we were, and no matter what amazing, complicated thing I had managed to whip up for us to eat that weekend, Lucy always insisted that we end our Saturday nights the same way— tater-tot hot dish and movie rentals from the local Blockbuster. It was her favorite. It was our ritual, and it went on until the day that Cheri and Lucy moved away to New York.

I sat down on Lucy's bed. "Scooch over," I said, kicking my way under her covers and placing the warm casserole between us. "I should have thought of this days ago."

She eyed the dish warily. "I don't know," she said. "You can't go home again, Bill."

"Fuck that," I said, handing her a fork and starting up a movie. "Take a fucking bite of the fucking tots, my friend."

And she did.

And then, as we sat back and admired Tim Robbins's naked ass pumping away in the opening scene of *Bull Durham*, she took another bite. And then another. And before I knew it, Kevin Costner was dancing in Susan Sarandon's kimono, half the dish was gone and pushed aside, and Lucy was curled up asleep, her cheek pressed against my arm, her breath smelling ever so faintly of fake cheese and tater tots.

chapter 25

The River House
Kingston

Sarah, Lotta, and Sage showed up two days later. All at once.

"Brian left me," said Sarah as she swept into the house. "Well, first he lost his job, which actually happened like two months ago, but he didn't want to tell me. But when he did tell me, I said that it was fine, to look on the bright side, that it would be a great plot point for the show. And *then* he left me. He said he didn't want to be on TV. He said he had no intention of his failures being splashed all over for public consumption, that he didn't even recognize who I was anymore, and then he just got the hell out of there. I think he's living in the W on Union Square."

I shot a desperate look at Lotta, who was staring at me with a shell-shocked look on her face. "I just thought we were meeting for lunch at Wagamama," she whispered to me. "But, voilà, now we are here."

"Are you guys all staying?" I said, eyeing the pile of luggage that had been deposited by the door.

She raised her hands helplessly. "Omari will be home soon." She looked around, taking in the room. "But, ooh, I like your house. Maybe he can come up here and stay, too?"

"Uh, hi, Sage?" I said to Lotta's stepdaughter, who had her phone out and was waving it around in the air.

"Don't you get reception here?" she said in response.

"I couldn't leave her alone in the Hamptons," whispered Lotta. "She has this terrible new boyfriend. It will be good for her to take some time away from him."

"Billy?" called Lucy from the kitchen. "Sarah says she needs something to eat, like, right now."

I turned around, trying to sort my thoughts.

"Okay. Um. Okay. There are three extra bedrooms upstairs. Lucy's already using the one on the river side, but Lotta, you and Sarah can take the others. Sage, do you mind sleeping on a pullout in the parlor?"

"Does it have a door I can lock?"

"Well, one you can close, anyway. And a flat-screen."

She grimaced but nodded. "I guess so, then."

"Okay, well, that's right down this way—on the left. The reception is better out on the porch!" I called as she dragged her suitcase down the hall.

"Billy!" bellowed Sarah. "I'm starving!"

"I'm not sad," said Sarah as she shoveled chips and salsa into her mouth. "I'm mad, and I'm a little freaked out, but I'm not sad."

"I'm sad," volunteered Lucy. "And mad. I'm pretty much still totally both."

We were sitting around my kitchen island, and I was basically emptying my refrigerator out in front of Sarah. Olives. Hummus. Some fresh mozzarella. Half a Tupperware container of mushroom pâté. A jar of pickled carrots that Ethan had made. Cold chicken. A stick of duck sausage . . .

"What are you going to do about filming, Sarah?" I asked.

She shrugged, furiously biting into a chicken leg. "My agent said that once we figure out what to do about Brian, it might be the best thing that could have happened. He said I'll go from being this season's villain to being this season's It girl."

"Wait, you were the villain?" said Lotta. "When did that happen?"

Sarah waved the chicken in Lotta's face. "I don't want to talk about it."

"Wait," said Lucy. "So your agent is actually happy that you got dumped?"

"It's good for the show. It makes me more accessible. He says it's a better plotline than me having a baby."

"But," I said, "didn't you actually *want* to have a baby?"

Sarah crammed her mouth with pickled carrot in response.

"Wine?" asked Lucy.

"Wine," I said. "Or, you know what? There's a bottle of tequila. Get the tequila."

"Maybe we should go out tonight?" said Lotta, eyeing her stepdaughter, who was lying on my couch, an angry look on her pretty face as she waved her phone in the air. "Or invite those girls over for Sage? What were their names? Tai and Mary?"

"Kai and Marta," I said. "And they're working tonight. We could go out, but I doubt that Lucy or Sarah are really up for it."

Lotta shook her head. "I can't fucking believe that Brian finally grew big enough balls to leave her. But he'll be back, right? I mean, this can't be a permanent thing."

"I don't know," I said. "It was kind of a long time coming. He never could stand the TV show."

"*I* can't stand the TV show," said Lotta. "You know that she asked if she and the crew could visit us on our honeymoon?"

I laughed. "I can't believe you said no. What a bitch you are, Lo."

"How's Lucy doing?"

I shrugged. "Bad and good days. I mean, how long do you grieve when your husband kills himself, right? It's not like there's a set amount of time."

Lotta nodded dreamily. "I think things used to be easier," she said. "Death was easier. There were rituals. Wakes and viewings and mourning clothes. People respected grief. You were allowed to pass through the stages, take all the time you needed. You weren't expected to just take a weekend off for the funeral, pop some Zoloft, and then get on with your life."

"Well, nobody is asking her to do that," I said.

"I know," said Lotta, "but I have this feeling that Lucy might need more time than most. Titus was a big man who led a big life. She must feel like the sun went out."

"Maybe," I said. "Or maybe she finally feels free."

Lotta looked at me, surprised.

"He could be a real bastard, Lo. You know that."

She shrugged. "He was an artist. I've never known a great artist who also wasn't a selfish piece of shit. At least to some degree. And he did love her, Billy. You can't deny that."

"Yeah, well, offing yourself is a fucking awesome way of showing your love," I said in return.

Lotta squeezed my hand. "I forgot that you have your own history with this."

"Lotta," whined Sage. "Just how long are we going to be here, anyway? My phone doesn't work and I'm missing very important messages!"

Lotta rolled her eyes and lowered her voice. "And by 'very important messages' I think she means that pizza boy she's been seeing. Or maybe her pot dealer. I have got to get that girl out of the house. I don't think she's even moved from the couch since this morning."

"I was just getting ready to go down to Huma for a bit. I guess I could take her with me," I offered.

Lotta turned to me, pleased. "Oh, yes. Anything to get her off her ass. Thank you." She looked over at Sage. "Sage, honey, you want to go see those nice girls you met the weekend of the beach party? Martha and Di?"

"Marta and Kai," I corrected again.

Sage looked over at her stepmother. "I'm not six, Lotta. You don't have to make playdates for me."

"I'm happy to take you," I said.

She flicked a disgusted look at her useless cell phone. "I guess I don't have anything else to do."

"Okay, just give me a few while I get ready," I said.

I didn't go upstairs right away, though. Instead, I wandered out onto the porch and took out my phone. I had been thinking about Brett more than I wanted to admit since I'd seen him at the funeral, and I kept hoping for a call. Instead, there was a text from Ethan, telling me that he would have lamb necks and breasts and turnips, carrots, and potatoes to give me for that weekend's Rosendale Food Truck Fest. And another message from Sarah, apparently from my upstairs bathroom, asking me if I had any better shampoo or did she have to use the icky organic stuff I had by my tub.

Scotch broth? I texted Ethan. Or maybe we can do mini shepherd's pie?

And Buy your own fucking shampoo if you don't like mine, back to Sarah.

My finger hovered over the screen for a moment, wanting to call up Brett's number, but I hesitated and then finally put my phone away. I knew that I should just go down to the city and see him. This was really something that needed to happen face-to-face. But with all the girls here at the house, I didn't see that happening anytime soon.

I went upstairs and took off the sweats and tee I had been wearing all day. Everyone but Lotta had woken up hungover, and we were all acting accordingly. I had cooked a huge, greasy breakfast, which everyone (including Lucy, I was happy to observe) quickly inhaled, and since then, Sarah had been soaking in the bath, Lucy had gone to take a nap, and Lotta and I had spent the morning sitting at the kitchen island, me drinking cup of coffee after cup of coffee and Lotta watching Sage battle her cell phone.

"You ready?" I asked Sage, who nodded and got up off the couch.

"Have fun!" trilled Lotta.

"Your reception should be better now," I said as we drove into town. "It usually kicks in for me right around here."

Sage quickly whipped out her phone and started scrolling. "Yes," she said happily. "Much better. Oh, man, I missed, like, ten messages."

"Boyfriend?" I asked.

"Kind of. I mean, I hope so, anyway. He's really cool."

It was funny, but away from Lotta, Sage suddenly stopped acting and sounding like a recalcitrant teen and actually turned into something resembling a normal human.

"So you're done with school for now?" I said.

She looked up from her phone. "What? Sorry. Just sending off a response."

"I said, are you done with school for now?"

She put her phone down. "I guess? I mean, school totally sucked, but I probably need to figure out something else to do before I actually decide that, right?"

"Are you really asking my opinion?"

She cocked her head and looked at me. "Yeah. Sure. I am. Lotta said that you didn't go to college or anything, and you've been supporting yourself since you were super young, right?"

"Right. But that wasn't by choice. If I could have gone to college, or at least culinary school, I definitely would have. I just didn't have the money."

"Oh, well, money." Sage waved her hand dismissively. "That's not really the problem."

"So what is, then?" I asked.

She shrugged, her pretty face suddenly clouded. "This is going to sound dumb, but I've always had a really hard time making friends."

I considered this, thinking about how quickly Sage had offered up drugs to Kai and Marta, and then how, later, the older girls had ridiculed her for her food sensitivities. She was a beautiful, rich, and obviously smart girl, but a little desperate to be liked.

"So you were lonely," I said.

"I told my dad I needed an assistant just because I wanted someone to talk to," she answered.

I looked at her, surprised she was being so frank. "And did he get you one?" I said.

She shook her head. "No. He said I should join the volleyball team. So I dropped out."

"I thought you got kicked out because of your grades."

"Hard to study when you're sitting in your dorm room alone night after night feeling sorry for yourself."

"So you'd rather live with your dad and Lotta than stick it out at school."

"They were assholes there," she said. "A bunch of rich snobs."

I looked at her sideways.

She laughed. "Dad and I weren't always superrich, you know. This is kind of a new development."

"Really," I said. "I didn't know that."

"And Lotta's not all that bad."

"Oh, wow," I said. "She'd actually be thrilled to hear you say that."

"Oh my God. Don't you dare tell her I told you so."

I laughed. "Why are you so tough on her?"

She looked down and fiddled with her phone for a moment. "I dunno," she finally said. "Did Lotta ever tell you about my mom?"

Only that she's a fucking nightmare.

"Not much," I hedged.

"She's crazy," said Sage flatly. "Like, really clinically crazy."

"Ah," I said. "I had one of those."

"You did?"

"Yeah," I said. "It wasn't easy."

"But see, my mom wasn't always like that. I mean, she was never totally normal, but she used to be kind of okay, you know? And my dad, I think he really tried to take care of her. He really did love her. I know that. But then she got worse. I mean, like, a lot. And she would refuse to take her meds or see her psychiatrist. And my dad went through hell. Like, I didn't know whether to be more worried about him or her, sometimes. And finally, he just couldn't do it anymore and they got a divorce and then he met Lotta . . ."

"But what's wrong with that? Your dad and Lotta seem really happy."

She shook her head, frustrated. "No. I mean, I know they're happy. I just . . . Look, I know that Lotta seems pretty normal and everything, but I heard that she used to do some really out-there stuff. I mean, it's not so hard to Google someone. She had to be hospitalized, right? She almost died. She was wack."

"But that wasn't because . . . I mean, Lotta is normal—"

"And my mom used to be sort of normal, too. I know it sounds stupid, but what if Lotta gets like my mom? What if she gets sick, too? I don't think my dad could take it again."

"Oh," I said. "Oh. No. Listen, Lotta had to go to the hospital because she was in rehab. I mean, she's a recovering addict. She's not mentally ill."

"Okay, but what if she starts using again? That would be just as bad."

I thought of Lotta and her 98-percent-sober plan; then I thought about the way she talked about Omari and Sage. "I don't think she will," I said. "I think she's pretty determined not to."

Sage sat back in her seat and chewed on her lip. "Maybe," she said. "I mean, I hope that's right. I guess she's pretty okay most of the time. Maybe even cool, right?"

"Well, not on a horse," I reminded her.

She laughed. "True that."

Huma was slow that day. It was a Tuesday and no one was coming in. Ethan said this often happened just before the holidays. Nobody was taking time off from work, nobody wanted to spend their money on a nice restaurant, the tourists dried up . . .

Marta, Kai, Sage, and I sat in the back storage room, drinking beer and waiting for customers. I had finished up my planning with Ethan, who was in the kitchen working on a special he wanted to serve tomorrow, but we were hanging around because I felt bad for Sage, who just seemed so happy to see the other young women.

Sage was staring at her phone with a frown.

"Boyfriend-to-be?" I asked.

She nodded, then looked up. "Is porn normal?" she said.

"What kind of porn?" said Marta.

"I mean, is it normal when a guy sends you porn?"

"Oh, totally," said Marta. "Totally normal."

"Sure," said Kai. "Even I get it sometimes."

"Um," I said. "But, wait, Sage, you guys aren't even dating yet, right?"

She wrinkled her nose. "Not really?"

"So, I would have to disagree. Not normal."

"Well, is this normal?" she said, shoving a blurry dick pic right in front of my face and then waving it around for everyone to see.

"Ugh," said Kai. "Not necessary."

"And not very well done, either," I said.

Marta rolled her eyes. "Don't listen to them. She's a lesbian, and she's old. Everyone does dick pics now. That's how men communicate."

"Wait, ew," said Kai. "Is this how Ethan communicates?"

"Well," said Marta, "most men."

"That is not true!" I said. "Or if it is true, that is super ridiculously fucking sad. There are a million better ways to communicate."

"Like how?" said Marta.

"Like, haven't any of you ever received an actual love letter?"

"What," said Sage, "like an old-timey pen-and-paper thing?"

I gaped at her. "Oh, for fuck's sake. 'Old-timey.' You sound like I'm talking about a Model T."

"You might as well be," said Kai. "No one writes letters anymore. No one even calls. Just text or Snapchat. In ten years we'll probably all only communicate via emoji."

"Some people call," I said.

"Oh, you mean like Brett?" taunted Marta. "Your hunky non-boyfriend?"

"Well, yes," I said, surprised that I hadn't realized this sooner. "He almost never texts. He calls me. Or I call him."

"That sounds like a nightmare," muttered Kai. "Who the hell actually talks on the phone anymore?"

"It's nice," I mused. "He has a nice voice. I like hearing it."

"'He has a nice voice,'" mocked Kai.

I ignored her. "So, no letters? No phone calls? I actually feel kind of sorry for you guys. You don't know what you're missing."

"Well, at least I have this!" squealed Sage, and thrust a picture of a guy's hairy asshole at me.

"Jesus fuck!" I cried. "You're not actually going to date this guy, are you?"

"Not after seeing that," said Sage. "In fact, I think he might have turned me off all white boys forever. Who the hell wants to think about that mess? This cannot be the way to a girl's heart."

"Oh, I dunno." Kai shrugged. "Depends on the girl, I'd say."

When we got back, we found Omari and Lotta making out on the living room couch. He'd rerouted his jet back from Germany to the Newburgh airport and then driven straight up.

"Daddy!" squealed Sage, immediately inserting herself between her father and Lotta. Lotta rolled her eyes but moved over good-naturedly.

"Good flight home, Omari?" I said.

"Yes, thank you. I hope it's okay that I've crashed your house party. With everything that's going on, Lotta wanted to stick close to you guys, but we can absolutely take a hotel room in Rhinebeck or at Mohonk if that's easier for you."

"No, no, there's plenty of room. And it's good for Lucy and Sarah to be around people right now. Where are they, anyway?"

"Out on the porch," said Lotta. "I think they're actually playing cards."

I smiled, thinking of my two glamorous, heartbroken friends, wrapped up in blankets and playing gin rummy.

"Have you guys eaten?"

"Not yet," said Lotta.

"Come into the kitchen." I waved everyone in. "I'll make us some dinner."

"Billy?"

I opened my eyes. Sarah was standing over me in the gray light of dawn.

"Sarah?"

"I'm sorry to wake you up, but I can't get your stove to light. And I desperately need coffee."

I switched on my light and yawned. "What time is it?"

Sarah had the grace to look a bit shamefaced. "Five a.m."

"Jesus. So early. Why are you up so early?"

She shrugged. "I just woke up and couldn't go back to sleep."

I pushed the covers back and got out of bed. "Okay, hang on. I'll come down."

The sun was rising over the river when I wandered down into the kitchen. Sarah sat at the island, wearing a black silk robe and eating an apple.

"You actually have to light this stove," I said, putting a match to the burner. "It's not the most modern technology."

Sarah wrinkled her nose. "That seems dangerous. Why not get a new one?"

I filled the kettle with water. "I enjoy the little explosion when I put the flame to the gas."

"That sounds like something Brian would say. Brian always made the coffee. Neither of us can cook, really. But he made the coffee."

I looked at her. She had put the apple down and was gnawing on one end of her long, dark hair extensions. "Do you miss him?" I asked.

She shook her head. "No."

"Not at all?"

She shrugged. "This isn't any different than when he was still living with me. He was gone all the time. He checked out a while ago."

I poured some coffee beans into the grinder. "What was he doing, though? I mean, when he was gone every day? Looking for a new job?"

She picked her apple back up. "I don't know. Maybe. I guess he fucked up pretty badly at his old job, though. It sounded like he lost a lot of money."

I raised my eyebrows. "Your money?"

She shook her head. "We kept our money separate. I didn't use him as a financial manager. Actually"—she looked at me—"I use Brett. He's very good."

"I'm sure he is." I turned on the grinder.

She waited for me to stop. "We were just about to try IVF, did you know that? I wasn't getting pregnant the normal way."

"I thought you guys weren't even having sex?"

She waved her hand in the air like she was swatting away a fly. "I mean, we had enough sex to know it wasn't working."

"Oh." I dumped the coffee into a filter and then poured the boiling water over it. "That sucks. Sorry."

She shrugged. "Maybe it was his fault. Anyway, we were going to do a procedure. It was scheduled for today, actually. But of course, now that he's gone . . ."

I poured more water into the filter. "You could still do it without him."

She shook her head. "No way. I'm not doing the single-mom thing. Besides, my producers wouldn't like it. We're talking about a whole new arc for me—on-the-prowl party girl. Tinder, Match. The whole online thing."

I put a cup of coffee in front of her. "Is that something you actually want to do?"

She picked up the cup and blew. "It'll make good TV."

chapter 26

It only took a few days before we settled into a routine. Sarah and Lucy were always up early, so they started taking walks on the paths by the river while the rest of us slept in. I still kept restaurant hours, more or less, and Sage slept like a teenager—nine or ten hours at a time. Lotta and Omari liked to linger upstairs doing things I tried not to think about too much, but we were all in the kitchen and around the island by ten or so. Then I'd make breakfast.

Sometimes it was virtuous. Oatmeal laden with pumpkin seeds and almonds and dried cherries, slices of fresh orange cut in rounds and drizzled with honey and cinnamon, thick homemade yogurt, and steaming pots of green tea . . . But other days I fried up the fat local pork sausage that Ethan had dropped by for us to sample, or sandwiched bacon and fried eggs and grilled tomatoes between two thick slices of buttered white bread. I made sweet-potato pancakes studded with chunks of bittersweet chocolate and a breakfast bread pudding that practically used up my weight in cream.

Everyone was appreciative, and everyone ate, and then at least Omari and Lucy would help with the dishes. Sarah, Lotta, and Sage never really grasped the idea that the dishes didn't wash themselves.

After breakfast, we'd all go our separate ways for a bit. I usually ran a few miles on the rail trail, and I was preparing the Airstream for the upcoming food truck event in Rosendale. The show had put Sarah on hiatus until they could sort out what they were going to do with her character now that Brian wanted to break his contract and be off-air altogether. Her entire plotline was blown since he refused to be filmed, so she spent her mornings e-mailing back and forth with the producers and her agent, trying to figure out a new approach.

Lotta and Omari were exploring the area. Lotta said they were interested in buying a horse farm that specialized in dressage on the other side of the river. (This made Sage roll her eyes in gleeful annoyance.) And Sage was actually helping out down at Huma. Ethan had called saying that one of his busboys had quit suddenly, and that Marta had recommended Sage to temporarily fill in.

"This is the first job she's ever had," whispered Lotta to me as she and Omari watched Sage gather her things to leave for work. "I can't believe she wants to do it."

"It's a good kitchen," I said. "She'll feel like she's part of something bigger than herself."

Lucy was still drifting. Maybe a little less than in the beginning, but she was definitely in her own world. She slept less, but she still spent a lot of time on the porch, or down at the dock, adding more and more layers as the days got shorter and colder. And if she wasn't at the water, she was generally in her room.

Everyone was on their own for lunch (though I kept the refrigerator well stocked just in case), and then we all came together again for dinner.

I found that I loved shopping and cooking for a crowd. It was entirely different than cooking for one, of course, but it wasn't the same as cooking in the truck, either.

I made mostly comfort food. Soups and braises and roasts, big baked-pasta dishes, batches of ramen, roasted vegetables, enormous tossed salads, slightly retro dishes like spaghetti with Bolognese sauce, garlic bread, meatloaf, and fried chicken. I made desserts, too. Enormous sheet pans of chocolate cake, apple bars, lemon tarts, rice pudding with raisins and almonds, peanut butter cookies, and homemade ice cream.

Everyone oohed and aahed and groaned and then complained that they were going to get fat eating my food, but everyone, even Lucy, always ate.

After dinner we'd watch movies, people taking turns choosing what to download, or sometimes Omari would play for us on the slightly out-of-tune upright piano in the living room, and we'd sing along. Sage, like her father, had a beautiful voice, and Lotta surprised me with her smoky contralto, but Sarah, Lucy, and I just went with loud and off-key when it was our turn.

This was meant to be a family home, Portia had said when I'd first seen the house.

And it was true. The house easily absorbed its occupants. I never felt overcrowded, or that I couldn't find a space of my own when I needed it. Maybe it was the way it was designed, wide open to the view, with all these window seats and little cubbies that felt like separate rooms within the rooms. And, of course, there was the porch, which someone was invariably using, no matter what the weather.

But the house was full, and it seemed happier that way.

One afternoon, Lucy came to me in the kitchen and asked to see the portrait that Titus had given me.

I had told her about it when she first arrived, of course, about how he had come up to see me, and what he had said. But when I'd offered to show her the painting, she had refused.

"You saw what I did with the last thing he was working on in his studio," she'd said, smiling grimly. "I still have a scar on my foot."

But now she said she was ready. "He left me a note," she said. "But it was terrible. It was dry and technical, mainly instructions about how to dispose of his possessions, whom to notify, what to do." She shook her head. "He was always better with pictures than with words. Maybe it will help to see the painting."

I led her up to my room and took it out of the closet where I had stashed it. I wasn't quite ready to see it on a regular basis, either.

The picture seemed even more charged. The emotions he had painted into it looked different now, knowing that he had created it with the burden of his sickness and looming death on his shoulders. The expressions on our faces, which seemed so particular to the two of us, now felt more universal. My hands weren't just clenched against my mother's death anymore.

Lucy stared at it for a long time, tears in her eyes.

"It's his version of an apology, I guess," she finally said.

I nodded. "I think so, too."

"It's worth a lot of money, you know. Especially since it was the last thing he completed before he died."

"I wouldn't sell it, Lu," I said quickly.

She shook her head. "You can if you want. I don't care." She sat down on the bed, still staring at the canvas. "When we first got together, he used to paint me all the time. God, there's a whole series out there—mostly nudes, of course. Me eating an apple. Me stretched out on a Turkish rug. Me holding a taxidermied fox. There were like five different versions of me in this hat with a veil that he absolutely loved. I don't know who owns them now. They're long gone. He probably traded them for a case of wine or a jar of caviar or some stupid thing. But he never painted me again after we got married. He had so many models. Woman after woman. And I'm sure he fucked more than a few of them. But he never asked for me to sit for him. That part of our love affair was over. I was there to run his life and make his breakfast and be on his arm when we went out. He used to joke that I was one of those rare things that were as ornamental as they were functional. Like an Eames chair. But I don't think he wanted to look too closely at me anymore. He just liked to think of me as I was when we first met—a dumb, innocent, seventeen-year-old on a plane."

She stood up and looked at the portrait for another long moment, and then shrugged and turned away. "Maybe now that he's gone, I can finally grow up."

chapter 27

Rosendale, NY
Food truck festival

This Rosendale place is so cute!" said Sarah as she stuck her head into the truck. "Why didn't you tell me about this cute, cute town?"

Rosendale *was* cute. It was tiny. Main Street, which snaked above Rondout Creek, was only about five blocks of "painted ladies," shops, and restaurants, crowned at one end by a small stone chapel that now served as the town library, and at the other with the towering steel buttresses of an old railroad bridge that had been converted to part of the rail trail.

There were about ten food trucks, and a revolving series of live bands playing in front of the movie theater. They had shut down traffic for the festival, and people all wrapped up in their winter coats, hats, gloves, scarves, and boots were drifting from truck to truck and shop to shop.

"That's the 'People's Republic of Rosendale' to you," said Kai. "Everyone who lives here is either an artist or an anarchist."

"I think there're some people from Brooklyn, too," Marta pointed out helpfully.

"Well," said Sarah, "it doesn't look like a hive of Communist activity. It just looks like a cute little Victorian postcard. I like all the purple and pink houses."

"What are you serving, B?" asked Lucy.

This was the first time Lucy had really come out in public since she had left the city. I knew that she was uneasy. She had told me that, mainly, she was afraid of bursting into tears for no particular reason. She never knew when she was going to cry. She said she felt like she was walking around with her heart oozing outside her chest. There was no protecting it.

But Lotta and Sarah had promised to keep close to her while they were there, and Omari had offered to bundle her into his car and drive her back to the River House the minute there was even one tear.

"I'll throw you right over my shoulders," he'd said. "I'll take off at a dead run. I used to be the quarterback of my high school football team, you know."

So Lucy had agreed to come, but she looked fragile and hesitant, peering through the window of the Airstream.

"Miniature shepherd's pie," I said, pointing to our chalkboard. "With lamb or spiced cauliflower and sweet potatoes."

"The Republic of Rosendale must always have a vegetarian option," said Kai.

"And I'm making warm molten chocolate cake cups with prune compote and whipped cream," said Marta.

"Jesus Christ," said Omari. "I'll take one of those right now."

"You just had a brownie, Dad," said Sage.

"Yes, but it was gluten-free. So now I can have this."

Marta passed him a paper cup of warm cake.

Marta, Kai, and I were basically a well-oiled machine at that point. We'd done a couple more events since Halloween and tried to get the Airstream out for lunch in different towns at least twice a week.

And it was working. It was working on every level. We were using up all of Huma's kitchen scraps. We were selling out nearly every time we served, and we were getting excellent word of mouth.

I should have been satisfied. It felt good to be serving my food to happy customers. It felt good to have Marta and Kai call me Chef. We'd already had a few repeat patrons that I recognized, who tracked us from village to village through the little website that Ethan had set up. It was going exactly as I had hoped it would go.

"What do you think?" I asked Lucy after I handed her a bowl of the lamb shepherd's pie.

I knew it looked good. I had layered each bowl so carefully, meat and/or vegetables, the mashed potatoes piped in a perfect crested pattern. Then I'd baked them and afterward used a blowtorch to get a golden-brown crust. I'd pressed a crisp, deep-fried sage leaf into the top of each serving. And I knew it tasted good. I had tasted and seasoned, seasoned and tasted, every step of the way.

She took a bite, chewed, and then swallowed, considering.

"It's good," she said. "It's really good, Bill."

"Tell me the truth," I said.

She took another bite. "No, really, it's good. It's just that—"

"What?"

"It's not as good as what you've been making at home."

I blinked. "What do you mean?"

She shook her head, confused. "I can't explain it exactly. I mean,

like I said, it's delicious. It really is. It just seems a little more generic . . . somehow. The stuff you've been cooking for our dinners
and breakfasts—it's just better."

"Like, the ingredients are better?"

She pursed her lips. "No," she said slowly. "I don't think so. This
lamb is great."

"The technique, then? Or maybe the venue? Because you're eating it out of a paper bowl in the street instead of at a table with a
view of the river?"

She shook her head. "No. That doesn't seem right, either."

I frowned at her.

She frowned back. "Don't be mad, Billy. You said you wanted the
truth. And I'm not saying it's bad. I'm just saying it's not *as* good."

I shook my head. "I just don't know what to do with this information. How can I fix it if you can't explain what I'm supposed to
fix?"

She took another bite and shrugged, helpless.

Kai bumped me with her elbow. "There's a pretty long line behind her, Chef. Maybe you should stop worrying and just sell your
fucking food."

I sat in my kitchen the next day, poring through my old cookbooks,
reading and thinking.

I was thinking about the best dishes I had ever cooked. The best
meals I had ever eaten. I was thinking about the chefs I'd worked
under who'd made a mark on me.

I remembered a meal an ex-boyfriend had made me. I could hardly
remember much about the man, except that he was English, but I remembered him making me eggs and soldiers: soft-boiled eggs with

the tops cut off, and strips of crisp, buttered toast to dip into the bright orange yolks. The playfulness of the meal, the Anglo eccentricity, the way it was designed to encourage a reluctant young child to eat—it had made me nostalgic for a childhood I'd never actually had.

Great chefs talk a lot about memory and inspiration. They see themselves as artists. They love to discuss what moves them to create, where their drive comes from. I had met more than one chef who could talk for hours about the woods they played in as children, about the dreamy landscape they inhabited, the quicksilver streams full of trout, the berries and mushrooms they gathered. The way their mothers or grandmothers taught them to bake a loaf of bread or plant a garden with their own loving, beautiful, arthritic fucking hands.

I wondered where that left me. A rat-ass child of Midwestern suburbia—no babbling creeks and deep, dark forests for me. I had malls and cul-de-sacs. No generational culinary secrets passed down, no handwritten recipes inherited, just a fervent desire to get the fuck out and never come back.

When my father had died, I was overwhelmed with a shameful feeling of relief. Not because I didn't love him or was happy that he was gone, but because I knew it meant I would never have to *go back*. I didn't want a reason to keep returning to the house where she had purposefully choked herself to death. I didn't want to have to continue walking through the same doorway I'd seen her sheet-draped body carried out of, I had no desire to inhabit the rooms she'd haunted every day of my interminable, hungry, lonely childhood. When I cooked, it wasn't ever to return to some halcyon days of the past: it was to make as much space between me and my fucking youthful pain as I possibly could.

Sage came home from the restaurant and found me in the kitchen, taking notes from an old copy of *Leone's Italian Cookbook* I'd found at a used bookstore in New Paltz.

"Hey," she said.

I looked up, not bothering to remove my reading glasses. "Hi. You look beat. Can I get you anything? Tea?"

She nodded and sat down at the counter. "I'm so tired," she said. "And sore, and smelly. And I know the best possible thing I could do is take a shower and go straight to bed. But I'm just going to sit here like a lump for a moment instead."

"You like the job?" I said as I filled the kettle.

She smiled. "Yeah. Isn't that weird? It's total scut work. They make me do all the worst stuff. But I don't mind. It's fun."

"It can be," I said, "when you work at the right place."

"And all those food sensitivities I thought I had? It's strange, but I eat at all the family meals, and nothing Ethan cooks gives me hives or makes me sick."

I hid my smile. "Well, he's a great chef. And his ingredients are all pretty much impeccable."

She laid her head down on the island for a moment. "I feel like I want to do something to thank them," she said into her arms. "You know, for letting me work there. I hardly know what I'm doing but they've been so nice about it."

"Well," I said, "the day after tomorrow is their night off. Why don't you invite them over here for dinner?"

Her head popped back up. "Oh, I couldn't cook for them. That would be total humiliation."

"I'll cook," I said. "We'll do something simple. And you can help."

"A dinner party?" said Sarah doubtfully at the breakfast table the next morning. "With those hipster kids?"

"It will be fun," insisted Sage. "They're so cool."

Sarah curled a lip. "Exactly."

"Well, I think it's lovely." Lotta beamed. "Omari and I will buy the wine."

"Absolutely," concurred Omari.

"I'll get flowers," said Lucy.

"It's not going to be very fancy," I said. "I was thinking about chicken pot pie."

"Oh, man, that sounds good," said Omari.

"You just ate," said Sage.

Omari shrugged. "Doesn't mean I'm not hungry."

"I guess I can buy a dessert?" said Sarah.

Sage shook her head. "I'm sure Marta will want to bring something."

"Well, what am I supposed to do, then?"

"You can set the table," I said.

"Speaking of tables, what are we going to do about Thanksgiving, by the way?" asked Lotta. "It's coming up. We'll have it here, I imagine?"

I looked at them, trying not to show how pleased I was with the suggestion. "Don't any of you have anywhere else you need to be?"

I looked at Lucy, and she laughed. "I don't have another place to go even if I wanted to."

Sarah pursed her lips. "Well, I'm sure I'll have to get back to the show eventually. But it's fine for now."

Lotta looked at Omari. "Nope," he said. "We're good."

"But maybe Sage would rather be at her mom's?" asked Lotta carefully. She turned toward her stepdaughter. "I would love to have you here, of course, but it would be no problem to fly you out to be with her if that's better for you."

I saw Sage study the naked look of yearning on Lotta's face. "No," she said slowly. "Mom has a new boyfriend. I think it's fine to do Thanksgiving with my dad . . . and you, Lotta." She turned her eyes away and mumbled, "I guess that could be cool."

Lotta glowed.

"Well, then, okay," I said. "Thanksgiving here. Why the hell not?"

Sage bolted up suddenly. "Oh my God, what time is it? I promised I'd come in early today. Marta's going to teach me to make piecrust! Oh, shit, I didn't wash my whites!"

Lotta waved her hand in the air. "I did," she said. "They're folded on top of your bed."

Sage stopped in her tracks and looked at Lotta. "Um. Wow. Thank you. That's super helpful, Lotta."

Lotta went pink with pleasure. "It was nothing," she said. "I was doing a load of delicates anyway."

Sage wrinkled her nose. "Ew. TMI." And ran out of the room.

Omari put his hand over Lotta's. "You are going to be the most amazing mom. If you can win that girl over, a baby is going to be a piece of a cake."

The room went still.

"What?" said Sarah. Her face was pale. "What did you just say?"

"Lotta?" I said slowly. "Holy fuck."

"A baby?" gasped Lucy.

"Oh, shit," said Omari. "I didn't mean to tell everyone. I was just so emotional about Sage. Oh, shit. I'm so sorry."

Lotta went even pinker. "This isn't how I meant to tell you guys." She looked around, her eyes alight. "Believe me, we were just as surprised as you."

"Wait," said Sarah. "So, you weren't even trying? How did you—I mean, you're forty-eight, Lotta."

"Very aware of that, Sarah, thank you," said Lotta. "It just happened in the way these things just happen, I guess. I'm sure everyone here is familiar with the process."

Sarah stood up. "Well, congratulations," she said stiffly. "I'm very happy for you." And then she marched out of the room.

I looked at her plate. "She didn't finish her sausage."

"Pass it on over," said Omari. "Gotta keep my strength up. Gonna be a daddy again, after all."

chapter 28

I started with cubes of bacon. There was a smokehouse in Sauger-ties. It took about forty-five minutes to drive there, but it was worth it. I liked their uncut slabs, double-smoked.

Then I added shallots, sliced in half and peeled cloves of garlic; then the cut-up chicken from Jack's, still on the bone, because the meat is always sweeter if you cook it on the bone; whole cremini mushrooms; and chunks of carrots and parsnips. I stripped in stems of fresh thyme and added golden, gelatinous chicken stock that I'd cooked and frozen the last time Ethan had given me leftover car-casses.

It all cooked down for a couple of hours, and then I let it cool and skimmed off the fat, and had Sage skin the pieces of chicken and pick the meat off the bones.

"Do it carefully," I said, throwing a piece of schmaltz to an ea-gerly waiting Chicken. "Nothing worse than a bite of flabby skin or an accidental bone."

We made the dough next, using a combination of lard and butter, mixing in more thyme as we rolled it out. We were making a slab pie as big as a sheet pan.

"It looks so pretty," said Sage, all eyes as I fluted the edges of the crust and then applied leaf shapes cut out from the extra dough.

We would put out warm spiced cashews to start with. I made a giant bowl of bitter-and-sweet salad with radicchio, fennel, and oranges and sautéed a pan of creamed kale. Marta had promised to bring her stickiest, richest, very best brownies.

We didn't often use the dining room. The view was better from the kitchen, but we wouldn't all fit around the island, so we put the leaf in the round, claw-foot table and threw a heavy white cloth over it. I was delighted to realize that the cut-glass chandelier, which I had never bothered to turn on before, acted like a disco ball, throwing dancing glimmers of light all over the walls and ceiling.

Sarah had gone out and bought bags of tea candles and mercury glass holders, which she proceeded to place not only in the dining room, but all through the house. She set the table with the good, sturdy white ironstone and slightly tarnished silver plate that had come with the house, and Lucy added a round tray of succulents and moss that she had put together. Kai, saying she was sick of watching us drink our wine out of tumblers, was bringing her own set of glassware.

It was a cold and rainy night, and fog was rolling off the river, so Omari lit fires in every fireplace, including the one in the dining room, put his own personally curated dinner party mix on the stereo, and then the house was ready.

"This is overkill for millennials," said Sarah. "We should have had some pizza delivered and served ironic Coors Light."

We all went upstairs to change, and before I could put on the simple black dress that I had laid out earlier, Lotta, Lucy, and Sarah were in my room, each with a contribution to my outfit.

I shook my head. "I really don't need to borrow clothes from you guys anymore," I said.

"Actually, these are our gifts to you," said Lucy as she handed me a dark blue cashmere sweaterdress. "For putting up with us."

Lotta tossed me a pair of Ferragamo booties and Sarah gave me some heavy silver hoop earrings and a pair of Wolford tights.

"You guys," I said, "you didn't have to do this!"

"Just put it on," said Sarah. "Even hipster millennials deserve better than whatever sad Gap thing you were about to wear."

They were forty-five minutes late. Kai forgot to bring her glassware so she had to suffer through watching us drink all of Omari's carefully selected wines out of inappropriate glasses. Ethan brought cauliflower fritters that I was immediately convinced would taste better than anything I was serving. And Marta's famous brownies turned out to be even more "magic" than we'd originally been informed.

"We can eat them now, or wait until after dinner," said Marta.

"Let's give it a moment," I said.

"You look beautiful, the house looks beautiful," said Kai to me, making my mouth drop open in surprise.

"I told her to say that," said Marta.

Kai was wearing formfitting plaid pants and a black V-neck tee, Marta was wearing a pleated miniskirt and a denim jacket, and Sage had changed into a red shift dress. They all looked unbearably gorgeous, cool, and young.

"Wine!" trilled Lotta. "Wine for everyone!"

"Not for you," said Sage. They had taken her aside the day before and told her about the baby. She had been ridiculously thrilled.

"Oh, well, in Europe, they let pregnant women have a glass or two," said Lotta.

"We're not in Europe," said Sage, snatching the bottle from Lotta's hands.

"I'll drink her share," said Sarah, thrusting her glass toward Sage.

The conversation was a little stilted at first, but after the second pour (third for Sarah), we all trooped into the dining room and sat down. Everyone exclaimed over the pie and the beautiful table, and Sage offered a toast to her friends.

"I just want to say thanks to you guys for letting me hang out at Huma, and not yelling at me when I fuck up, and for making me feel like I'm, maybe, just a little bit good at something." She lifted her glass. "So thanks! Here's some chicken pot pie!"

"Hear! Hear!" everyone answered.

I passed around the salad and kale and served the pie, dishing out squares of the savory pastry. There was a gratifying silence as everyone dug in.

"Billy," said Ethan after a moment, "I'm stunned. This is the best thing that you've made."

"It's mind-blowing," said Marta. "It's so good."

"Why aren't you serving this at Leftovers?" said Kai. "How come you've been holding out?"

"Sage helped," I said.

"Mere scut work," said Sage. "It's all Billy."

"She's been doing this every night," said Lucy. "Seriously, you guys. She's been cooking at this level every time she makes us dinner."

I shook my head. "It's nothing special. It's just family-style food. I put a lot more effort into the menu for the truck."

Ethan shot me a curious glance but kept eating.

Sarah poured herself another glass of wine and then quaffed it down. "Did everyone hear about Lotta's baby?" she said a little too loudly as she grabbed at the wine bottle again.

Marta, Kai, and Ethan turned toward her.

"Wow," said Kai. "I mean, how old are you, anyway?"

"Forty-eight!" crowed Sarah as she guzzled her wine. "She's forty-eight and they just frigging *made* a baby without even meaning to. I mean, how crazy is that?"

"Sarah," Lucy murmured.

"Well," said Ethan, "congratulations. That's awesome."

"Thank you," said Lotta. "We're very excited."

"I am only forty-two," said Sarah. "And I couldn't make a baby when I tried."

"Sarah," said Lucy again, a little louder.

Sarah turned to Lucy. "What? You know, just because your husband offed himself doesn't mean you get to boss everyone around."

"Sarah!" I yelped.

"I lost a man, too, you know! And he was way nicer than Titus! Titus was an asshole!"

She poured herself another glass of wine.

"Jesus," said Lotta. "Maybe someone should cut her off."

Sarah gave her an unfocused glare. "I can drink all I want. I'm not pregnant."

Lotta sighed. "Listen, Sarah. I'm sorry if this is hard for you—"

"Hard? Why should this be hard? I think it's great! It's a modern miracle! Unwanted baby delivered to super-ancient mother!"

"Hey," said Omari, "this is a very wanted baby."

"And I'm not that ancient," said Lotta.

"Eh," said Kai, screwing up her face. "You are pretty old."

Sarah turned to her. "Right?" She turned back to us. "See, she gets it! Di—"

"Kai," corrected Kai.

"Kai gets it!"

"Who wants brownies?" cried Marta. She sounded a bit desperate.

"I do!" trilled Sarah. "Bring them on!"

Maybe it was a mistake, but we all, except for Lotta, ended up eating a brownie. I'm not sure why everyone else chose to partake, but I just figured that if I was going to get through a night with Sarah and Kai being cunts, Marta and Ethan pawing each other under the table (which I unfortunately discovered when I dropped my fork), and Lotta and Omari being all radiantly pregnant, a little chemical help was not uncalled for.

Plus I missed Brett.

I had been missing him all night. He loved dinner parties. He'd once told me that some of his favorite memories of his family were of the dinner parties his parents would throw. At least once a month, he and his brother would eat early and then be hustled into their pajamas and allowed to watch movies in the den while the adults would sit around the table, talking and laughing and eating and drinking. And then they'd all have dessert together and his mother would put him and his brother to bed, and they'd fall asleep listening to the roars of laughter and the drift of grown-up voices. He said that he couldn't *wait* until he was old enough to stay up and be part of the crowd, but that there was something that made him so happy even just hearing it from the other room.

The brownie took some time to kick in, but once it did, it didn't make me miss Brett any less.

I turned to Lucy. "I think I'm going to call Brett. Should I call Brett?"

"No!" said Lucy. Then she blinked her eyes. "I mean, I don't think so. Actually, maybe? I'm not sure."

"Lotta? Should I call Brett?"

"Absolutely!" said Sarah.

"No, honey, do not do that," said Lotta at the same time.

I looked between them. "Well, now I don't know who to listen to. Omari, what do you think?"

Omari stood up. "I'm going to go play the piano," he said as he wandered out of the room.

"You know," said Marta very seriously, "that's Omari Scott who is going to play piano. He is a very famous musician."

"We should go watch him," said Ethan, lurching up.

"We should record him on our phones so that we can put him on the YouTubes and everyone can see him!" answered Marta.

"No!" said Lotta, following them out. "Do not do that! Give me your phones!"

Sarah looked at Kai. "You're very pretty. Billy told me you're a lesbian, is that true?"

Kai smirked at her. "Yup."

"I was a lesbian once," said Sarah. "Back in prep school."

Kai nodded. "Most everyone was."

"Do you want to go dance to Omari Scott's piano playing?" asked Sarah. "He's very famous, you know."

Kai looked at Sarah and her normally sharp blue eyes grew a little softer. "Okay," she said. "I'd like that." She offered Sarah her hand and pulled her up.

Then it was just me and Lucy, sitting in front of the remains of the pie.

"More pie?" I asked her.

"Dang. My hands are so big," she said in return.

"Well," I said, helping myself to more pie, "this is all as weird as fuck."

Lucy laughed, shaking her head. "Which part? Me being a destitute widow? Sarah about to become a lesbian? Lotta about to have a baby, or all of us getting stoned with a bunch of kids?"

"Any of them." I threw up my hands. "All of them!"

Lucy looked at her hands again. "I mean, remember dragging Lotta's ass home from every bar in Manhattan? Remember when we were all wondering just how soon she was going to die? And now she's going to have a baby? I mean, who knew she'd be the only of us to get her shit together?"

"Hey!" I said, stung. "She's not the only one with her shit together. I believe I have my shit together."

Lucy laughed. "You are currently as stoned as I've ever seen you."

"Yes, but aside from that."

Lucy blinked, a thoughtful look on her face. "No, you're right. You're doing good, too. You've got your truck and your cooking and your awful dog and your hipster teenage friends. You're running your riverfront home for the damaged and miserable . . . It all seems to be working for you." She stuck her finger in her glass of champagne and then sucked on it. "It's funny, I guess I always thought that if you made any decisions without me, they were bound to fail."

"Well, that's not codependent or anything."

"And you know what? I always thought that I was the center of our little klatch, but really, it turned out to be you."

"You brought us all together," I said.

"Maybe at first. Not anymore. You're the den mother now, Bill."

She poked sadly at the moss in the centerpiece. "I guess you don't need me after all."

I shook my head. "Of course I need you, Lulu. I was miserable the whole time we weren't talking. In fact, half the time I was running around going, 'What would Lucy do?' I had all these conversations with you in my head."

She smiled. "Me too. I talked to you, too. And even in my head, you've got a mouth like a sailor, Bill."

I squeezed her hand. "Having you back is way better than imaginary conversations."

"Let's go watch those guys dance," she said, laughing. "I hear Omari Scott is very famous."

"Jesus," breathed Lucy as we peeked into the living room. "What is Sarah doing?"

"Dancing?" I said. "Which I definitely do not believe I have ever seen her do quite like this before?"

"Do you think she was a stripper back in prep school, too?" said Lucy.

Sarah was locked up against Kai, grinding on the younger woman's leg, her torso bent back, her boobs thrust up, her hair brushing the top of her ass.

Lotta walked over to us. "I'm going to bed. I'm sober, and I'm pregnant, and I'm very tired, and I am absolutely not babysitting you all tonight. Sorry. Don't let Sage do anything worse than whatever she's already done, okay? And don't let any of those kids drive home. And maybe peel Sarah off that poor girl before she breaks something?"

"Oh." Lucy giggled. "I'm not sure that's possible."

Lotta sighed. "Well, as they say, not my circus, not my monkeys. Good night, girls. It was a very nice party."

"Lotta went to bed early," Lucy breathed. "She really is pregnant!"

"Should I call Brett now?" I answered in return.

The night was unseasonably mild, and Lucy and I fell asleep wrapped up in down comforters on the wicker chaise longues on the porch. It was still raining, and the sound was particularly loud on the metal roof. Marta slept on the couch, while Ethan slept next to her on the floor. Sarah and Kai ended up sleeping in Sarah's bed, but Sarah told us later that, from what she could remember, she didn't *think* they did much. Maybe just some above-the-waist messing around. Sage made it to her own bed, and Omari eventually found his way back to his and Lotta's room.

It should have been nice to wake up on the porch. The sun was rising over the water, and it was clear and bright after a night of hard rain, but my back was killing me and I was hungover as hell.

There were a lot of hangovers in the house that morning. I offered to make something greasy and helpful, but Kai, Marta, and Ethan had to open the restaurant, so they couldn't stay for breakfast.

"Thanks, Billy," said Marta on their way out. "It was so fun!"

"Yes, thank you," called Ethan. "We had a blast!"

Even Kai managed a begrudging thanks. Right after she kissed Sarah good-bye.

"She was kind of sweet, right?" said Sarah, gazing at Kai as she walked away.

"I'm pretty sure that is the first time that word has ever been applied to Kai in her entire life," I said.

"Man," said Omari as we watched them through the window, picking their way down to Ethan's truck. "To be twenty-five again. They weren't even feeling it at all this morning, were they?"

"I think that was pretty much a normal Tuesday night for them," Lucy said.

"You couldn't pay me to go back," said Lotta fervently as their car pulled away. "Not in a million years."

chapter 29

I realized the other day," said Ethan as we drove over the Kingston-Rhinecliff Bridge, "that you have never actually eaten a meal at Huma."

"What?" I was looking out the window at the river below us, which uncoiled in a glittering, bright blue swath, almost perfectly reflecting the color of the sky above.

"Billy, you've never eaten a meal at Huma."

I looked over at him. "Of course I have. The first time I came."

"You mean when we gathered the chanterelles?"

"Oh. Right. I guess that doesn't really count. Well, I've had about a billion family meals."

He shook his head. "Those are different."

I thought for a moment. "Huh. I guess you're right. That's weird."

"It needs to be corrected. Come tomorrow night, there's not much booked, we'll do the tasting menu. Just five courses."

"Oh, I'm not sure that will work. Omari and Lotta have tickets to Levon Helm's studio in Woodstock, and I think Sarah and Lucy were planning on an *Orange Is the New Black* marathon."

He smiled. "I didn't invite them. I am just inviting you."

I laughed. "How exclusive. Okay. If you say so, Chef."

We were heading back from Germantown, a village on the Dutchess side of the river. There was a farm there—Turkana—where they raised and sold Ossabaw Island hogs and Ethan had been hoping to source directly from them for the restaurant.

The farm had been beautiful, run by a couple of expatriate Manhattanites named Peter and Mark, and it turned out that they did way more than just pigs. Their barns had been filled with heritage breed animals—Royal Palm turkeys, Toulouse geese, British White beef cows . . . They had loaded us down with paper-wrapped samples from their freezer, and Ethan had been thrilled with the possibilities.

"You know, I read this book about a CSA in upstate, Essex Farm," he'd said as we'd left Turkana and were driving alongside the undulating stone walls that separated the riverside estates from the road. "They produce everything their members could possibly need for all four seasons. They do meat and dairy and fruit and vegetable crops. They do grains and honey. They pickle and can and dry and preserve and keep a root cellar. And their members come by every week and are given enough seasonal produce and meat to last them through. It's the dream, right? Supplying everything your restaurant needs from your own farm?"

"That sounds like a fuck-load of work," I said. "How could you possibly farm like that and keep a restaurant going?"

He nodded. "Yeah. It's when I start wishing there were, like, ten of me. I mean, Dan Barber manages, right? At Blue Hill?"

I shook my head. "He doesn't just grow at his own farms. He

sources out locally, too. And he's certainly not doing all the work himself. He's got an army of people at this point."

Ethan pushed his hair away from his face. "That's true. I guess there's something to learn from that. I mean, that's when you know you've really made it as a chef, right? When everyone else is cooking and you're just standing over their shoulders telling them what they're doing wrong."

I smiled. "Somehow I can't ever see you getting to that point."

"The best chefs have a vision," he said, "but they are also trusting. I mean, cooking is a collaborative art. Even if you shop for and cook the entire meal yourself, you have to buy your ingredients from someone in the beginning, and you always want to have someone else to feed it to at the end, right? The process isn't over until the meal is finished. I mean, I don't ever really cook alone at Huma. Even if I dictate the menu, everyone who touches the food adds their own spin."

"Sure." I nodded.

"It's all about connection," he said as he pulled up to a traffic light. "Not just the people working in the kitchen, but the farmers who grow the ingredients, the people they learned from, the earth it's grown in, the animals we're consuming, the customers who consume. You can't be a chef in a vacuum."

"Well, yeah," I said. "The essential nature of a restaurant kind of precludes that. But most great restaurants that I've been to kind of begin and end with their chef."

"No, but see, that's what we chefs want you to think. That it's all about us. Only our genius, our vision. We hire and fire based on who most perfectly follows our every command. But Huma isn't just an expression of my own personal ego. It's my home. And my staff are my family. And you can't have a family of just one person. I have to trust every single worker in that kitchen in order to make it all happen."

"And how is it now that you and Marta are together?" I felt a little uncomfortable bringing her up, but I was curious. His words were striking something in me in a way that I couldn't quite explain yet.

He paused a moment, thinking. "Well, you know, we started the restaurant together. Even before anything happened between us, we dreamed it up. And it's always been as much hers as mine."

He pulled up in front of the River House, bringing the truck to a stop but not turning it off.

"The first time I cooked for Marta was a few days after we met in a level-one baking class. We were paired up to work on a basic chocolate cake. Man, she was already so much better at baking than I was. She was kick-ass. She kept looking at the recipe and saying, 'But what if we just changed this one little thing? What would happen?' She kept twisting it, trying to make it a little more provocative. A little more memorable. And she was pissing off our teacher, because he just wanted her to master the basic recipe. But she was already so much further ahead than that."

He drummed his hands on the wheel of the truck.

"Anyway, I liked her the minute I met her, and I guess maybe my macho pride had been kind of wounded by just how much better she was than me in our baking class, so I told her that she should come hang sometime and I would cook for her. I wanted to show her that maybe I sucked at cakes, but I was good at other things, you know?"

I smiled, imagining a teen version of Ethan trying to impress the teen version of Marta.

"I had an apartment off campus with its own kitchen, which was a big deal, because if you lived in the dorms, you had to share the kitchen and everyone was always jostling for space and fighting over cleanup. It was a pain. So she and Kai came over. It was the first time I met Kai, too. And I made them this artichoke stew. It was hard-core Iranian food, no deconstruction, no new spin on it or anything. Just something that my dad cooked when I was a kid that I had always loved. And it probably wasn't that good. I was using supermarket, frozen ingredients, and actually, I definitely wasn't that great of a chef yet. But I was homesick for my folks and L.A. and Little Persia, and I kind of just poured all that feeling into that stew and served it up in mismatched bowls and waited to see what would happen."

"Let me guess," I said. "Kai hated it."

He laughed. "Totally. Kai turned up her nose. Her dad was a diplomat and she had grown up rich and living all over the world and had probably already had the best artichoke stew possible in some ancient grandmother's kitchen in Tehran. She was already a total food snob. My pathetic bowl of stew was just not going to impress her. But Marta . . ." He smiled, remembering. "Marta ate the whole bowl and then asked for seconds, and then she turned to me and said, 'I'm not Iranian, or anything, but this—this tastes like home to me.'"

I closed my eyes for a moment. My heart ached. "So Huma isn't just your family. It's your love story."

"Yeah," he said softly. "And it's our home. It's not just my home. It's hers, too."

The four of us walked the rail trail together. The grass was frosted, bent, and brittle, and gleamed like glass. The bare ground was frozen and unyielding. The woods were silent, all the noisy hum and buzz of insects and frogs having been extinguished by the first hard freeze. Only an occasional cardinal or blue jay flashed through the air. The sky was shrouded with heavy, slate-gray clouds. There was a skim of silvery ice on the slow-moving stream that bordered the path. We could see our breath in the air.

Chicken ran ahead of us, wearing a little red sweater that Lucy had bought for him, his nails clicking against the frozen ground, bravely snuffling at every fallen log and suspicious rock formation.

Lucy, Lotta, and I had proper winter hiking boots, but Sarah had only brought her lightweight running shoes, and she was poking along behind us and complaining that her feet were cold.

"Well, if you'd walk a little faster, you'd warm up," I said, rolling my eyes.

"I can't walk faster," she whined. "I'm too cold!"

"What do you guys think of the name Alfhild for a girl?" said Lotta.

"Alf-what?" I said.

"It means 'battle of the elves.' Omari doesn't care for it, but I think it's very poetic. Or Hjalmar for a boy? That means 'fighter with a helmet.'"

"I didn't realize the Swedes were so bloodthirsty," I said.

"So, there's an offer on the brownstone," said Lucy suddenly.

We all turned toward her, surprised.

"I didn't even know it was up for sale yet," said Lotta.

Lucy shrugged. "It helps to have a mother who's a real estate agent."

"Is it a good offer?" I said.

She nodded. "Probably as good as it's going to get. There won't be anything left over, but the sale will pay off all the debt, anyway."

I looked at her. "So you're going to take it?"

She sucked on her lower lip. "Do I have a choice?"

"And then what?" asked Sarah.

Lucy shook her head. "I can't live off of my writing. At least, not yet. And no one is going to hire a forty-four-year-old model, no matter how well-preserved she might be. I have the money I saved, but that would only buy me a couple of years—less, actually, since I have to rent a new place to live—and then I'd end up with no savings . . . I guess I could move back in with my mom?"

We were all silent, thinking about Lucy and Cheri living together again.

"Well, you can stay here as long as you like," I offered. "I have plenty of room, obviously."

"Or Omari and I can loan you money," said Lotta. "As much as you need. Pay it back whenever."

"I have a guest room in my place," said Sarah. "Trust me when I say I'm not looking forward to going back to my empty apartment. You'd be doing me a favor if you moved in."

Lucy smiled, a little teary-eyed. "Thank you, guys. I'll have to think about it. Don't worry, I'll figure it out." She paused for a moment. "Maybe I should move to Brooklyn?"

We all laughed.

"I hear the booze is incredibly cheap out there and the lumbersexuals run wild in the streets," I said.

"I hear that you see Matt Damon on every corner," said Lotta.

"That place in Ditmas Park was really nice." Sarah sighed. "Remember the courtyard?"

We kept walking.

A snowflake fell.

And then another.

It stormed that night. The first snow of the season. It blew in over the river, beating against the windows, falling in tiny, icy flakes and coating everything it touched in a shimmer of rime.

We lit fires and candles against the cold. I cooked a pot of black-bean soup and made cornbread and a big spinach salad with goat cheese and candied pecans and roasted sweet peppers, and we ate in front of the kitchen fire, drinking valpolicella and watching the landscape change from fall to winter outside.

After, we went into the living room, and everyone sprawled out and listened to Omari play piano, but nobody sang. Sage hooked her legs over the arm of the big upholstered chair in the corner and fiddled with her laptop. I paged through an old copy of *Gourmet* magazine, remembering the glory days of Ruth Reichl. Sarah and Lucy huddled in front of the fire, playing a fierce game of gin rummy. Lotta sat on a cushion on the floor, her head resting against Omari's knee, her hand unconsciously cupped under her barely protuberant belly.

Finally, the storm stopped, and we all put on our jackets and boots and trooped outside into the yard. The snow had mounded in icy piles and drifts. Omari and Sage tried to make some snowballs but the snow was too fine and wouldn't pack properly. It just dissolved when it was thrown, leaving a shooting cloud of glister hanging in the air.

We made our way down to the river, skidding through the virgin snow and beating a path to the dock, which floated like an iceberg on top of the black river. We stood at the water's edge, our feet cold, the sky now brilliantly clear and shining with stars, the fine, icy powder all around us reflecting back their glittering light. We breathed in the sharp, cold air and looked at the way the world was something it hadn't been just hours before.

chapter 30

Huma had changed since the first time I had walked through the door. Anissa and her ear gauges still greeted me up front and led me to my seat, but the blue mason jars were gone, replaced by small, twisted arrangements of yellow and red bittersweet berries on their stems in silver bud vases. The cutlery was heavy and solid, the stemware actually matched, and, I noticed, as I ran my hand over the wood, that the tables had been sanded and sealed.

No more splinters.

The restaurant was nearly empty. Just a solitary couple in the corner, sharing a dish of pasta.

Kai came out from behind the bar, a drink in her hand.

"The Kingston," she said as she put the glass down in front of me.

I blinked. "Did Ethan tell you to give me this?"

She gave me a shrug and a little half smile as she headed back for the bar. "Nah. I remembered."

I sipped the bright, lemony drink as the good-looking waiter—whose name I now knew was Chuck—brought me the menu.

"From Chef Rahimi," he said with an exaggerated little bow.

I squinted. It was, I saw, handwritten in the same cramped, messy penmanship as the first time.

I looked at the handsome waiter and then sighed, fishing out my reading glasses and popping them on.

Huma Tasting Menu:
Created for Billy Sitwell

1) The Wedding
Persian melon, blanched almond, harissa, and cucumber soup
Basil, mint, and lovage herb square

I'd had this before, of course. The cold, elusive soup, the brilliant surprise of the melting herbs exploding in my mouth. It wasn't new to me anymore. Ethan had since taken me through the steps to make it, listed all the ingredients, shown me the melon vines he had crossbred himself, told me the story behind him creating it. It was demystified. But this time, with every bite I took, I wasn't thinking about how it was made. I was thinking about the day I had first tasted it. I was thinking about how eating the soup had sent me up and out of my chair to hunt down the chef who created it. I was reminded of the four of us eating caviar and drinking Negronis and toasting Lotta's marriage. How beautiful Lotta had been in her blue dress. The way Titus had pulled Lucy into his lap. Sarah talking about moving to Brooklyn and Brian looking like he was already halfway out the door. How Brett had laughed at me and rolled his eyes when I'd been so mean about turning down his offer of help. The second kitchen.

Ethan with his arms full of roses. Marta cheerfully telling him off. The whole day came back to me, intact.

2) Billy Gets the Job
Heirloom beefsteak tomato sauce with charred cipollini onions
over lemon-garlic tagliatelle
with double-smoked slab-bacon bits

I smiled. Ethan had told me later that the only thing he would have changed about my sandwich was that it needed bacon.

3) Lost in the Maze
Coffee-rubbed British White beef tenderloin
House-made hominy
Concord grape coulis

I was almost embarrassed to eat it. It seemed too intimate. As I bit into the chewy, flavorful beef, his face flashed back to me, the way the sun and shadow had played over his skin. I tasted the supple, earthy hominy and I could smell dried cornstalks and mud, feel the way the coffee he had handed me had warmed my cold fingers. Then the sweet and acidic coulis, and it was the scent of his skin, the taste of his mouth, bitter and creamy, how his hands had slid down the sides of my rib cage and settled on my waist.

He was correct about that kiss. Maybe it hadn't been right, exactly, but it also hadn't been nothing. It was something that we had needed to try. It had led us both to bigger things.

4) Chicken Pot Pie
Double-smoked slab bacon; Krempl Farm chicken thigh and stock;
cremini mushrooms; shallots; garlic; carrots; parsnips; thyme;
house-made lard, butter, and thyme pastry crust

I wrinkled my nose when this dish was put down in front of me. What was my homely cooking doing in a parade of haute cuisine?

Of course, he had deconstructed it. It looked different. The chicken and mushrooms and vegetables were arranged in a few perfect bites, the sauce was drizzled and dripped just so, the pastry was broken in craggy pieces and scattered over the top.

I took a bite, thinking that he must have improved upon it. Surely there would be surprise truffles or some miraculous trick he had played with the pastry. Maybe it only looked like my chicken pot pie but would taste altogether different.

But it was exactly my recipe. He hadn't missed an ingredient. It tasted exactly the same.

I looked at it for a moment, considering. Then I slowly brought another bite to my lips and closed my eyes, attempting to taste what he was trying to tell me.

The pastry shattered in my mouth, I could feel the way the fats and flour had combined to make airy pockets, the way the lusciousness of the butter and the earthy taste of the lard lingered to coat my mouth. I chewed on a bit of the bacon, felt the smoky brine pop in my mouth. The chicken was moist and savory and tenderly slid apart under my bite. The sauce was deep and round on my tongue. I could taste the flecks of thyme, the sweet depth of the roasted alliums, the umami of the mushrooms . . .

None of these flavors or textures was new. Someone had written this recipe years and years before me. It wasn't surprising or mysterious. It didn't push the envelope in any way. But it was, perhaps, the best version of these flavors and textures I had ever eaten. There was not a thing I wanted to change.

And it wasn't out of place in this amazing meal at all.

5) *We're Not Talking About the Soup*
Mini pumpkin and apple tarts
Crème franche

I laughed when I saw Marta's contribution. I remembered the way she had told me off. Her normally sweet face thrust into mine, so fierce and flushed. The little haunts and ghouls running all around us. The harried mother drinking the borscht in the middle of the street.

But I hadn't actually tasted Marta's tarts that day. I had clicked off my phone after talking to Lucy, and I had looked at Ethan and Kai and Marta, my mouth dry, a dizzy wave of shock and sorrow crashing over me.

"I have to go to the city," I had whispered. "I don't know when I'll be back."

And they hadn't needed another word. They hadn't asked for an explanation. They had waved me off, saying not to worry, promising to finish out our day, saying that they would break everything down and get it all back home.

"Do you need someone to watch Chicken?" Marta had asked as I dashed around trying to gather my things.

"We can just keep the little shit at our place, right, E?" said Kai.

And that's when the tears had come. That's when I had stopped to fiercely hug each one of my new, young friends and then rushed off to help Lucy.

Kai brought me a glass of sauternes and I sat for a long time after dessert was cleared. I couldn't bring myself to see Ethan and Marta yet. I was too moved, too full, too touched.

I was the camper that evening, the customer who sits there until the candles are blown out, until the lights are turned back up, until someone brings out the push broom and starts sweeping the night to a close.

Late that night, alone in my room, I thought about how this would end.

I had a family of sorts filling this house, and I had a family of sorts at Huma, and it felt right. But hopefully, eventually, naturally, Lucy and Sarah would heal enough to get on with their lives, and Lotta, Omari, and Sage would return to their home to prepare for their new baby. I would learn what I needed to learn from Ethan and Marta and even Kai, and then we would all be separate again.

And then what? Tuesday girls' nights? Texting and e-mails and liking each other's Instagram photos and Facebook updates? Seeing each other's lives from afar?

My mother had been alone in her own family. Her illness had kept her isolated and apart. Eventually she couldn't take the solitude any longer, and so she'd done what she had to do to escape it. And of course, by doing that, I'd always believed that she'd handed down the exact same curse to me.

But I wasn't sick like her. Or, at least, I had better ways to fight the illness. If I was isolated, if I was lonely, it was because of my own choices.

I did not have to be alone.

I turned on the light and got out of bed, shivering in the cold night air as I rifled through the little desk at the window for a pen and paper.

B—

Hi.

Hello.

It's been a while.

The other day, Lucy told me that the food I have been cooking at home is better than the food I've been making professionally.

And now I imagine you're saying, "Yes, Billy, and so the fuck what?" We don't talk for weeks (or has it been months? It feels like months) and the first thing I do is get all whiny about Lucy being mean to me.

But bear with me. It might not look like it yet, but this is a love letter. (And I'm only telling you that now so you don't give up in disgust and tear this thing up before it gets juicy. I swear, it will eventually get juicy. There is a chocolate center! A prize at the bottom of the cereal box! Just keep licking this Tootsie Pop! Don't tear it up yet.)

So, anyway, Lucy told me that my home cooking was better than my professional cooking and I kind of wanted to strangle her. But, she's a widow now, and I'm not the kind of asshole who attacks pathetic widows, so I didn't. But I did go home after she said what she said and sit around my kitchen for a long fucking time muttering angrily to myself and trying to figure out how to prove her wrong.

Because she had to be wrong, Brett. She had to be wrong! I am so careful with the food I make for the truck. I plan every detail. I apply every technique. I used a goddamn blowtorch! How could she say that my stupid workaday pastas and soups are somehow better than these recipes I have been making myself fucking crazy worrying over?

And then I was driving around with the chef I work with now, and he said that to be a really great chef, you have to understand connection. He kept going on and on about how you have to be able to connect with your staff, your suppliers, and the farmers who grow your food, and most importantly, you have to be able to connect to the people you are feeding.

(Yes, still a love letter. I swear to fucking God. Be patient.)

And what he said didn't piss me off, per se, but it did kind of make me stop in my tracks. Because... he's probably not wrong. And suddenly it made me understand why Lucy might have been right. Because the people I'm cooking for here are the only people I've allowed myself to really love since my mom died.

I mean, I'm sorry to pull the dead-mom card here, but I was taught pretty early that if you allow yourself to connect to someone, you stand a very good chance of being kicked in the emotional balls when they decide to disconnect. So I keep things relatively simple. Lotta, Sarah, especially Lucy—they are all the family I allow myself to have. And when I cook for them, I know how to make them happy. I know what they need. I know how to connect to them.

But those three are one thing, right? I can connect with them because I know them and love them. But how am I supposed to apply that philosophy to a bunch of random customers? How do I take this connection, this love, and apply it to every person I feed, every stranger who comes through the door?

I mean, I know this probably all sounds like mystical bullshit. I know that I should probably just make my stupid shepherd's pies and tomato sandwiches and sell them and call it a day, but I have to say—there is a part of me that knows, deep down, that this is The Thing I have to master before I can become the chef I want to be.

And then tonight, I was lying in bed thinking of you (see! love letter! Here it comes!). I was thinking that I miss you. I was thinking that I wished you were here. And suddenly, I realized that I might know a way to fix the problem with my cooking.

What if, when I cook, I was cooking for you?

I fought our connection, Brett. I did everything you said I was doing. I kept you at arm's length. I pushed you away. I refused to acknowledge that there was something between us. Because (again, dead mother) I thought that if I pretended it wasn't happening, I wouldn't be putting myself at risk. Because if I admitted just how much I hungered for you, I was only going to end up starved when you inevitably left.

But here's the truth—I felt joy in your arms. Even when everything else I was feeling was pale and faded. When we would lie in bed, tangled up in each other, and I would touch your skin with my tongue, taste the salt of your flesh, the sweetness of your kisses, I knew, deep down, that you were just as important to me as anyone has ever been. Maybe even more so. We were—we are—connected.

So what if I cooked for you, Brett? What if you were the person I imagined when I add salt, sugar, spice? What if you were at the beginning and the end of every meal for me? What if every dish I touched was connected to you, everything I made was with you in mind? Then I couldn't help but cook with my heart and soul. I would be connected. And anyone who eats what I give them would feel that connection, too.

I think that this is the only way I can become the chef I want to be. I honestly believe this. Because you are my family. Because you are the man I love, and that love will make my craft better.

And I'm sorry it took me so fucking long to say this to you. And I hope that I'm not too late. I know you've been patient. I know I've kept you waiting for longer than anyone should rightfully wait.

But... come back to me, Brett. Come back to my bed. Come back to my arms. And come back to my kitchen.

I promise, I'll feed you. I'll feed you butter and honey and pomegranate seeds. I'll feed you marrow and ripe figs and the heart of the artichoke. I'll feed you violets and fresh cream and yes, borscht and pho. I will feed you with my heart and soul and my very bones, my love. Give me the chance to show you.

Come back and let me cook for you.

Always yours,

—B

chapter 31

It was past midnight and I was putting the last pie into the oven.

"Apple, chocolate pecan, pumpkin, pumpkin, quince, buttermilk," I recited to myself.

The air smelled like cinnamon and cloves and roasted nuts and melted butter and caramelizing fruit. The kitchen was a pool of light in the otherwise dark house. The fire had burnt down to embers and everyone else had gone to bed, but I was determined to finish the pies before morning. My little stove would never get everything else done on time, otherwise.

I knew I could have used Huma's kitchen, or asked Marta to bring all the desserts, or even just bought pies from one of the very good bakeries in the area, but I wanted to do this myself.

I was a forty-two-year-old chef and I had never made Thanksgiving dinner before. My kitchen had been too small in the city, and I usually just joined Lucy and Titus at Craft or Union Square Cafe. Growing up, I had itched to try, but my father always insisted that we visit his elderly aunt at her nursing home instead, saying that she'd be alone otherwise.

Personally, I think Great-aunt Dot could have given a shit. In the early years, she'd spent most of the cafeteria-grade meal peering over at us, slowly shaking her head, and whispering in her cracked and girlish voice, "Now tell me, just *who* is this little person again and *why* is she here?" And in the later years, she said nothing at all, just sat and stared off into space as we forced down slimy turkey, canned gravy, and reconstituted mashed potatoes.

But I knew the real reason why my father hadn't wanted me to cook Thanksgiving dinner at home. It had been her holiday. The one time, every year, that we could guarantee that my mother would show up in full.

My mother said that Thanksgiving was the best holiday because it wasn't about presents or candy or religion. It was about family. And love. And counting your blessings. And turkey and pie.

She had always stayed up late the night before, making at least half a dozen different kinds of pie. And every Thanksgiving morning I would wander down to the kitchen and she would be bent over the stove, sautéing the onions and apples for the stuffing in her big cast-iron pot, and there would be the pies, all perfectly lined up on the kitchen counter.

"You're almost big enough," she'd say every year, deftly steering me away before I could ruin anything by sticking my finger where it didn't belong. "Maybe next year you can stay up and help me, Wilhelmina."

She was the only person in the world who ever called me by my full name.

We'd have dinner on the table by four, and there was always a strange group of odds and ends who came as guests. My mother didn't have any friends, and her family lived down south, but she liked to invite lonely checkout boys and spinster waitresses and anyone she could collect as the holiday approached. We always had a full table.

The timer went off and I slid out the apple pie and replaced it with the two pumpkins (one big can of pumpkin always makes enough for two pies).

I reset the timer and sat down at the island, going over my menu for the next day. I had planned on something simple and elegant, but then I had made the mistake of asking if there was anything that anyone wanted me to include. Ethan said he would bring ajil, and Marta wanted rice and beans. Kai made me promise to let her pick all the wine. Omari requested thyme-and-mushroom stuffing, Lotta had begged for mashed carrots as well as yams ("The baby wants them, Billy!"), Sarah had insisted that I make her mother's potato rolls, Sage said she wanted at least one can of cranberries, still in the proper can shape—none of that homemade nonsense—and Lucy had asked for green-bean casserole, complete with cream of mushroom soup and French-fried onions.

Brett had asked for marrow and violets but then laughed and said he just wanted mashed potatoes and gravy.

I sighed happily, looking at the menu, trying to draw the connections between each dish. I might not have a table full of random strangers, but apparently I had a table full of random dishes. But I thought I could see the story they had to tell.

"Still baking?" said Lucy as she entered the kitchen. She was barefoot, wearing her pajamas and my plaid shawl. Her eyes gleamed and she smiled at me like she had a secret.

"I thought you were asleep," I said.

She shook her head. "I couldn't sleep. I was just lying in bed thinking."

"Oh?" I said absently, glancing back down at the menu. "What about?"

"Billy," she said, and there was something in her voice that made me lift my head up and look at her again. "I know what I want to do next."

afterword

East Village, Manhattan
Café Wilhelmina
A year later

"Sage, fire up the mushroom soup!" I called over my shoulder as I fished the tangle of crisped thyme and rosemary out of the hot oil and sprinkled it over the two roast turkeys waiting on the counter.

"*Oui*, Chef!" she returned.

I rolled my eyes. "I hope that's not the only thing you learned while you were training in Paris," I grumbled.

She grinned at me mockingly. "*Non*, Chef!"

"Billy!" called Lucy from the front. "Are you coming? They're here!"

I pulled off my chef's hat and attempted to pat down my hair as I twisted my way past the staff and out of the kitchen.

I paused as I entered the front of the house, taking a moment to admire the way the tiny dining room had been rearranged for the holiday. All the two- and four-tops had been pulled away from the dark gray walls and placed together to make one long table in the center of the room. There was a haphazard line of bud vases holding short orange tulips, interspersed with flickering tea lights, miniature sugar pears, and tight bunches of caviar-size champagne grapes in their golden skins. The places were set with oversize silvery-gray napkins flopping off the sturdy white china, and enough delicate stemware, properly arranged in a diamond pattern, to meet even Kai's exacting standards.

Lucy was acting as hostess tonight, something she reserved the right to do when the mood took her.

"I don't see why I have to take the 'silent partner' thing literally," she always said.

She looked lovely and welcoming as she opened the door for Cheri. Her long blond hair was loose and flowing, a warm smile on her face as she kissed her mother hello.

She looked like this more and more often lately, I thought. Happy. Happier than I had seen her in years, actually. When she wasn't at the restaurant, she was working, writing a memoir of her life with Titus—she wasn't even sure she would try to publish it, she told me. But it felt like something she felt compelled to do.

I sometimes caught her staring at his portrait of us. It had a place of pride on the wall over the bar. We had talked a long time about where to hang it, or indeed, whether to hang it at all, but in the end we had decided it should go front and center. It was, after all, a true and beautiful version of us. It told our story. Or at least an important piece of it.

Lotta and Omari were in the foyer, taking off their coats and arranging their bags. Omari peeled the snowsuit off their fat-cheeked baby, Juni Rose, who wailed loudly as the sleeve caught on her hand.

"Oh, hush, hush, little one," said Lotta as she freed her daughter's hand and gave her a kiss on the cheek.

Sarah was sitting at the bar with Kai, the two of them huddled over glasses of wine, their respective dark and light heads bent so close they were almost touching. Sarah had come in through the back way earlier, hoping to outsmart the paparazzi who were lurking around the front waiting to see who she would bring to dinner. The new "party girl" version of Sarah was a huge hit—even if (or maybe because) she was the show's newest villain. Her producers set her up with a never-ending series of younger men, and their audience loved to see what wild exploits Sarah would get up to next. She was supposed to be dating a twenty-three-year-old hockey player at the moment, but from the way she was looking at Kai, I thought that the hockey player was probably shit out of luck.

Marta and Ethan arrived together. Marta had changed her hair from blue to purple and was even rounder than usual, her pregnant belly thrust out through her partially buttoned plaid coat. Ethan pulled his stocking cap off his head and looked around, taking in the little jewel-box-like space that Lucy and I had worked so long and hard to create.

Huma had exploded this last year. Omari had mentioned it in an interview he gave to the *New York Times* about his newest project. He and Lotta, inspired by Levon Helm's studio and Midnight Ramble concerts, were building a horse farm/recording studio just outside Woodstock. And now Huma had become a pilgrimage destination for foodies. Ethan and Marta were expanding into a second location on the Rondout, one that concentrated on more casual, home-cooked Persian food, and Kai had taken over my Airstream, turning it into a mobile wine bar.

The baby had been a surprise, I heard, but there was a wedding planned for the spring.

For a moment, Ethan's dark eyes met mine and I was nervous,

wondering what he'd think. This was the first time he had seen Wilhelmina's since it opened.

Then he smiled and kissed his fingers in tribute. "It's perfect," he mouthed to me.

Sage rushed past me from the kitchen with a little cry of joy, making a beeline for her baby sister, who she plucked right out of Lotta's arms and swung around until Juni Rose chortled with glee.

"Sage! Sage! Is the soup ready?" I yelled after her.

"*Oui*, Chef!" she said, laughing.

"Is that everyone?" said Brett, as he came up from behind and slipped his arm around my waist.

I leaned back into him, nodding, even as I thought of all the people who were not there.

One thing about having a restaurant is that you never knew who might take your OPEN sign as a literal invitation. A restaurant is an unlocked door. It can be a lost-and-found. New York might be a big city, but that doesn't make it any less of a small world. I was always expecting to face ex-boyfriends or half-forgotten restaurateurs I had worked with. I was always ready to paste on a smile and pretend I hadn't forgotten a name.

And sometimes I let my imagination run wild. I would place my father and Titus, laughing at the bar, matching each other drink for drink and story for story. I would put my great-aunt Dot at the corner table, her facilities magically restored, and give her a martini and some witty repartee with my funniest waitress.

And of course, she was always there. My mother, with me as she had been with me every day since she had left. She was at my station, whispering in my ear as I prepped. She was guiding my hand as I stirred and spiced and tasted. She was behind me as I greeted my guests and received their compliments on my food. She was standing by my side at the end of the night as I swept the floor and scrubbed down my chopping blocks with handfuls of salt.

She was not always a comforting presence. She was not always warm or wise or even welcome. But in my wildest flights of imagination, in my most perfect world, she was at least always there.

I leaned back into Brett for another moment, absorbing his warmth as I looked over the dining room filled with people I loved. They were laughing and talking and drinking, happy to be in the warm, beautiful space, happy to see each other, and anticipating the delicious meal I would feed them all.

And then I straightened up, put my chef's hat back on, and turned back toward the kitchen.

acknowledgments

Thanks to my amazing agent, Emma Parry, who supports me unconditionally, and who has given me a new life that I love. Luke Janklow, thank you for seeing me through your eyes. You allowed me to be myself, and I'm so proud to see where that takes me.

To Alison Callahan, who was open to books that explore women's issues and their voices. Women are the future!

To Tyler Burrow, for introducing me to Café Medi. To chef Vincent Chirico, who showed me how poetic slicing fish is and allowed me to shadow him and his epic staff. To Jared Boles, managing partner of Beauty & Essex, and Cadi, who taught me to bartend at her bar in Brooklyn and how to be the comic relief for the comics in Billyburg. I learned a lot about pouring beer and kept my Converse clean. To chef Marc Murphy, Jake Spitz, and Pam Murphy, for their incredible hospitality at Landmarc. I can't believe I made my own pasta and amazing lunch for my daughter! To chef Jon Feshan, Simon Huck, and Kola House owners Eric Marx and Lisle Richards.

I was so excited to show off my kitchen skills and so flattered to be in the same room with Jon. His staff is amazing, and my thighs survived the epic food with tons of SoulCycle classes with Stacey G., Akin, and Sam Y.

To Maia Rossini, who has taught me to love myself and opened my eyes to a world I didn't even know existed. Her enthusiasm is electric, and I'm honored to work with such a prolific writer. Every week was eye-opening as I ventured into the world of hospitality. I saw passion and compassion on a scale that only Billy can describe.

To my amazing right arm, Kevin M. Barba, who has walked with me every step of *A Dangerous Age* and now *The Second Course.* I'm just getting started, so don't think I'm going anywhere. And to Capezio, for their amazing bodysuits. I took the ballerina off the stage and put her in the kitchen with Rag & Bone or FRAME black jeans and my black Converse every day for months.

"Ask not what you can do for your country. Ask what's for lunch."

WHAT'S FOR LUNCH?

The Second Course

Kelly Killoren
with Maia Rossini

This readers group guide for The Second Course *includes an introduction, discussion questions, and ideas for enhancing your book club. The suggested questions are intended to help your reading group find new and interesting angles and topics for your discussion. We hope that these ideas will enrich your conversation and increase your enjoyment of the book.*

Introduction

Billy Sitwell has found herself at loose ends. Sales of her vintage cocktail book have fizzled, and her landlord is raising the rent on her apartment. Worse still, she's bored by the pretensions of city food. Financially stressed, she's only too eager to accept a magnetic young chef's casual invitation to dine at his restaurant in the Hudson Valley.

Upon her return to Manhattan, Billy resolves to start her life over in a brand-new place, working with a different type of food. But will the prospect of leaving behind her dearest city friends—Lucy, Lotta, and Sarah—as well as her on-again/off-again love interest, Brett, prevent Billy from fully achieving her personal and professional goals?

As Billy navigates uncertain culinary waters, she also must confront the family tragedy in her past that keeps her wary of settling into a profession or a committed relationship. Surrounded by foodies who carry secrets of their own, and without the emotional support of her best friend, Billy must face radical change and self-discovery head-on, with a chef's knife firmly in hand.

Topics and Questions
for Discussion

1. How does Lotta Eklund's newfound sobriety affect her long-standing friendship with Lucy, Billy, and Sarah? Why are her friends wary of her impending wedding to the famous music impresario Omari Scott?

2. "Food became my everything when I was six years old and my mother died" (p. 11). To wh at extent does the centrality of food in Billy Sitwell's life determine her relationships, her career, and her choice of where to live?

3. Why does Billy seem unwilling to commit to a serious relationship with her long-suffering paramour, Brett? Why does his love for her seem to destabilize her? To what extent do you think their relationship has the potential to be successful in the long term?

4. "You know how sometimes you see a house and it instantly feels familiar, like the place has just been waiting for you to show up?" (p. 29). How does Billy's visceral response to the River House in Kingston, New York, foreshadow her decision to stay there longer than a weekend? What aspects of the house seem especially appealing to the reformed Manhattanite?

5.   After Billy gathers mushrooms with Ethan Rahimi, the chef of Huma, and he prepares her a mind-blowing chanterelle pasta, she finds herself besotted by him and his transcendent food. What keeps Billy from getting romantically involved with Ethan? What role does Brett play in her calculations?

6.   Discuss the intense nature of Billy's friendship with Lucy. In what ways do they function more as sisters or family than as friends? What aspects of their very different personalities keep causing friction in their relationship?

7.   "You don't get it. . . . Everything has always just been handed to you. Everything gets dumped into your lap because you look the way you do" (p. 90). Billy, Lucy, Lotta, and Sarah are all invested in (and succeeding at) aging well and keeping up appearances. When Billy lashes out at Lucy, does she do so because she is—on some level—deeply jealous of her best friend's life? What are some other explanations for their epic argument?

8.   Discuss Billy's business pitch to Ethan. Why does she opt for simplicity in her sample meal? Why does her approach appeal to a chef like Ethan?

9.   How does Sage Scott act as the fly in the ointment when it comes to Lotta's marital happiness with Omari? What details about Sage's life make her a more sympathetic character than she appears in Lotta's accounts of her stepdaughter?

10. "The millennials are making merciless . . . fun of her" (p. 149). Throughout *The Second Course*, Billy is acutely attuned to the frustrations and humor of aging, particularly in her hilarious interactions with the twentysomething staff at Huma. Discuss some of

the social and cultural differences between Billy's fortysomething city friends and millennials Ethan, Kai, Marta, and Sage.

11. Why does Billy's impromptu dance with Ethan during the post-work staff drink provoke Kai and Marta to such extreme emotional outbursts? To what extent did the revelation of their secret love triangle surprise you?

12. Why does Titus's appearance at Billy's door shake her to her core? What does Titus's painting enable Billy to realize about her relationship with Lucy? What do you think prompts Titus's decision to choose his wife and her best friend for his final painting?

13. "It was the sweetness of feeding someone who really tasted what you had made for them; it was the pleasure of knowing you had just changed someone's day, even just a little bit, for the better" (p. 205). How does Billy's sense of food's significance evolve over the course of the novel? How is her discovery related to her serving as chef extraordinaire to all her friends at her house?

14. How do Lucy's friends come to her aid in the aftermath of Titus's suicide? Why do they repair to Kingston? What do Billy's culinary attempts to coax Lucy to eat reveal about her character?

15. How does the opening of Café Wilhelmina in the East Village bring Billy and Lucy's friendship full circle? Why do you think the author chose to end the novel with that particularly joyous scene?

Enhance Your
Book Club

1. In *The Second Course*, Chef Ethan Rahimi describes a memory palate: "Everything we've ever eaten is tied to emotion and context" (p. 221). Ask members of your book group to share their memory palates and recall foods that bring them back to a certain place or time in their lives. How do those foods make them feel when they eat them now?

2. Billy Sitwell's life is shot through with regret over the loss of her mother at an early age to suicide. So when Lucy Brockton's husband, Titus, unexpectedly takes his life and turns his wife's life upside down, Billy is in many respects the ideal companion to accompany Lucy through her grief. Even though the friends are estranged, Lucy reaches out to Billy for support. As a group, discuss the ways that tragedy can bring people together despite their differences.

3. In the novel, Billy comes to realize that her dislike for Manhattan's haute cuisine is in some sense connected to her growing appreciation for lovingly made, simply prepared food. With your book group, discuss Billy's conflicted feelings about leaving Manhattan for the bucolic Hudson Valley. How do her ever-changing opinions about

food relate to her place of residence? Why might the opening of Café Wilhelmina in Manhattan's East Village with Lucy as her silent partner represent the ideal outcome for Billy?

4. Billy, Lucy, Lotta, and Sarah undergo many significant changes, particularly with respect to their shifting romantic relationships. With your book group, explore how marriage, death, separation, pregnancy, and childbirth define these characters' lives. Ask members of your book group which character in the book most reminds them of themselves. Have them back up their opinions with evidence from the novel.